Heartache of the Hunter

John Charles

ISBN: 978-0-9825854-8-1

Published by:
CONVERPAGE
23 Acorn Street
Scituate, MA 02066
www.converpage.com

Keeping the presence of Bat Player with him, his thoughts drifted to the hour in the morning of moon low tide, of how cold the northeast wind was on the sand flats this early in April and how digging clams and drinking gin were the focus of his days. He wondered if one of the empty metal chairs in the dream belonged to his grandfather, Bat Player.

The skiff sat stern first in the back of Burningwater's pickup. The truck's rear wheels were parked in about six inches of water on the beach next to the fish pier. Wading the ten feet to the dock piling with the bowline, Charlie Bay watched the wind on the water. There was a system for the skiff during the winter digging season. He looked at it as part prayer and part common sense. His body was old. If things were done in a certain way, in a certain rhythm, the clams knew he was coming, they were ready to be taken and his bones gave him one more day. Tying the skiff to the pier on the outgoing tide and driving the pickup from under it was the opening. The flat bottom of the skiff slapping the water announced his presence to the clams. Dragging it crunching and grinding up the beach behind his truck to a perch in the dunes, ready to do it all again, was the closing. In more recent years, the sounds of skiff and sand were known by the local fishermen to mark the boundaries of Burningwater's livelihood. The last time he fished on the water was coming onto a third season. He called himself a lobsterman but he dug clams for a living.

For Charlie Bay this cold Maine morning was no different than any other in early spring. The half dozen Downeast lobster boats that dotted the small river harbor swung with the wind and the tide. There was heavy water moving through the moorings on the ebb. The combination of runoff from melting snow, four days of rain and a full moon left the river high and strong. Loading his gear into the skiff, Charlie Bay studied the current. As usual, his timing was perfect to ease across the tidal river basin that fishermen had used as a harbor for generations. Rowing fifteen yards up one of the shallow feeder streams, he was on a bar he had worked for a lifetime. It was an island of sand that remained the same through years of dredging, landfills and local politics. But, each time he set foot on the grainy earth exposed by the outgoing tide, it was new.

As Burningwater stepped from the skiff into the boot high river water, the sand showed only a few lumps and bumps, the evidence of yesterday's digging. He noticed the bar's edge was remodeled to a little sharper curve with the stronger current. He saw the same pale western blue sky against the light brown marsh grass. The same chilling cold crept inside his boots as he waded through the shallows and like always his nose dripped clear water onto his upper lip. Charlie Bay wiped his nose with the back of his hand, set the skiff's anchor in the shallows and trudged through to wet sand. And just as every other day, he wondered how long he could last.

In the warmer weather, digging clams meant finding a good crop of squirt holes in a small area of sand, pounding the ground a couple of times with a clam hoe and watching for the clams to spew. Once he found a good spot, Charlie Bay sat on his bucket and worked just one hole, ever widening the perimeter. This time of year, digging was more work. Clams were deeper and that required smaller holes over more territory. The extra effort was compensated by higher market prices and by fewer fools on the sand. Today he was one of three.

After digging for about four hours and leaving a fair number of sand mounds scattered across the bar, Charlie Bay's back told him no more, his knuckles told him no more and his feet were numb. He was at the turning point of his workday. The choice was either quit now, buy some gin and drink, or force himself to hang on, catch his second wind and go two more hours with the tide, then drink.

Most of the folks who lived and worked around the harbor thought Burningwater drank to kill the memories, memories of a family and an Indian Nation destroyed. No one really believed he was simply an old and drunk Indian. The locals knew him as an Indian who belonged to the Casco Tribe, what was left of it. They knew him as someone who never said much and spent his time on the water or the sand. They also knew that he had memories worth killing. For this, he was tolerated and at times forgiven.

Charlie Bay Burningwater was a full-blooded member of the Casco Nation and he did drink. But it was not to kill memories. He drank to eliminate a circle of time. The purpose of alcohol for Charlie Bay was to remove his time at night in the dream and his time in the day thinking about it. He wanted to get rid of both and he thought he was good at it.

Without much deliberation, Charlie Bay stretched his back and moved to start a new hole. He took a few steps to what looked like a promising spot, spread his legs, bent forward and drove the claming fork into the sand. With the thrust, he felt a hard object shatter. Thinking it was just another empty quahog shell, he turned over the ground. As his eyes focused, he recognized the sand-covered fragment of a human skull. For a moment he froze staring at the bone, then his legs buckled. Falling forward to his knees and reaching into the watery hole, Charlie Bay pulled the sandy skull toward his chest. The top was broken and gone. The two orbits and nasal opening, despite being packed with sand, were unmistakable. With a wet hand, Charlie Bay caressed the surface. Clutching the light brown bone, he rolled to the ground. His eyes clamped shut. The moist sand glued his clothes to skin. The fragmentary skull joined his day and his dream. Lying with his knees pulled to his chest, he cradled the physical remains of one who came before. Burningwater turned his head skyward and chanted.

"Sondaqua, Sondaqua soaring high above me.
Look down upon a son of the Nations
and call to Mother Earth that I might be forgiven.
I make this prayer to you Sondaqua, Sondaqua.

Sondaqua, Sondaqua soaring high above me.
Look down upon a son of the Nations

and call to Mother Earth that I might be forgiven.
I make the prayer to you Sondaqua."

His voice trailed off as his teeth clenched, "and call to Mother Earth that I might be forgiven."

Charlie Bay Burningwater fought it hard but failed. He cried an old and deep cry.

Thirty-three thousand feet in the air, six hundred miles per hour, satellite TV that includes CNN, all for a fare cheaper than driving, why not fly? One reason was Margaret didn't own a car and even if she borrowed one the drive from Philadelphia to Maine was at least eight hours. The choice was easy. TV was a bonus.

She set her laptop on the seatback tray but avoided turning it on by scanning through the forty-eight channels on the screen embedded into the headrest in front of her. An elderly couple in the adjacent two seats had settled into the flight with headphones and an early afternoon Soap Opera. As Margaret searched for CNN the woman leaned toward her during a commercial, "Isn't this great! I didn't have to miss my favorite story."

Margaret nodded with a smile and considered how she called the Soap her "favorite story". She turned on her laptop and entered the expression under dialog notes at the bottom of a long list in the file.

This was the fun part of writing for Margaret, listening to a phrase, catching a glimpse of a story line in some everyday event or conversation. The hard part was sorting through the files, the dictation, the character sketches and the plot lines to integrate it all into a play that worked.

Her first play took four years to complete by writing around a part time job turning out grant proposals for a university consulting firm and two nights a week as a waitress in a small South Philly bistro. She wrote most of the rest of the time and she did finish it, although, in her mind, now working on her third play, the first was never done.

During college, Margaret majored in Theatre and U.S. History. She considered herself a playwright and writing her profession. The history part was to appease her father and from his perspective, to keep the possibility of law school, an option. But, through the years and to her surprise, she developed a genuine affection for American history and at times, found particular events as points of focus for writing. Her first effort after college combined both disciplines and resulted in the play, *Overturn*.

The story line was a carry over from her senior thesis in history. Her college research focused on the Supreme Court's decision in the case of Plessy v. Ferguson and "Jim Crow" legislation for separate but equal education. Her ignorance of the law and her ignorance of supposedly separate but equal education embarrassed her. Since graduation, she never stopped reading, researching and writing about Plessy, later Thurgood Marshall and overturning Plessy with Brown

v. Board of Ed. Her work, *Overturn* with all the key players, chronicles the journey. It is four years of historical research and four years of writing. It is thorough, accurate and boring. It reads, even to her, like a history lecture.

So Margaret is on her way to Maine, sitting next to a woman watching her favorite story, to connect with friends, other writers, directors and actors, all doing summer stock somewhere along the southern Maine coast, to workshop *Overturn*, to see it performed and to rewrite it.

She isn't discouraged. She sees play writing as a process and has confidence in her ability to improve. She has faith in "write what you know" even if it is from the library archives. And Margaret Anne Garret believes, with all her heart, Arthur Miller's words, "plays should strive for a well defined expression of profound social needs". She will keep at it. This is what she does.

Keeping at it was not easy when it involved Maine and her family. Margaret fought for independence after college, living in a studio apartment in South Philadelphia, maintaining her own finances despite her parents' wealth and generosity and establishing herself as a writer. But in returning home, she was always weary of getting sucked back into the old ways, ways frozen in time. The trouble was she needed some of the old ways when she returned to Maine. On this trip she needed a place to stay and a car. Fortunately, her parents were away on an annual early May golf holiday in the Carolinas with friends. She had the keys to her father's

SUV, left for her to pick up at the airport and the house was empty, hers for the weekend. This was comfortable for both her parents and for Margaret.

On Saturday she was scheduled to meet a good friend and director to view some rehearsal sites she had lined up by email in Kennebunk and Ogunquit. Margaret wasn't sure what barn stage meant when it came to summer stock rehearsal theatres and even with attached photos, she needed to get a feel for the spaces. She also needed to rent or borrow digital recording equipment for the dates most people were available. Her hope was to workshop the play and get at least one complete run-through during the last two weeks in May. Then it was back to Philadelphia, rewrite *Overturn* and keep writing her current play, *Shadowcatchers*. She considered the holes in her plan as the plane landed.

With the lingering early evening sun, Margaret had no trouble finding the backdoor key hidden under an eve of the porch roof. Her leather sandals against the tile floor were the only sounds in the kitchen as she set down her carryon and opened the refrigerator, looking for nothing in particular but taking a bottled water. She glanced at the home phone out of habit and then to the photos held by fruit magnets on the white enamel door. Neither had changed. Her eyes drifted to the granite-topped island in the center of the room. There was a note and what looked like a shoe box wrapped in brown paper and tied with string sitting on the counter. Margaret read the block pencil letters in two lines on the paper covering. The letters were a mix of caps and small case, printed with childlike quality and the names spelled correctly. "Margaret" was the first line and "Charlie Bay Burningwater" the second. The note alongside the box was from her mother. "I'm off to meet your father at Hilton Head-please give me a call when you're settled in. Bud Walker dropped this package off for you. He's much better looking than I remember him when you were in school together. Maybe you should call him. Love, Mom".

Margaret mumbled, "Yenta lives. Bud Walker was always good looking… Charlie Bay Burning-water…what's...?"

The box was light but well wrapped. She got a knife from the draw below, cut the string and tore off the paper. It was a shoe box but an old one. Margaret didn't recognize the brand and growing up surrounded by retail, she knew shoes. Inside was a single audio cassette tape, standing upright and supported on all sides by crumpled white tissue paper. There was no note and no label on the cassette. Margaret was stunned. She hadn't seen or spoken to Charlie Bay in what had to be a dozen years or even more. Tumbling the tape slowly in her fingers and studying it for any hint of purpose, she flashed back to her view as a young girl from Charlie Bay's lap, nestled into his arms and looking up onto his weathered windburn chin speckled in white stubble. She thought about the high cheek bones that sheltered his squinting eyes and the brown stain filling the cracks of his worn teeth. He smelled like peanut brittle. She was amazed. This tape was from Charlie Bay Burningwater; the Storyteller.

"Where can I play it?" Mumbling to herself, "What am I supposed to do with this… it's a tape… what am I going to do with tape?"

Margaret knew there was nothing in her room. She used to have a disc player for old CDs but she had put everything on her phone and running MP3 mini, all useless. At one point, her brother had a boom box that she remembered seeing stacked in the basement storage room. It had a cassette player but she had no idea if the huge thing was still around or worked.

When she got to the storage room, it was apparent most of the stuff in there was hers. She saved everything. The first carton she saw was labeled "my so called high school life-or something like it, box #2 of 5". She was tempted to dive in but the tape in her hand was a reminder. There was no boom box on any of the shelves. She figured the garage was next.

From time to time, her father was known to recycle all kinds of old stuff; TVs, stereos, obsolete electronics, to his work shop in the third bay of the garage. The shop was separated from the rest of the inside space by a double sliding door. As Margaret slid one panel far enough to slip in and hit the light switch, she saw it. A 1983 red Cadillac Seville with a full Cabriolet roof, her father's treasure. She had forgotten all about the old fake convertible he garaged for preservation. She forgot his pride and joy but, she did see the boom box.

Margaret checked the plug and hit the on button. AM talk radio was a good sign from the speakers but when she pressed play on the tape deck the heads didn't move. She inserted the tape, selected the tape button and hit play again, nothing. Leaning back against the Seville she bumped the antenna. The Delco Bose Stereo Cassette was factory built into the Cadillac. He called it a must have option, "Just listen Margaret, just listen to this!"

She did and she remembered the cassette player. It should work. She needed keys. They fell from the visor as she remembered again. Dean Martin singing "Volare" came from all four bulging door speakers before she ejected the tape. He was consistent, "Dean Martin's Greatest Hits", long a favorite on record, tape and CD. She set the Volare' cassette on the passenger seat, inserted the unmarked tape and settled into the smooth leather seat.

"It happened, in a village pretty far from here, a Hunter was in search of a wife." Charlie Bay's voice was tentative and there was a pause. He cleared his throat and began again.

"He was not having success. This made him restless and often he left the village for long times to hunt the buffalo." Charlie Bay gained strength and volume.

"One day, hunting at the edge of the plain, he saw a beautiful woman standing on a hilltop. As he approached her his heart was taken. He knew this woman to be his wife. Her heart was also captured and in the

Hunter she knew her husband. As you might expect, soon they married.

Following custom of the people, the Hunter wished to meet the family of his wife and give gifts in return for their daughter as his bride. But the Hunter's wife said her family lived on a land far from his village. She promised someday she would take him there. She also asked him, as wives do, to be patient. Many days past, finally she told her husband in the morning they would travel to her family. With the sunrise, the two climbed their meeting hill. At the crest she asked him to roll on the grass three times. He obeyed her, rolled three times on the grass and turned into a buffalo. The Hunter's wife also rolled on the grass and turned into a buffalo. Together they ran to her people.

When they arrived at a great herd, Buffalo Woman searched and found her family. Her father, a Buffalo Chief, was pleased to see such a fine husband for his daughter. He immediately asked them to stay and spend their remaining days as buffalo."

Charlie Bay chuckled, his voice livened. "The Hunter didn't want to live his life as a buffalo! Oh no! He was upset and anxious about the request. He wanted to return to his village. Buffalo Woman again asked her husband to be patient and appease her father by suggesting a contest to determine his fate. Buffalo Woman's father agreed. The condition for their return to the Hunter's village was that he must outrun the fastest bull in the herd.

The Hunter had never raced a buffalo so he sought

his wife's counsel. She told him to be sure to use the wind and the hills to his advantage. He was never to run directly into the wind or over hilltop. He should weave his way through the valleys, allowing the wind and the hills to push him whenever they were willing. The race was never a contest. To his relief the Hunter defeated the fastest buffalo. For now anyway, the Buffalo Chief accepted his loss and bid farewell to his daughter and her husband. But, he did hope that they might reappear someday and stay with him for good."

Charlie Bay's voice had grown hoarse. There was a pause. Margaret thought she heard a clink. She recalled the sound; glass colliding with the blackened pipe ashtray that sat beside the storyteller's chair. Seconds later, she listened to a metal cap twist off the bottle. A few gurgles and the burp confirmed it. She was annoyed with the interruption. Another few gurgles and Charlie Bay continued.

"Returning to the hilltop, Buffalo Woman and her husband rolled on the grass three times. Back to human form, she asked her husband to tell no one of their journey. In the days that followed, the love between Buffalo Woman and her husband grew. Soon they shared their lives with a son. For all these seasons, the Hunter provided meat for his family. His success now also fed many of his relatives and friends. But, there was one among them who was very suspicious about how well he knew the buffalo heart. This suspicious mind belonged to his grandmother. She often told him that there was more to his success than he let be known. Of course, she did eat well for food was plentiful and life was good.

This didn't last. Mother Earth changed. The rivers and the land began to dry out. Where the Hunter and his people had known water, there was only dust. And with dust came thirst and hunger. Now more than ever, the Hunter's relatives depended on him for food. Life was hard. The Hunter's eyes saw the children stop growing and the old people in his village become thin. The drought also touched the buffalo. They were nowhere to be found. But the Hunter knew he must continue until he brought food for his family.

One day, the Hunter was away searching for buffalo, his son and the other children of the village were playing. Some pretended to be hunters, others pretended to be the hunted buffalo. It happened the Hunter's son acted like a buffalo and rolled three times on the ground. As he did, he turned into a buffalo. Seeing this change the children began to scream. Hearing their shrieks Buffalo Woman ran to find her son. When she saw him, she rolled on the ground three times and turned into a buffalo. With her son by her side they galloped fast away from the village. These events did not escape the watchful eye of the Hunter's grandmother.

Now it also happened as Buffalo Woman and her son raced across the plain, the Hunter caught sight of them. His heart soared like an eagle. He saw food for his family. The Hunter chased mother and her calf until suddenly they stopped, turned and faced his bow. The Hunter quickly killed them both and butchered them. Returning to his village, his heart raced with happiness.

This food would feed his people.
When everyone saw the Hunter's horse draped with meat, joy rang out in the village. Sharing with all, the Hunter kept only a small portion for himself, his wife and son. As he searched for them a midst the excitement of the feast, he saw only his grandmother waiting to give him bad news. He heard the tale and a loud cry leapt from his heart. The Hunter rode fast toward the Sun."

Again, Charlie Bay's voice grew weak. Hearing the sound of his deep breathing and the click of his recorder, Margaret pressed stop. She needed a break. The voice was a little thinner but the words were without hesitation. She sighed, looked around the interior of the car and let her head fall back to the red leather rest of the driver's seat. Margaret stretched out her right arm without moving her body, pressed the chrome play button and closed her eyes.

"After many days of wandering and not being aware of the world around him, the Hunter came to a cave in the foothills. He was tired, thirsty and wondered if he were in a dream. Approaching the cave he saw an old woman standing at the entrance. He sat before her and told his story. The old woman grew restless with the Hunter's self-pity. When he finished, she scolded him for believing that it was he, and only he, who brought food to the village. She reminded him that Buffalo Woman could've rolled three times before him and turned herself, along with their son, back to his loved ones! The old woman pointed a finger in his face and told him that he was stuck in his own sorrow and not thinking clearly about what had been given.

Humbled and stung at the old woman's tongue, the Hunter asked what he could do that his wife and son might live again. The old woman told him to return to Buffalo Woman's father. The Buffalo Chief would direct his future. The Hunter rolled three times on the ground, turned himself into a buffalo and raced to the herd.

The Buffalo Chief came out alone to greet his son. Quietly, the Chief said he understood from a dream that the Hunter had spoken to his wife, the Old Woman of the Cave. She demonstrated the sharpness of her tongue. Now the Hunter would understand the reason why most of his days were spent as a buffalo. The Hunter had no patience for the Buffalo Chief's plight and wanted only to learn what he must do for the return of his loved ones.

The Chief explained that to place the world around him in order, he must return to his people and gather the bones of his wife and son. He must bring the bones to their meeting hill and cover them with prairie grass. The chief warned that if the bones had been burned or broken all hope was lost. The Hunter would have no choice but to remain alone for the rest of his days. But, if he did as he was told, his wife and son would live again. The one condition was that he must come back to the herd and spend his remaining days as a buffalo.

The Hunter returned to human form and searched for the bones of his wife and son at the spot where he killed them. There were no bones. In heartache he rode to his village, gave away what little he had and prepared to spend his remaining days without his wife and son.

Before he departed, his grandmother found him and told him about an old woman living in a cave that came to her in a dream. The old woman asked her to gather the bones of the Hunter's wife and son before they were burned or broken and hide them. This particular old woman had a sharp tongue and because of this his grandmother gathered the bones as she was told.

Ha! The Hunter's heart soared like an eagle. He returned the bones to the exact spot on the hilltop and covered them with prairie grass. The Hunter spent the next two days watching from a distance hoping to catch one last glimpse of his wife and son. They never came. He knew that for the circle to be complete he must turn into a buffalo and fulfill the conditions of the Buffalo Chief. He rolled three times on the grass, turned into a buffalo and without looking back at his village, galloped off to spend his remaining days.

When he arrived at the herd the Buffalo Chief reminded the Hunter that he had always hoped to have him live as a buffalo.

“I'm glad you are here. It is a noble call to provide food and clothing for the Nations. It is also good to have a growing heart and not one stopped by heartache.

My son, to have a growing heart, you must choose your place on Earth and hold the ground that is yours. And you know, this doesn't often take the form one might expect.”

Turning to the East, the Buffalo Chief nodded toward his daughter as she galloped with their son down from a hilltop.

And so it was, Buffalo Woman, the Hunter and their son spent the remaining days on this Earth in a proud and noble manner."

Charlie Bay laughed a quick laugh; happy his voice and his memory made it through the whole thing.

"Storytellers know many legends, my child, and are always eager to tell one."

To the hum of the tape player Margaret considered why, after all these years, Charlie Bay Burningwater sent her this story. There was no note, no explanation. "Heartache of the Hunter" was her favorite. She was consistent and Charlie Bay knew.

After listening to "Heartache of the Hunter" two more times in the quiet comfort of the red Cadillac Seville with the full Cabriolet roof and Delco Bose speakers, she took the tape up to her old room and tucked it under some expired 20% off Bloomingdales coupons in her nightstand drawer.

When Margaret's head hit the pillow she was tired but her mind occupied by Burningwater, his home on Eagle Island and by Molly, the nanny who took her there.

"Let's ride to the wind", was her call to Margaret for a trip to Charlie Bay.

Molly's huge royal blue Mercury had slippery seats, push button everything, including the mirror on the passenger door, ashtrays and a dashboard full of knobs. Across on the driver's side, with one hand fixed to the top of a worn blue wheel and the other tapping something, tapping somewhere, sat her nanny grinning ear to ear. Together, they turned from a four lane onto the dusty dirt road running next to the railroad tracks and rolled to Eagle Island. The two of them, headed for Charlie Bay's with every window down, Molly's long salt and pepper hair dancing in the breeze as the rest of the world melted away.

Margaret fought sleep with images of the last quarter mile of a forty-five minute trip from her parent's house, Molly staring over the dash as the old Mercury rumbled its way toward three knolls in the middle of the marshland. She remembered crossing the narrow railroad tie bridge, turning up the sandy road and passing the blueberry patch to park just shy of Charlie Bay's backdoor. From the age of seven, for five or six years and as long as there wasn't snow, Margaret rode at Molly's side to Burningwater's Eagle Island.

The recollection of days spent with Charlie Bay brought her mind's eye to the long Casco Point beach at half tide and her search for skipping stones. Near sleep, Margaret was there; feeling the sun, smelling the wind, and seeing the fixed silhouette of Molly sitting on the rocks, on her rock, staring for hours to open ocean. A bit further up in the sand, Charlie Bay's beached dory was Margaret's refuge, her safe haven, where she and Burningwater always waited, without measure, for Molly. Nestled between the high walls of the dory's bow and dosing in a bed of salty old orange life jackets, visit after visit, Margaret listened to the Storyteller.

Without warning, a long forgotten image startled Margaret from sleep; Charlie Bay Burningwater slept when he was tired, wherever, whenever and usually without clothes. She learned this the hard way. A nap for Charlie Bay in the dory on a warm summer afternoon was no exception.

Margaret took a deep breath, slid a little deeper under the covers and considered the smell of pipe tobacco and the small pieces of peanut brittle that collected on the breast pocket flaps of the Storyteller's work shirt. After she had picked up enough pieces, the collection allowed her to place the candy on the tip of her tongue, curl into the lap of Charlie Bay Burningwater and let the slow melting pleasure of sweet and story linger.

She slept well.

Margaret knew Harry, now directing, better than most of the men in her life. They became friends in college and worked as interns together on Broadway shortly after graduating. Harry was a director's assistant on the revival of a safe, tried and true musical and Margaret was on the second run of August Wilson's *Fences.* Harry had a title, Margaret, a much better play. Wilson's ten part cycle of works about African Americans in his home town of Pittsburgh was an inspiration for Margaret. Her favorite of the ten plays, each set in a decade of the twentieth century, was *The Piano Lesson.* And the chance to hear *Fences* performed every day, she considered an extraordinary gift. It was because of August Wilson that

Margaret wrote any time she wasn't doing any job asked. Maybe because his play was a musical, Harry networked all the time.

This morning Margaret was the beneficiary of Harry's extensive contacts. She found excellent rehearsal space and met old friends and understudies willing to workshop the play. Harry connected her with tech support free and even a condo to house sit for as long as she wanted, also free. He would do anything for her and, down the road he wanted one of her plays. They both would know when and which one.

Margaret had the feeling Harry had already passed on *Overturn* by his persistent questioning about her current work, *Shadowcatchers.* He was glad she shelved the first draft of her adaptation for the stage of Dee Brown's Bury My Heart at Wounded Knee. Despite her passion for injustice and her drive to persevere with the story it became so complex and the history of Native American genocide so heartwrenching, even she thought it was too much too soon. But she also thought it was an important story to tell on stage. So did a Chicago publishing company whose Native American playwright had already adapted Dee Brown's book for the theatre. Margaret stumbled onto the play after she had stopped rewriting but couldn't let her play or the research go. In the meantime, a period piece love affair between a nineteenth century female photographer and an older artistic publisher eager to work with new glass plate photo techniques kept Harry interested. The irony with the project was Margaret's uncertainty about love. She had fallen in love acouple of times but wondered if she had ever been in love. When she doubted love, *Shadowcatchers* stalled. It was presently stalled. But today, *Overturn*, thanks to Harry, was moving with a lot fewer holes in the plan.

Driving back to her parent's home, reviewing it all, she was ambivalent about the day's successes and it surprised her. Charlie Bay's hold on her with "Heartache of the Hunter" did not. The new plan was to change her flight from Sunday to Monday and find Burningwater.

Chapter Two

It wasn't Molly's blue Mercury that turned onto the dirt road running next to the abandoned railroad tracks but, with the windows down and the salt air it smelled the same to Margaret. Her father's SUV bounced in and out of the ruts as she took the only route to Eagle Island. When the bumpiness increased, she was forced to slow down and appreciate the contrast of the pale blue sky against the light brown sea grass in the May sun. Margaret enjoyed returning to this flat open space. Acre after acre spread before her until her eyes caught only marsh surface blending with woodlands to the west and the tidal Casco River melting with the ocean to the east. Straight ahead and due north rose the island home of Charlie Bay Burningwater. Her heart was pounding.

Charlie Bay lived on the ocean side of three mounds known collectively as Eagle Island. They were elliptically shaped patches of farmland that ran from east to west across the marsh. Each eighty plus acre plot, joined by two tidal causeways formed the Casco Indian Reservation's northern third. The whole reservation, with the exception of Eagle Island and land to the west along Rt. 1, was comprised of about sixteen hundred acres of sand flats and wetlands. The middle third of the territory was a scattering of seagrass islets and marshes that shored the Casco River. The southern third was a series of sandbars and clam flats. At low tide, mile after mile of corrugated sand and at high tide, a ten foot bay of saltwater poised to turn and rush back to the ocean. This was a federally recognized Indian Reservation. This was land, at the end of the 1960's, nobody wanted. This was the last remnant of the traditional homeland of the Casco Nation.

It wasn't always just the marshland and Eagle Island the Casco Tribal Nation called home. At the beginning of the nineteenth century about six thousand acres of woodland to the north was also Casco land. The tribe's main settlement bordered the Casco River to the south and was the center of the hunting and fishing activities of the Casco people. In more recent generations, Charlie Bay's family drifted from the community's village on the mainland and occupied the three mounds of Eagle Island. His grandfathers still hunted the northern forest season after season. For a good part of the 1800's they shared with other members of the Casco tribe in the resources provided by sea and woodland. At the turn of the twentieth century, thousands of acres, once home to the

Casco Nation, were parts of two small Maine towns and all of a State Park.

The dirt road seemed to go on forever before Margaret approached the narrow bridge that crossed the Casco River to Eagle Island. Easing the SUV up to the succession of rail ties that formed its surface, she peered down over the railingless edge into the rushing out-going tide. Margaret aimed the truck to the center of the bridge, glanced again at the churning current and headed to the other side. Once on solid ground, she turned east up the hill to Charlie Bay's.

The grass in the center of the winding road to his home was a brown stripe amid the white sandy tire paths. The course was still a little soft; even this late in the spring and the truck surged side to side as she made the climb. To Margaret, it appeared so much the same, so unchanged. She drove past the collapsed walls of the salt marsh hay barn and noticed the wind and weather exposed just a few more beams. Beyond the barn was the single, loan-standing chimney, anchored to the fireplace by its inlaid beachstone mantel, beauty in tact. She never saw the farmhouse but heard the story of the fire many times. The sharp and straight vertical line of the chimney cut the sky to the hill crest and pointed the way to Charlie Bay's back porch. She pulled the truck up to the house, shut off the engine and listened for the distant muffled rhythm of rolling waves against the Maine coast. Opening the truck door she looked from the hillcrest back to the west. The marshland unfolded almost at her feet. The panorama was startling. It had changed. Her memory held the image of large sandy white patches linked with green islands and strung together by small blue waterways. The white islets of her past, produced by years of dredging, were now completely overgrown with seagrass. The tiny meandering streaks of blue had also disappeared, leaving only an enormous stretch of golden marshland, bordered on each side by the North and South branches of the Casco River. The straight running ribbons of blue join to pool at the western end of Eagle Island. A view that Margaret remembered as a maze of sand and grass, scratched with estuaries, now ran before her as a solid swath land straight to Rt1. She considered the differences until she felt the wind and heard the waves.

Margaret didn't head up the steps to the backdoor. Through force of an old habit, she passed the plum rose bushes and walked around the south side of the house. As she turned the corner to face the ocean, the wind, the water and the warmth of the early afternoon sun brought her back to Charlie Bay Burningwater. She climbed the front stairs, pushed the wooden screen door inward across a crescent shaped bare spot on the porch floor and eased inside. The brown wicker furniture on the screened-in porch was untouched. Margaret remembered the smell of the musty cushions and another place where she and Charlie Bay waited for Molly. Charlie Bay rocking and puffing his pipe, dull thumping sound of wood on wood, rickety rocker to rickety floor, salt ocean air and pipe smoke, it was all here.

The dark green paper shade on the window of the front door was drawn about one third of the distance to the bottom of the pane. Margaret moved toward the door and bent forward until the reflection of her squinting eyes and wrinkled nose came into view. Her own image startled her. For just a second she froze, holding her breath. Almost as fast, she gathered herself and raised both hands to her face and reduced the glare. Peering between shade and frame, she saw Charlie Bay's home unaltered in time. The center oak staircase was dark and bare with a small pale braided area rug at its base. To the left of the stairs was a black straight back rocker with a faded red corduroy pillow. Beyond the rocker, was an end table with the metal pipe ashtray tucked in the corner next to Charlie Bay's overstuffed chair, arms stained and worn. Sliding to the right on the window, she increased her view of the room. As she moved, her eyes glanced past the beachstone fireplace on the outside wall and focused on the light blue sofa set parallel to the porch. She froze. It wasn't a full view but it was enough; the pile of work clothes on the floor, the pint gin bottle next to the clothes and the naked wrinkled bronze body next to both.

It seemed to be a gentle thud as her entire body tipped forward into the front door and she expected things to be quiet enough for a quick exit. But, while pushing herself up and back from the door, she heard, first the rustling of tired spring cushions and then the shuffling of footsteps on the hardwood floor. In an instant, a naked torso flashed across the window. No sooner than the unclothed form passed in front of her, it reappeared, headed in the opposite direction. Margaret edged closer to the window. Without warning, once again, a bare Charlie Bay Burningwater dashed by the door. This time, he was carrying pants.

Just seconds after disappearing from sight, Charlie Bay reappeared, wearing baggy khaki work pants, without a belt or shirt. He opened the door slowly. Only his left arm moved. The rest of his body remained rigid; he was locked on the woman's face. Recognizing her large dark brown eyes and auburn hair, Charlie Bay knew exactly who stood before him. In a soft hoarse voice, he was the first to speak "I'm a little slower than I used to be ... you know; the pants." Without changing his stoic expression he continued, "I, ah, I...."

Thinking he had no idea who this was at his front door other than someone who had just seen him dash naked across his living room, Margaret reached to say something, anything to break the moment. "I, I'm older. It's me Margaret, Margaret Garret."

"I know." Charley Bay responded, still focused on her eyes. "Come in." He opened the door a little further and turned toward the clothes that remained scattered on the floor. As Margaret stepped into the house she immediately noticed the skin on his bare back was scarred. The scars ran from the base of his left ear, at an angle across his neck, to just below his right shoulder blade. From there the light and irregular skin covered his back, only to disappear at the waist of his pants. Charlie Bay bent over, picked up his shirt and faced Margaret to expose additional scars on his arms and the left side of his stomach. Hesitating for a second, he saw her stare, "My legs also got burned too."

Margaret didn't remember the scars. Charley Bay didn't want to lose her. He did what he did best; he told the story.

"When I was about twelve, I was named Seal Swimmer. The name came in the summer while I was working as a tailman, a lobsterman's helper."

Continuing to talk, Charlie Bay put on and buttoned his shirt. The buttons and holes weren't matched and he tucked in only the front. This caught Margaret's attention. Unaffected, Charlie Bay motioned for her to sit in the rocker as he eased into the faded green stuffed chair in the corner.

His voice had the same rhythm and tone as on the tape, raspy at first, then stronger. She slid into the rocker and felt her body relax.

"It was a hot day in August, not a breath of air. Looking back on it, ol' Abe Jordan was a little hungover, never spoke much anyway, but on this day he didn't say a word. At around ten, with no wind and no current, he just went below and to sleep. I sat on the fantail of his old wooden thirty-two foot Friendship sloop as we drifted in the sun for awhile, until I got so boiling hot that I finally decided to strip down and jump into the biggest, coolest swell I could find. When I popped my head up out of the water and opened my eyes, about fifteen feet away, a harbor seal had come up with me. We just floated there, face to face for a few seconds until, without so much as a ripple the seal slipped back under water. I put my face into the water, opened my eyes... floated dead man's style and watched that seal swim right under me; big dark eyes, watching me, watching him. When I came up for air, there was two or three more of them, right there in front of me. As soon as I'd dead man float, they would cross underneath me, but an arm's length away. And when they would pass their big round eyes rolled right back to the top of their brow without a blink. Before I knew it, I was surrounded by harbor seals. At my next breath I found myself in the center of a circle of seals, each focused on this scrawny naked little human being, not of their world, giggling in boy's pitch, with no fat to keep from shivering and treading water...working hard to stay afloat. I have often thought of how curious a being I must've been to them."

Charlie Bay paused and considered the event, distant from Margaret. Catching his own drift, he cleared his throat, looked at his gin bottle and chuckled, "Well it didn't last for long, Abe came topside, called me Seal Swimmer and mumbled about getting back to work. The seals were gone in a heartbeat but I was called Seal Swimmer....'til the fire."

Margaret was puzzled by Charlie Bay's reference to the fire. Recalling the fire story, there was never a mention of him burned or injured when flames took his uncle's farmhouse on Eagle Island to the ground. She watched as Charlie Bay settled deeper into the Storyteller's chair. She had never heard this one.

"At that time, I was working my own boat, bought from Abe's brother, Sparky Jordan. He was given the name because he installed engines in fishing boats. It was sunrise and just a few boats had left the harbor. There was no air, quiet. I was starting to salt bait and make room for more red fish I brought with me in the skiff. I figured I'd let her warm up a bit and pushed the starter. Out of nowhere, I heard a thundering boom. My ears blocked. The bones of my legs jolted and the cold, cold water was all I felt around me. When I finally came to the surface everything was burning, including me. I was surrounded by flames, couldn't see a thing 'cept up. When the fire got close I'd duck under, look through the water for sky then pop up again for air and try to find a way out. They say I was among the burning water as it moved with the current the whole length of the harbor. I don't remember being pulled into a skiff by my Uncle William, but when they finally reached me, I was lying on my back, my stomach burning and I was gasping for air. It was right then and there my uncle William changed my name."

Looking at the gin bottle, Charlie Bay squinted to see how much remained. He looked back to Margaret knowing two quick stories had broken the uncertainty. Grinning, he rolled open the palms of his hands with a warm welcome expression. It was a reception that she knew well. He looked to her eyes, "Bay Burningwater to this very day. Charlie was added a little later, as a first name for the American folks outside the Casco...make it easier for the locals to call me an American name...don't know where it came from."

She smiled. After a moment, Margaret leaned forward in the rocker, curious about the fire but even more curious about the tape.

"Why did you send me "Heartache of the Hunter"?"

Charlie Bay continued to grin. He appreciated her intensity and her directness. He was happy she came.

"I can't write. But I heard you do...heard you were good at it.

I need a writer...you're from university. You know university people...how they write back and forth."

The words, "I can't write", came from his mouth with a matter of fact quality that expressed no guilt or shame; he simply stated a just reason for a common sense way to meet his need. In her everyday world of e-mail, texting, blogging and all the others, the ability to write was never a question. She glanced toward the small oak table adjacent to Charlie Bay's chair. Not a book, magazine or newspaper was in sight. There wasn't and, in her recollection, there never had been a lamp in that corner of the room. Charlie Bay followed her response.

"Can't read either, but I can print my name. Bud helped me with yours."

She sat back into the rocker.

"I don't have a telephone, an address. I don't have a driver's license or a mail box."

The list of don'ts and didn'ts progressed through all of the state and federal institutions he knew. He made his point by ending with, “in the American world, I don’t exist.”

But practicals aside, she sensed that there was another reason he sent her “Heartache”. For his part, he was aware his choice to send her favorite story was more than a charming use of an electronic device in an old storyteller's attempt to reconnect with a relationship of his past. But for now, in his own way, he chose to be blunt and pragmatic.

"And I need your help with the university Americans."

Margaret whispered, "university Americans".

Without speaking, he stood up, walked to the staircase and climbed the stairs. She watched his bare feet shuffle against the oak steps and his left hand slide along the rail. His action was rote and rhythmic, his eyes wide with purpose.

For a few moments after he left the room Margaret didn’t move. She considered his phrase, “university Americans” and reached to dictate into her cell. She stopped. She would remember this one.

The quiet was interrupted by the thumps and thuds of his rummaging around under a bed, in the back of a closet or somewhere else she only imagined by the sounds.

When he returned, Charlie Bay was carrying a small wooden Clementine crate containing an unopened box with a picture of a portable radio on the outside and a pair of binoculars without a case. The printing on the side of the wooden crate was faded but the orange stencil of the fruit was clear. Sitting back in his chair, he set the box gently across his knees. With dark brown eyes, he looked to Margaret.

"Years ago, as I became a young man, the western most mound of Eagle Island was called the Western Door."

Hesitating for just an instant, Charlie Bay glanced at the pint gin bottle and then returned to her face.

"The Western Door is the burial ground of my people. For as long as I can remember, a grandfather, one who kept the dead, would bring me with him whenever he traveled to tend this place. As my grandfathers died, on a certain day, I became one who kept the dead." He paused, his voice cracked, "The circle of the dead has been broken." Then in words never spoken, "I am the one who broke the circle."

Charlie Bay dropped his head in shame. Burdened by guilt built over decades, he sat slumped and motionless. Margaret was lost.

"What do you mean? What happened?"

Feeling some relief in finally speaking the words to her face to face, Charlie Bay raised his head, took a deep breath and began another story.

"The marsh, the sand flats, the tidal water, all are beautiful places, rich and fertile places. They had been so for many generations. Two generations ago these places were thought to be useless...just places to dump waste from factories, from humans. Places to bury old cars and oil drums, to leave old boats and barges to rust and bleed into the river until they were no more. The fish left, the birds left, the clam beds closed and the marsh became like it was thought to be, useless. All that remained was the harbor in the Casco River, but it was filling up with sand and mud and the boats of summer people. Some of the people, who make decisions about these things, decided to dredge the river to make the harbor better for the summer people and for the fisherman. The marshland to the west and the north, the homeland of the Casco Nation, was the chosen place to dump the mud and the sand."

Margaret hung on each word.

"Decisions were made by American men and money. It was no good then."

Charlie Bay's explanation touched her passion for injustice. She was right where he expected her to be.

"The dredging piped all the sand and mud that they sucked up from the bottom of the river and harbor and took it to the western end of the marsh, filled it all in to make land along Rt.1. You know where the golf is?"

She knew the area and businesses along the highway and nodded.

"That's where they began dumping everything and from there...they worked their way east, back toward Eagle Island. The Western Door used to be shaped like the tip of a harpoon with prongs sticking out on each side and waterways and eddies running on both sides like this."

Balancing the Clementine crate on his thighs, Charlie Bay held up his hands before his face. With arms outstretched, he spread his fingers apart widely, palms toward her and touched his index finger tips together but not his thumbs. Peering through the opening, Margaret saw the pronged shape he formed. She nodded.

"After about eight months of filling up the marsh the engineers and the dredgers said that to hold the sand and keep the water away, all of these little rivers must be made into one river with branches from the north and south and the Western Door reshaped like this."

Bringing his fingers together, he tucked his thumbs over against his palms. This altered the shape to a narrow wedge and demonstrated the western tip of Eagle Island as she knew it.

"When they widened the channel on the north and south by cutting into the Western Door, the bones of my ancestors were torn from the earth. After the very first morning of digging and dredging, there were pieces of my people sprinkling the sand and burping up from the ground. They stopped only long enough for university Americans to come. Then the scrapping and probing began, by groups with shovels and picks and brushes. But it was digging all the same, like dogs scratching in the dirt for the bones of my grandfathers. It happened very fast, the tents and the tables, the bags and the boxes of bones, the papers and the promises to return everything to this place, their rightful place, with their people.

But that's not what happened. The study that was to put the bones in proper order and make a record for my people passed from months to years. More promises came with gifts and more letters with promises.

The circle of the dead has been broken. Too much time has passed. I no longer trust any of them. Theirs is not my world. And that's why I need your help. You are of a university. You know them. You are a writer."

In formal fashion, Charlie Bay stood up, walked over to Margaret and handed her the Clementine crate. In it she saw an unopened portable weather radio, clearly out of date, binoculars, apparently unused and some sheets of stationary with the letterhead of the Anthropology Department for the State University. Removing the letters from the bottom of the box, she skimmed their contents. One apparently came with the gift of the weather radio. The patronizing tone annoyed her. She searched through more pages for the name of the individual in charge of the Casco field research and found it. The head of the excavation project was Dr. Sandra Walsh. Without returning to his seat, Charlie Bay stood straight, his pants sagged and he followed her survey of the papers. As she lifted her head, he spoke, "Walsh, she's the university American you want. Walsh."

Margaret had no sense of the logistical complexities and the political implications of his request. All she had was an instinctual urge to leap, to do whatever he asked. But, she was aware enough to recognize that the distance between where she was as a playwright and what he needed, an attorney, was a big gap. The big gap didn't stop her from saying yes.

Less tense, Charlie Bay eased back into his chair, mindful of his urgency and her hesitancy. He became cautious. At least for today, he was not going further. He didn't say a word to her about his dream.

"I was chosen by my grandfathers to keep the dead of my people. I lost sight of my gift and let it slip away." He let his hands rest on his thighs, his shoulders rolled forward, his body still. Considering one another for a few moments in silence, neither was uneasy.

Charlie Bay was the first to move. He slapped his knees in unison, leaned forward and stood. As his back straightened, there was first a crack and then a moan. Gesturing for Margaret to set the crate on the floor and at the same time jerking his head toward the back door, he motioned for her to follow him. On the back porch, he slipped his bare feet into his shin high clamming boots, hobbled out the door and down the back steps with Margaret in tow. The fresh salt air felt good to both of them and was quick to renew conversation.

"How did you make the tape?"

"Bud Walker."

Margaret smiled. "He dropped the box off at my parent's house."

"You know, he graduated high school with you. He works on the fish pier at the co-op and fishes. He sure remembers you. It's your figure he remembers anyway, because I could tell by the smile on his face and the glint in his eyes. He was right, you turned out pretty good."

Charlie Bay mumbled to himself about sex and love.

"He also let me borrow the tape recorder; well gave it to me really. He said he didn't use it anymore. Learning which button did what wasn't easy. I almost gave the damn thing back to him. But, I got use to it, buttons, batteries and all."

As they walked past the south side of the house, out onto the bluff at the end of the island, Casco Point and the open ocean stretched eastward. Charley Bay removed his pipe and tobacco pouch from his breast pocket. Before packing the bowl he reflexively offered small pinches of tobacco to the four directions, then to the sky and to the earth while whispering an inaudible prayer. The ground leaves were carried on the wind. Studying him, Margaret saw a spiritual side she knew but didn't remember. Uneasy with her focus on his movements, he turned away and into the wind.

"The wind's picking up from the southwest, third day in a row ... pretty early for May. If this holds the water will warm and the lobsters will be running on shore a week or two sooner come the end of July."

It wasn't often that Charlie Bay made conversation about the weather. Margaret wanted to talk but, not about the weather. She eased off. Facing east and both squinting in the horizon's reflected light, they made their way down separate paths onto the rocky beach.

As the eastern tip of Eagle Island narrowed, it seemed the focal point in every view was a large solitary grey boulder. It was a waist high, arm wide rock with a concaved top among less than foot size sea worn flakes of slate and granite. Misplaced, unmatched and just barely licked by the ocean during storm surges, it was the bow pulpit of the island. It was where Molly spent hour upon hour, still and staring seaward. Both their thoughts recalled her silhouette against the water.

"How's she doing? I haven't seen her in a long time."

Margaret knew Charlie Bay meant Molly and was surprised he hadn’t seen her. She turned to his face. He had his pipe clenched between his teeth, the same spot as always, notched and brown.

"I'm not sure. It’s been a while...saw her only a few times before high school...none since then."

“Hmmm”, Charlie Bay murmured and let it drop.

A few moments later, they turned away from the Point and walked along the northern shore of the island, side by side, slices of sun and puffs of wind, now at their back. As they left the sea worn stones behind and meandered onto a sand-covered beach Charlie Bay spoke.

"For years, when I would walk along this beach and the sand flats too, I found those damn yellow golf balls from the driving golf. I'd dig them up all over the bars, never picked 'em up, but after awhile I got used to it. Never liked it, but got used to it." He spoke with a troubled voice. "You see the ocean doesn't care. She is an indifferent being who will pick up and drop off on the tide. It used to be golf balls. Now, it is the bones of my people."

She stopped walking, so did Charlie Bay one step later.

"At the beginning of last month, while I was digging on the bar, I uncovered the skull of one who had come before. I pierced the bone with my hoe. I broke it more than it had already been broken.

The dead from the Western Door are once more burping up from their earth, this time from cutting tide waters instead of scratching people. I can never accept either the ocean or the university Americans scattering the bones of my grandfathers. They're both too indifferent beings." He took a deep breath. He was angry.

"I've taken the bones that I found from the Western Door and moved them to a new place. I pray that it will be a safe place for all those who are to be returned to it. Now you and I must gather the missing and make sure that they are reburied."

Dignity and determination continued in his gate as they walked the shore line up to his fishing shack.

The shack was set on a small dock and work platform a few feet off the sand. It was scattered with barrels, stacks of wooden lobster traps and red and blue buoys. Next to the work dock was his beached dory. Its light tan hull and red bottom were as she remembered. Entering a path marked by a large tree stump that served as the anchor for the dory, they made the steep inland climb, back toward the house in single file. Margaret let Charlie Bay walk ahead. A short distance later, she caught him standing on a small rise near some blueberry bushes and looking west. It was a beautiful place.

"This is it."

It wasn't a question, she knew. There was no response from Charlie Bay.

"I'll help you Charlie Bay. I'll help you get the remains of your people back here, to the island."

Charlie Bay dipped his chin and squinted without a word.

Instead of heading back to Rt. 1 and her parent's home, Margaret found Rt. 9 and wound her way to the fishermen's co-op on the Casco River. She parked in the town lot and walked the half mile through the dunes to a public beach and open ocean. Rewriting *Overturn* had somehow fallen from the top spot on her list of summer priorities. She wasn't sure why. Sitting on the cool sand, she considered Charlie Bay. She said yes to his request and she meant it. But, she wasn't sure what yes meant. She watched the water. Charlie Bay was in the one spot.

That evening Margaret returned to her parent's home by default. She had expected to be on an early Sunday afternoon flight and taking a Bistro evening shift. Because of Charlie Bay, with a couple of rescheduling calls, she was out on the 8:05 in the morning and tonight crossing paths with her parents.

During the Philly years and on her own, she was more aware that her ability to dive into a situation on instinct alone took its emotional toll; generally fatigue and collapse. Charlie Bay Burningwater exhausted her. Having no idea of how or why, she took the physical drain as an outward sign of an internal bull's eye. Her capacity to integrate the experience was on overload and sleep was her answer.

Passing the refrigerator in the kitchen, Margaret remembered her parents planned to return in time for her mother's monthly Sunday night dinner date with friends from the nail salon. "Nail Gossip" was the notation written on the calendar stuck with a banana magnet to the freezer door. She assumed that her mother wasn't home, decided to leave on the microwave night light and shuffled toward the staircase.

As she approached the top of the steps, she saw the light in the hallway shining from the half open door of her father's study and heard the hum of his computer. Listening for the keyboard, she wondered if with luck, he was out to join business friends, at his golf club networking. He called them "Moose Hunts" and they usually coincided with "Nail Gossip". Tonight, she wasn't in the mood to be interrogated. Facing a carryover from adolescent curfew checks, she moved into the hall and found the gatekeeper at his post, waiting.

"Hey Margaret, how are you doing?"

Her head dropped, just what she hoped to avoid. But, it was still good to see him and in the hall she resigned herself to the inevitable. The thought that she was twenty-five and entitled to some measure of adult equality was her hope. She pushed open the six-panel door and peered inside, her father already moving to the doorway. Margaret stepped into the room. They hugged and with her chin on her father's shoulder, she looked around his space. It hadn't changed for years.

A large antique oak desk and leatherback swivel chair faced the door. They were set between two windows with long dark forest green drapes and white shades. Next to each window was a tall oak bookcase filled with file folders, binders and portfolios. There was not a hard cover, paperback or magazine anywhere in the room. On the floor was a red Oriental rug with one of its corners fixed by a brown leather winged chair and a brass floor lamp. A half dozen or so manila folders were strune at the circular base of the lamp. This room always made Margaret uneasy. It was not neutral territory. It was not the kitchen table and her mother was nowhere to be found. Her father kissed her cheek.

Jim Garret, a stalky man with natural jet-black hair, no grey at the temples despite entering his fifties, drifted back to the swivel chair and pointed to his computer, "Brand new laptop, not perfect but it's the best on the market. It’s wireless with the fiber optic cable to the router downstairs, plus that whereever card...you know. The thing runs like a rocket ship."

She smiled, expecting nothing less of her father than a rocket ship.

Jim Garret had a physical presence exuding strength and energy, the combination of genes and a home gym replaced twice in the past ten years. His outstanding business instincts, good management skills, terrific timing were enhanced by usually being in the right place at the right time. At any level, he observed and understood the reciprocal relationships between the players. This kept him where he enjoyed it most, behind the scenes, watching and building. Jim appreciated the monetary rewards of his success; quality education for his children, country club membership to soothe his passion for golf and the power associated with cash and assets. And within this strategy of construction, he never exceeded the bounds of buying the best and keeping a low profile.

Wondering out loud, "What happened to your old laptop?" were the first tired words that tumbled from Margaret.

"Donated to St. Mary's school, same as every year. Why, are you looking for a new one?" He didn't wait for a response. "Because you're due. I could order online for you and have it sent down to Philadelphia. Ya, I think it's about time for a new one. Yours has got to be almost two years old."

Again, she smiled at his words. Words which always indicated an eagerness to solve a problem, to buy something, to do something, to go somewhere and in a heartbeat to make everything better for one of his children. She shook her head no.

Without hesitation or any indication of disappointment, Jim reached down behind his chair next to the bookcase and picked up a plastic shopping bag from the floor. "I got this today, for you, if you're around this summer." As he spoke, he removed a top of the line GPS from the package. "The truck is a little old and the only vehicle without a GPS and I thought for travel it should have one. It has all the location features and if you end up commuting to the State House

Offices...." He was uncomfortable and his words trailed off knowing the plans, for him anyway, were still undecided. "I downloaded the satellite info and had the adapter put in the truck, so it's all set to go. All you have to do is plug it in." Reaching over his desk, he handed her the box. Margaret didn't have the heart to tell him she had voice activated GPS on her phone. So, she stepped up to the desk, took the gift to make him happy and understood it required her to talk. Questions were to follow.

"So what did you do today? You stayed the extra day." was his first. A subtle start, he was trying not to be too direct.

Margaret was waking up. "I drove out to Eagle Island to visit Charlie Bay Burningwater."

Taken aback, Jim left the thought of directing the conversation to Margaret spending the summer on a law school resume builder. Despite calmness, he was annoyed.

"Charlie Burningwater? Why did you go to see him?" Jim shook his head. "What in the world would you have to talk about with him?"

Within the ambiguities in the taxonomy of sin, Margaret was always very clear on this one; the Sin of Omission. GPS or not she had no intention of telling him much about anything.

"It had been so long since I'd seen the ocean, I thought I should. I ended up at the Casco River co-op so I drove over to Eagle Island. I saw Charlie Bay. He and I talked for awhile...a little about the old days when I was a kid, visiting him. He asked about Molly, how she was doing?" She hesitated, "Where is Molly? What ever happened to her?"

For days Jim Garret had been having this conversation in his mind hoping he would see his daughter. For days he had been planning how to get her permission to make the one phone call it was going to take to place her with the Governor's legal team, boost her resume and focus her career goals on law. Being a playwright was all well and good but, for Jim Garret, his daughter needed a profession. In his scenario, this was a key meeting. Now it was a conversation headed in a direction he never could have anticipated. Now he wasn't prepared. But, most of all, with the mention of Charlie Bay Burningwater, he was not happy.

Walking around to the front of his desk and motioning for his daughter to sit down, he leaned the back of his thighs against the oak edge and folded his arms across his chest as she slid into the winged back chair. His voice was soft, serious and loaded with emotion, "First of all, you need some background on Charlie Burningwater...he's one of a long list of people that Molly cared for and who misused her kindness. Molly was like that; she tried to help a lot of people like Burningwater, people who were just lost souls. She always seemed to attract them, people she felt needed her. She built a social circle of these kinds of people; all these lost souls...Charlie Burningwater is a manipulative drunk who only took from Molly and never gave to her in return."

Jim paused. It was obvious to Margaret Burningwater made her father angry.

“When your mother and I found out Molly was taking you on her trips to see these folks...ah, when she was taking you to see Burningwater, when we thought she was taking you to the ocean. Well, that's when she stopped taking care of you. That's when we hired a new nanny." Jim Garret was also familiar with the Sin of Omission.

"But what happened to her?"

Familiar with her unrelenting tone, Jim stood still and silent. He had lost. He wanted to leave without saying more but it wasn’t possible. It was time.

"Margaret, Molly was a sick women, depressed, confused. She became one of her own. She was broke, on and off medication, alcohol and in and out of the hospital. Finally I had her placed in the State Mental Hospital.”

“You had her committed?”

“I had to. She stopped eating...talking." After pausing, he spoke more softly, "She passed during your last year of college". His eyes looked to the floor.

"What? She died over four years ago and I never knew?" Her father didn’t respond. "How come you didn't tell me Molly was...?"

Waiting for her to finish, he finally answered in a low monotone "You had been away. I didn't want to have to explain why I was taking care of everything...." He raised his head, wrinkled his brow in an apologetic expression and stated clearly. "Margaret, there are some things I never told you. Molly was my half sister."

Looking into her father's watery eyes, Margaret knew, despite all her unanswered questions, their conversation was over.

Jim rolled open his palms, “Sorry Margaret.”

Without another word, her father left the room.

Chapter Three

One-way streets always gave Margaret trouble. It was routine for her to watch a destination, so close, disappear in the rear view mirror because she was following directions. Today was no exception.

Margaret watched in frustration as the Social Science building faded from view and section after section of metered visitor parking on the one-way street was filled. Anticipating the meeting with Dr. Walsh, she was anxious. The poor planning with campus directions and the GPS telling her, with a British accent, that it was recalculating wasn't making it any easier. Moving further from her destination and almost late, she decided to return to a faculty lot next to Dr. Walsh's office building. She was prepared to take the ticket and pay the fine. It was worth whatever the cost. Margaret parked in a spot reserved by a green and white sign for the Assistant Dean of the College of Social Sciences and wiped her moist palms on a napkin from under the driver's seat.

The meeting with Sandra Walsh was set up without deception but some ambiguity. By identifying herself as a researcher from the University of Pennsylvania and interested in the Casco skeletal collection, both true, she responded from experience to the questions from Dr. Walsh's secretary. Despite her vague and general answers, Margaret was given a time suitable for their overlapping schedules. Sandra Walsh planned to leave for the State of Washington and a summer research project in five days. This was her only day for office hours and Margaret planned to be in Ogunquit tomorrow working on *Overturn*.

As preparation, Margaret decided once the usual introductions were exchanged, she would be direct and ask up front for the immediate return of the Casco skeletal collection. Nervous but confident, she believed the less she knew about the political and academic ramifications of the situation the better. Charlie Bay Burningwater wanted the remains of his ancestors returned now. Her strategy was to keep it simple. For she and Burningwater, it was simple.

In the lobby, Margaret checked the directory and found Sandra Walsh's office in the Anthropology Department on the seventh floor of the eight story office and classroom high-rise. Glancing around as she walked to the elevators, she saw a stack of outdated daily university newspapers, a bulletin board with a flyer for last March's Spring break and tear away coupons for inexpensive contact lenses. The Greek letters scratched on the elevator doors caught her eye as she stood impatiently waiting for them to open. As she stepped into the elevator, the universality of academic life gave her a sense of security. Charlie Bay was right, she knew this world. He did not.

When the doors closed it hit her again. The loss came in waves, sometimes fast, without warning. She missed Molly. She missed someone who had been dead for more than four years. The measure of time meant nothing to Margaret. Her experience of Molly's death was the moment she heard the words. She was angry and edgy. To engage Dr. Sandra Walsh for the return of the Casco ancestral remains was welcomed.

In the Anthropology reception area, she announced her name to the secretary and apologized for being a few minutes late with the excuse of a parking problem. Dr Walsh's secretary was a thin-wristed woman with several large gold colored bracelets on each wrist. She was cordial and told her in a loud voice that it happened often. Hearing Margaret's answer to her question of a final parking spot, she laughed and joked about towing. Margaret forced a polite smile as the secretary escorted her into Sandra Walsh's office and was thankful the small talk ended. She worried about the towing.

Sitting in a wooden straight-back chair, one of three next to a round maple conference table, she was told Dr. Walsh was on her way and to make herself comfortable. Margaret was determined to remain focused; she refused coffee but used the smell of a fresh pot. As the secretary left the room, Margaret's eyes followed her through the open door with painted black block letters: Sandra Walsh, Ph.D., Chairperson, Department of Anthropology, Maine State University. From the door, she scanned the room.

It was not a large office but, it did have an alcove. Three of the walls were masked by oak and maple bookcases stacked with colorful hard covers and paperbacks. Loose journals and bound periodicals were scattered among the shelves and any available additional space was lined with artifacts and photographic memorabilia documenting a lifelong academic career. Dr. Walsh's desk was a simple wooden rectangular table with another straight back chair. The center of her desk was buried by a mound of papers. Student papers were piled in two small cardboard file boxes. One was on the left corner of the tabletop with a second on the floor to the right of the chair, each marked by course and number. Behind the desk, the fourth wall of the room was a series of glass panels framed in aluminum casings. There were two bird feeders, chest high, attached to the external glass surface by suction cups that symmetrically aligned with the corners of the desk. The most curious piece in the room for Margaret was a card catalog cabinet, well worn from years of library use, now apparently recycled to Dr. Walsh in obsolescence. It was situated at a right angle to the left-hand side of the table, and to Margaret's eye, clearly in the middle of the only corridor to the desk chair. About six of the fifty or so catalog drawers were open with a number of index cards tipped vertically.

Without a computer, a printer, a scanner, a copier or some other everyday generic box of technology that does something remarkable, this office was of a different time.

The alcove, between two bookcases of one wall, however, was home to two desktops, multiple laptops, printers, a scanner, cameras and carts all strung together with a bird's nest of cable and wire. It was a technical walk-in closet and it looked dangerous.

Sandra Walsh separated her two worlds without a door. As Margaret sat in the oak and unplugged, it appeared to her, the digital world Dr. Walsh tolerated, the analogue she cherished.

Edging closer to the peculiar card catalog, she read the labels on a row of drawers. Casco was printed on the front of three draws, one open and marked halfway through the tray by a vertical index card. As she leaned in for a closer look, she heard someone enter the room behind her. Startled, she tensed, sprang up and faced Dr. Sandra Walsh.

Sandra Walsh was a round woman with closely cropped gray hair and silver rimmed bifocals resting half way down her nose. She was wearing a tan full-length lab coat over a high button white cotton blouse and a mid-calf purple skirt. Her stomach bulged below the waistline. With her right hand extended, she burst toward Margaret. Her bright blue eyes darted from side to side and her lips parted in a broad smile. Margaret shook her hand and watched the anthropology professor speed around the room to deposit printed material, most of it journals and file folders, in various locations. In a broad sweeping arc, she placed file after file, in strategic positions. Along the way she spoke a quick personal introduction. As she placed the last collection on the table, she gestured for Margaret to be seated.

“I miss paper, bound journals...hard to find. If I hear from one more jackass publisher telling me this or that journal is going paperless, I’m going to horde, horde every bound journal I can get my hands on! These piles are going to get a lot bigger that’s for damn sure.”

Sandra was an individual of intelligence and intensity. Margaret liked her immediately.

"So Margaret, I'm glad we could get this meeting scheduled. As you may have heard from my secretary, I'm headed away from all this administrative chaos for the summer. Thank God." Sandra slapped the pile of papers as she spoke and then mumbled audibly, "I'd like to get away from it for good. But that's another matter. What's your interest in the Casco Collection?" Sandra sat down to listen.

Surprised at how fast she came to the point, Margaret removed a letter-sized envelope from her leather briefcase and leaned toward Dr. Walsh.

"I come at the request of Charlie Bay Burningwater to formally ask for the immediate return of all the bones of his ancestors, bones that were removed from their burial ground on Eagle Island."

At the end of her statement Margaret maintained eye contact and handed her the letter. It was the same message as a formal written request and signed by Charlie Bay. The block letters, in pen, were much larger than the text. As Sandra Walsh read the letter, Margaret perceived a change in the pallor of her unmade cheeks from rose to white. Margaret's cheeks were flush.

After reviewing the content of the letter, Sandra Walsh folded the single page, inserted it into the envelope and placed it on the table. She collected her academic demeanor, sat back in her chair and delivered a direct professional response. It was a familiar one.

"The policy of this University, as well as the anthropological research community in general, has always been one of repatriation considerations in the context of active ongoing research. That is to say, that if a collection housed at this institution was affording scholars and students the opportunity for continued study and publication, which resulted in significant contributions to the literature, then the retention of the collection in question was more than justified. As you may or may not be aware, I have a personal and professional affinity for the Casco Collection. I was a part of the excavation and the occasion yielded a specification that has defined my career. Along with colleagues, I have written numerous papers and designed many research projects focused on the investigation and the reconstruction of various aspects in the lifeways of the Casco. The Casco skeletal material has been an enormous resource for many very interesting and significant contributions to the literature. The difficulty has been and is true today, as new investigatory methods and technologies are developed, the research intensifies and productivity increases. The advances in CAT scan availability, 3-D cone beam technology, chemical analysis and SEM techniques make the sample even more valuable than it was forty years ago."

Sandra was successful. Margaret was intimidated. She was clearly out of her discipline. She did the only thing possible; she bluffed.

"The request is a simple one and despite all that you've said, it stands. Should you choose not to respond immediately and favorably, we are prepared to take further actions."

Margaret raised her eyebrows and implied in her tone and body language that there was a team of legal professionals supporting them with a specific, well-planned strategy. Margaret and Charlie Bay had neither. Thinking only about leaving before her stage presence collapsed, she knew this wasn't going any further.

From the other side, this late in her career, Sandra Walsh also had no choice, she bluffed. But she wasn't as good an actor.

"I am not in the position to make the decision. It will involve all of the powers that be in the University system, so, we will need to talk again. Call me on Friday. I will be at this number all day."

Margaret nodded, took her card and left the office. A pensive Dr. Walsh closed the door behind her.

Sandra Walsh received her doctoral degree in the early sixties, as the only woman in a strong anthropology program. Even though her dissertation amounted to nothing more than a very long and dry biography of Ales Hrdlicka, her presence and contributions were, at the time and in that environment, remarkable achievements. Ironically, the desire, which she acquired during her early years in academic life, for the equal opportunity and professional recognition of women, was initiated in researching the contributions to anthropology of Hrdlicka. He was a man who saw no place for women in the field. To her credit and with astute political shrewdness, Sandra looked beyond the Victorian worldview of the physician and physical anthropologist. She focused on the methods and techniques he developed for the discipline of physical anthropology, how he brought it into the fold of respected scientific investigation and carved a place for himself and others at the Smithsonian during the first half of the twentieth century.

First and foremost, Hrdlicka was an avid collector. Collecting human crania and skeletal material from burial sites all over the world, his primary focus was North America. At the time of his death in 1943, some fifteen thousand Native Americans had their skeletal remains housed at the Smithsonian as a direct result of his efforts. Sandra Walsh's insight into Hrdlicka's contribution to anthropology spawned the clarity and direction of her own vocation. She recognized at an early stage of her career that it was necessary to not only collect and analyze specimens as physical anthropologists had done in previous decades, but to also synthesize, interpret and reconstruct past lifeways from the bones of those who came before. Her affection for the Casco Skeletal Collection was genuine. It was the opportunity.

Sitting alone in her office, Sandra remembered the day she received the call from the project director of the Army Corps of Engineers on Eagle Island like it was yesterday. At the time, she was the only anthropologist in the Sociology Department of Maine State University. There was no state archeologist and one was not appointed until three years later, in nineteen-seventy. Placed in charge of the excavation and in control of the specimens from the Casco Nation burial site by default, she was given the task of harvesting, cataloging and archiving the human skeletal material from what was perceived to be a significant burial ground of some antiquity. The Corps of Engineers outlined the boundaries for their reconstruction of the western tip of Eagle Island and she had ten days in which to clear the field of human remains. They were ten days that began a forty year journey linked to the Casco Collection.

In an academic climate of publish or perish, she thrived with her research of the Casco and produced a succession of well received papers on the diet, diseases, dentition and lifeways of the inhabitants of the region surrounding Eagle Island. Casco studies on dental enamel as an indicator of environmental stress carved a place in the anthropological literature for the University as a research center on Native American skeletal material and established her as a recognized authority.

With academic success came leverage. Her positions and actions, in the late seventies and early eighties, on admissions committees and editorial boards altered the gender injustices, which she identified as a graduate student. They were also altered by time. Sandra's initial zeal for equal opportunity was tempered by a commitment to produce the highest quality of scholarly research with individuals of either gender having similar goals and standards. She viewed her own progress and her profession's in equal opportunity with great satisfaction. Her ease in many arenas, with diverse groups of colleagues did not go unnoticed. In nineteen-ninety Dr. Walsh was named Chair of Anthropology department and a year ago she was offered an Associate Deanship. All of this she took in stride, never letting administration disrupt the primary focus of her career, her one true passion; the Casco Collection.

Recently however, she came to realize, the work recognized as her greatest academic strength, was a source of personal anguish. The Casco Collection troubled her. With increasing frequency, she found herself searching for a means to address the haunting responsibility for and the possibility of, Casco repatriation.

As a method of coping, Sandra outwardly attributed the whole struggle to guilt acquired through a strong parochial education. She had learned guilt and was good at it, Casco included. During times of reflection, she frequently thanked, with expletives, her parents and the nuns. At the same time, she acknowledged a genuine inner need for reconciliation. Hunting for the opportunity to attain it, Margaret's request from Burningwater was now a part of the search.

Dr. Walsh slid to the edge of the straight-backed wooden chair, dragging it along the floor as she leaned and stretched toward her office door. Opening the door only a few inches and balancing herself with the knob, she called to her secretary.

"Connie, get Max Sorensen on the phone. I have to speak with him today, so I want you to keep trying until you get him. Try Boston first."

Closing the door, she sat back in her chair, stared blankly at the floor and waited.

After Margaret turned off the ignition and set the brake, she picked up the fifty dollar parking ticket that she had shoved up onto the dashboard before leaving the Assistant Dean's parking spot. Folding the ticket into her pocket, she thought how the fine for the violation and money in general, in Charlie Bay's quest, were irrelevant. Margaret was uncertain about how much to tell Burningwater. She spotted his truck on the other side of the fishermen's co-op lot. Walking to the pick up, she was replaying her meeting with Dr. Walsh. She toyed with different angles in the presentation to Charlie Bay, each one positive. She was unsettled and thought a backup plan was needed if Sandra Walsh and the University continued to stall. But, backup plans implied lawyers and she felt it was best to leave lawyers for another time. Margaret knew Charlie Bay wanted no part of another plan. It wouldn't come up, not today.

The afternoon sun felt good on her face as she leaned against the warm hood and searched the harbor for a sign of Burningwater. The air was easy to breathe as it bounced off the river. Unfamiliar with the schedules of the waterfront, she decided that finding his truck was enough for now and sat on the bumper to watch for him in the harbor. Margaret used the break to consider the library catalog cabinet in Sandra Walsh's office and dictated a description into her cell recorder. She rambled on about the piece as a prop until his battered blue skiff appeared off the stern of a much larger lobster boat. With oars gently breaking the surface to direct the boat, Charlie Bay was guiding the small skiff effortlessly to shore. He sat with his back to the bow, his face away from hers. Seeing the labors of a workday in two five-gallon buckets of clams nestled in the boat as it struck the beach, she was hesitant to approach him. As she stepped away from the truck her movement caught Charlie Bay's eye and he nodded. The compressed and curved body of the clam digger was all business as he pulled the bow up onto the sand and walked to the pickup. After backing the truck down the beach, he looped the eye of the bowline over the ball of his trailer hitch and dragged the skiff crunching and grinding its way above the high watermark into the dunes. He was loading the two buckets into the back of the pickup when she gave him the condensed version.

"I saw Sandra Walsh this morning and gave her your letter. I am supposed to call her back on Friday for an answer."

She waited for a response. There was none. Charlie Bay was an angry and impatient man. His eyes squinted out onto the harbor. His lips pursed as he took his pipe and tobacco pouch from his breast pocket. Clenching the stem between his teeth, he pinched a small bit of tobacco with his thumb and index finger and made an offering in the four directions, then to sky and earth. The prayer was inaudible and she waited. As he filled his pipe and lit it, Margaret continued with more difficult news.

"The other thing I have to tell you is that Molly has passed away." She looked up toward his eyes. "She died almost five years ago. I'm sorry that you didn't know sooner."

The muscles in his cheeks flexed repeatedly as he bit down against the pipe stem. Continuing to stare at the water, he asked, "Where's she buried?"

Margaret's eyes filled with tears. For the first time sorrow overcame anger. She had no idea where Molly was buried. She turned her head away from Charlie Bay and tried to control her tears.

"I don't know."

Chapter Four

It took Sandra's secretary three days to find the elusive Maximilian Kolbe Sorensen. Sandra Walsh was not happy. The delay meant she had to reschedule her flight west. When she finally spoke with Max on Thursday night, she arranged to meet him the following Tuesday at her home in Maine and gave him no information. As ridiculous as it seemed to her, he was entrenched for the Memorial Day weekend with his son and two other college athletes somewhere in the Mid-Atlantic States for an NCAA Lacrosse Tournament. She had very little patience with and even less understanding of sports, the game of lacrosse was a complete unknown to her. However, Max was the biological anthropologist she wanted for the reburial and waiting for him was all she had.

There were many reasons why Sandra Walsh picked Max Sorensen to implement her abrupt decision to repatriate the Casco skeletal collection. Two dominated her thinking; instinct and trust. Her instinct told her there was something in him, some intangible that made him the one and she trusted him, heart and soul. However a worry and sometime problem was the characteristic of his personality she perceived as both a gift and a curse. Max disappeared. In his nature, without conscious choice or intention, he was often so taken by a concept, a project or his passion that the world around him no longer existed. It was invisible and irrelevant. She identified this trait as the primary factor in the disintegration of his personal life and his inability to obtain a tenured track university faculty position. As for the repatriation of the skeletal collection that comprised her life's work, she needed him to disappear and get it done. Like it or not, she stayed until Tuesday.

Heading north on the New Jersey Turnpike, Max was a half hour behind the morning rush hour traffic into New York City. He was relaxed and reliving the weekend with his youngest son. It was a good weekend; with laughter, with friends and with Max paying the bills. He felt happy, young and even as if he were, at times, one of the guys. But knowing he was the father, the financial resource and old kept his daydream in check. Max enjoyed the tournament, even though his knowledge of lacrosse was limited and acquired by observation. He never played. But, on occasion, he felt the athletic experiences of his son as coming close to being his own.

This was the second consecutive year they attended the Lacrosse National Championship weekend. Max hoped this and other tournaments around the East Coast were now father and son traditions. Anticipating the chance to watch his son play in regional games, he was looking forward to the summer's Connecticut Lacrosse Tournament and in October, Baltimore's Fallball Tournament. All of this made Max, the fan and the father, smile as he cruised the highway in his faded ultramarine blue '99 Volvo sedan.

Just shy of the City, he was approaching a well-established family tradition, sometimes bittersweet, but always a necessary stop; the Vince Lombardi rest area on the New Jersey Turnpike. Glancing at his watch, he calculated his estimated time of arrival at the Lombardi. He also figured how much time he had for food and when to be back on the road to make the scheduled late afternoon meeting with Sandra in Maine. For Max, time was linear, divided into a sequence of events and for the most part, he was totally dedicated to each moment. The increments of his time fell between the extra few minutes on his snooze alarm and the fifteen weeks of a semester. Today, Max thought he had a twenty-minute block to eat but he was unsure about the remaining ten weeks of summer. The ten indeterminate weeks of his teaching hiatus bothered him as time uncertain.

When Max turned onto the ramp for the Lombardi, without his wife and without their two squirming boys of younger years moaning for the men's room, it hit him. He was alone. But still, it was a family tradition. This stop in

New Jersey gave him the constancy he sought, even now, in solitude. So on the marshland surrounded by ten foot Cat and Nine Tails, he drove to a spot in the car parking lot and for this segment of time, Max Sorensen's world was in order. Once outside the car, he stretched skyward with a grunt, tugged at his sagging pants and started across the hard top to the entrance of a familiar place in an unfamiliar territory.

Max had reached the stage in his life where he was getting crusty on the outside and soft in the middle. His waist and age increased in parallel increments. Despite his denial, there was no going back. From time to time, he made halfhearted attempts to keep his weight in check during the non-holiday intervals of a calendar year. As a result, he found new appreciation for pretty much every ethnic holiday celebration. Like other men in their fifties, his chin fought gravity and his hips rolled at the crest enough to be noticed even by his own subjective standard. Max's perception of his appearance and his appearance to others were two different and distinct views. Describing the color of his thinning gray hair as brown, he thought of himself as much closer to thirty than seventy.

As he walked across the lot, the pain in his back, knees and ankles from the past four hours of driving was overridden by hunger. An early start made this mid-morning stop lunch, and he knew exactly what he was going to have; dogs. Max Sorensen subsisted on a diet dominated by hot dogs. For a good portion of his adult life, even through the married years, the true staple of his menu was the hot dog. The initial attraction was utilitarian. For him, it was an efficient food; four bites, in any environment and it was gone. With cheese and ketchup he argued to anyone who would listen, it contained the four major food groups. Now, completely focused on food, as he approached the Lombardi building, his mouth watered, his stomach called and his pace quickened.

The sun was warm as he stood on the walkway entrance to the red brick Georgian Colonial. With one dog done, he savored each bite of the second. People passed before him. Diverse human beings surrounded him. His love of the Vince Lombardi was renewed. He was the anthropologist, the consummate participant observer, planted at the entryway of a turnpike stop and watching people. For Max this rest area was a remnant of an American assimilation lineage. It was a link to Ellis Island. Travelers were passing through, headed for somewhere, anywhere in America. It didn't matter. He finished eating and watched. To him, participant observation was almost as good as skeletal material. He delighted in observing America's ethnic faces, a country with people from all over the world, looking like they came from all over the world. People seeking something: opportunity, education, belief, wealth and most of all American stuff. Sitting off to one side on the steps, he studied the physical characteristics of the passersby and thought of great American stuff: land, homes, cars, debt, credit cards, lap tops, flat screen LCDs, tablets and smart phones. Revisiting an old and favorite hypothesis, he considered how rapidly generational assimilation homogenized cultural diversity and American stuff was the medium. He thought about the irony in Coach Lombardi's drive to win, how much these individuals milling around him were driven to win and whether or not the great American mean was a victory. As usual, he gave himself a headache. Walking back to the car overwhelmed by the distraction, he was at least full. Settling back into a warm worn leather driver's seat, he wondered what was on the mind of his mentor and his friend, Sandra Walsh. He wondered what the summer held.

The route from the highway to Sandra's home was like other parts of the Maine coastline, fixed with landmarks from four centuries of European settlement and fresh with the promise of new enterprise. Even though Max hadn't visited the area for five or six years, he remembered the way until he was distracted by the smell of the ocean. The sea breeze renewed his tired body. As he rolled down the window and drew in the salt air, he lost his focus and missed the turn to Sandra's. But, he kept going east to the sea because it didn't matter. He was early, restless and six hours after the hot dogs, hungry. Scanning the streets, a small seasonal front yard fried clam stand caught his eye. Maybe it was the salt air or maybe it was the anxiety forever associated with the chair of his dissertation committee but, whatever the reason, fried food was the solution. With a pint of clams in crumbs and a side order of onion rings, he wove his way through the narrow roads until he found an access to the beach. It was a long day's drive and he hadn't been to the ocean for almost a year.

The cool, fine white sand felt good against the soles of his bare feet as he walked to a large driftwood log and sat down cradling two grease spotted containers. No drink, no ketchup, no utensils, just salt and he devoured the contents of both boxes. Full again, he stared toward the open ocean; eyes fixed on the horizon. The beach on a weekday, late in the afternoon and so early in the season was deserted in every direction. He burped freely and wondered if he should have taken an antacid before the food. Then he wondered if he should take one before the meeting with Sandra and his part in a project unknown.

Regardless of what Sandra had in mind, Max was concerned about being committed to more writing. Writing didn't come easily for him. He acknowledged its necessity, but found it to be an intense and laborious task. Max didn't like to write. He had been putting off writing all year. The summer was supposed to be scheduled as a time to catch up and complete two research papers on his field site and laboratory work with Nubian skeletal material. The one redeeming aspect, in generating these publications, was their focus on a location and a skeletal collection he enjoyed.

The core of a rather erratic academic career was Max's research in the Nile Valley. The lives and social organization of the people of pre-dynastic Egypt intrigued him. The attraction to identify, reconstruct and understand the lifeways of individuals with a complex and stratified society existing seven thousand years ago remained constant in an otherwise meandering career. The current aspect of his Nubian study was no exception. The non-metric trait analysis of the physical characteristics of the region's inhabitants supported his hypothesis of an elite ruling class in place as precursors to the dynasties of the pharaohs. An aspect of the research that excited Max was the change in analysis methods afforded by the advance in technologies. Non-metric traits, the unique physical characteristics of individuals which were interpreted as evidence of an isolated gene pool, possibly a ruling class, had the potential to be traced with DNA. All the years of recording and analyzing the lumps and bumps on bones were, in some cases, verifiable with DNA. For Max, it was a great time to be a scientist. His mind was racing with a new project, using DNA samples from archived skeletal collections. He intended to trace the migratory patterns along the Nile, beginning in the Sudan and progressing to Cairo, by plotting gene flow. But, he knew all too well the principle that was so often his downfall; he had to finish one project, including the writing, before he was able to start another. Troubled by the sense that he was about to be interrupted, he rubbed his distended stomach, burped again and considered how food was becoming the focus of his days.

Two large suitcases stood adjacent to the front door as Max entered the winterized cottage. Sandra Walsh called this small frame house, with a slightly larger lot, just one block from the ocean, home for the last forty years. The water was visible through a row of cottages from one corner of the backyard. You had to stand on a chair to see it and Max knew the spot.

The inside of Sandra's home was well worn and comfortable. On the first floor, a large main living area was decorated like an early twentieth century reading room, oak cases and cabinets, every available space filled with books, journals, and papers. Bolstered by Sandra's warm embrace, in this environment Max was at ease before the door closed. As she led him to a stuffed beige chair in the combination living room-study-office, he felt good, even relaxed. Without any hesitation, Sandra sat opposite Max in a rocker a few feet away. She made no offers of cordiality and came right to business. He was neither surprised nor offended.

"Max, I never told you or anyone else the whole story of the Casco excavation. I know you are familiar, or at least you should be familiar with the material, because I made you read all of my research. And I know it was a long time ago, but what you recall about the Casco doesn't matter as long as you recognize how much that skeletal collection has meant to me. It has been my life's blood and it is time to find a way to put those bones and all that goes with them to rest."

Max was lost but didn't speak. Sandra was boiling with energy. He knew she wasn't going to stop until he received the full measure of what was on her mind. Without any expression of confusion, he listened, no longer relaxed.

"I'll never forget that first day. Max, there were bones everywhere! When the Army Corp of Engineers took off the sea grass on the northwest corner of Eagle Island, it was like they were jumping out of the ground. My heart was pounding hard as hell. My dissertation research on Hrdlicka took on new life and I understood how he must have felt on the Aleutian Islands when he was collecting specimens. All that I could think was gather, gather...gather and record. We had so little time. The engineers gave us only a few days and it was a frenzy of gather and record with whomever I could roundup on short notice. But, you have to remember, it was the late sixties, the methods were weak, protocols varied and people were scattered all over the place but the harvest...the harvest was wonderful. And I knew it was going to be great from the moment I laid my eyes on the tip of that island. In that instant, I saw what that collection could become, what it could mean and from then on, my career has been dedicated to the fulfillment of our obligation to those bones; to insure that the Casco story was told. I had to tell the story of a people who were basically rubbed out!

The problem is; I am not done. But, it's done. It is done because of the law; the law, Max."

Sitting back in her chair, Sandra wondered whether she made any progress in convincing herself, let alone Maximilian Kolbe Sorensen, a colleague and more importantly a friend that the law was the reason for her forthcoming request.

For his part, Max wasn't sure what was going on and he wanted more information. He was certainly familiar with the Native American Grave Protection and Repatriation Act and its five-year compliance deadline to return skeletal collections. Using the acronym, he figured he'd let her go some more.

"NAGPRA?"

"Yes and I have a request for reburial and yes it has been well over five years. The request comes from a remnant, one member of the once large Casco Nation.

When we were doing the excavation, with trowels and shovels, disorganized manpower and all sorts of equipment he was one of the few Casco in the area. He sat poised on top of the island knoll watching us harvest his past. And there we were bustling around flush with scientific promise for the future. He was there day after day; Charlie Bay Burningwater. Last week he made a formal request for the return of all the Casco skeletal material. The man is a known lineal descendant."

The Native American Grave Protection and Repatriation Act required the expeditious return by Federal agencies, museums and institutions of Native American remains and associated funerary objects when requested by lineal descendants, by tribal members or by other individuals asserting some degree of cultural affiliation. The NAGPRA legislation gave the strongest recognition for repatriation to lineal descendants. In the years since the law's enactment, litigation delayed the return of material from some institutions by exploiting the ambiguity of the term cultural affiliation. However, the courts were quick and consistent in their support of return based upon lineal descendency. The precedent established in the judicial system made Sandra's legal options non-existent and Max knew it immediately.

"Max, we don't have a leg to stand on. Without an immediate and definitive response this will be costly and a public relations nightmare for the University. I am committed to the Washington project for the summer so here is what I want. I want you to handle the skeletal inventory and the reburial for me."

Sandra did not give Max a chance to respond. "The lab space was set up on Friday, you can stay here for as long as required and I am only a call or an email away if you need me. All my numbers: cell, office, email ...all of it's on my desk." She paused and then continued in a very unbusiness-like tone. "Max I need you to do this for me."

The look on her face expressed the reciprocal relationship, which existed between Max and Sandra through the years. He owed her and it was time to repay. He got the message but his debt was not to be repaid without an argument.

"It's like burning books! I love books!"

The words shot from his mouth with the thought of performing such a repulsive task. As always, he spoke before he considered the depth of her request and the depth of their relationship.

Anticipating the need to vent his frustrations with the concept and implications of repatriation, she hoped for a logical and rational discussion to follow. Her first expectation was correct. Max was off on a verbal tirade. Having had no idea for how long, she wondered how to pace the conversation. Her flight was in three hours.

"Sandra you know that this contradicts everything that I believe as a scientist. How in the world could you, you of all people, ask me to do such a thing? You can't be serious about me....I abhor the thought of putting those bones back in the ground. You are asking me to torch a library." Max leaned forward in his chair, his face wrinkled with an incredulous expression and his outstretched arms begged for an alternative. "Just think of the wealth of information that material holds; the stories, with the right technologies and in the right hands, new stories that will jump out at us again and again. Those bones still have a lot to tell us, you and all the researchers to come after you. You've just begun to uncover the secrets of the Casco lifeways. Now you are willing to bury them away. Think of the bigger picture here; we are a part of the European migration that ruthlessly wiped out millions of Native Americans. Our European ancestors destroyed their homes, their traditions, and their lives. We have exterminated culture after culture.

It's only been four hundred years since a way of life that existed for maybe three or four thousand years was ruined. Eliminated! You've only been working with that collection for forty years; think of what we'll learn in the next forty or eighty or the next hundred years from those bones. We've an obligation to reconstruct and understand what our ancestors destroyed! How can you turn your back on such a responsibility? Hell, now we're; because you're dragging me into it, we're going to rub it out again!" He took a breath but he wasn't done. "Sandra you know laws are just social constructs. They can be changed, amended, skirted, or even broken but this; what you have and what it can be, this is an irreplaceable treasure of human existence. This is something that, once in the ground, will be no more forever."

She loved his passion. The driving force in Max's life was a quest for understanding; an understanding of those who came before, who they were. How they lived. What they believed. What gave their life meaning and what was their relationship to the world around them. All of which, Sandra found ironic in a man who, at times, seemed so disconnected from the world around him; a world which appeared to be passing him by. As she listened to his plea, she took consolation in his passion, a search for understanding in the process of human existence and the torment in his own. It was also her passion but it was a different path.

Before Sandra responded, Max began again. "You know all this skeletal material is simply objective data, signs in the archeological record like any other artifact." He was less emotional and more logical in his rebuttal. "The spirit which gave the organic components its humanness departed with death. The remains are inanimate and quantifiable materials. The skeletal remnant is this objective vessel which once housed the being. Now, it simply endures to tell the story. And don't forget, the tools that allow the story to unfold are growing by leaps and bounds. The techniques for replicating DNA sequences have opened the door, in just the last five years or so, for me to trace Nubian lineages in ways that I never dreamed possible. And best of all, from archived skeletal collections! Think of what lies ahead for the Casco. Sandra, please don't ask me to bury it away." Max was annoyed that he was in her debt and that repayment superseded science.

Sandra responded in the context of her initial position; the law. But, she didn't repeat the NAGPRA requirement that all archived skeletal material of known tribal lineage be repatriated to descendants within the five years. Nor did she state that the University, at her direction, had intentionally missed the deadline by years and years. Checking her watch, she gave him a different tack and perspective.

"Max do you remember the Settlement Act of 1980, that whole land dispute and claim with the Passamaquoddies and the Penobscots, the one made against the State of Maine? How the Tribes laid claim to thousands and thousands of acres of Maine land based on past treaties. And how, in most people's mind, they won; coming away with land, money and among other things Federal Recognition as Tribal Nations?"

Max was familiar with the case and the resulting Settlement Act. He smiled and nodded in affirmation that some Native Americans finally got something in compensation for the long-standing injustices. Remembering that the two tribes received considerable amounts of land, money and only lost gambling privileges, he nodded.

"Well, with all the notoriety and recognition afforded the Passamaquoddies and the Penobscots, it is important to remember that there are three Federally Recognized Tribes in Maine. Don't leave out the Casco.

Because of their continuous presence in the region since European contact, on land which nobody else wanted, they also argued successfully for federal recognition but a few years after the Passamaquoddy and Penobscot Settlement Act. They used the same strategy in citing the Non-intercourse Act, and that somehow the State of Maine either took land or brokered land deals of Indian Territory illegally. But the Casco, very shrewdly I might add, went through the Bureau of Indian Affairs for federal recognition. There was no cash or land claim. It was interesting, that whole thing. It's kind of a mystery how that all happened so quietly, no press, no publicity.

The Casco population numbers were much higher in the first half of the twentieth century, then dropped dramatically. By the time of their federal recognition, whole family lineages had died off and there were just a handful of Casco left. You know it was the same old story. They were relocated, assimilated into other Native American groups or the State's mainstream. The small number of Casco, who chose to remain through those years, were politically and legally passive, almost non-existent. The only exception was this BIA federal recognition that came out of the blue.

But to the point, the Casco have always been considered, throughout the historic record and by our current standards, as impoverished fishermen; the remains of an indigenous group of predominantly marine hunter-gatherers destined to disappear, become extinct. Because they were in such a dramatic state of decline in the second half of the century, the Settlement Act, along with all those attorneys arguing for money and land, passed them by. But their federal recognition stands as powerful as any other tribe's, even though they haven't used its strength, until now, until Burningwater. The law says that as federally recognized they get the bones no matter what the size is of the tribe, even if it's just this one member, Charlie Bay Burningwater. They clearly have the law on their side Max, that's all it takes."

Twirling his wedding ring with the thumb and index finger of his right hand, Max slumped in his chair with a facial expression and the body language of a man in submission. Sandra, familiar with the look, was quick to take advantage and outlined her request.

"The lab space for the inventory has been set up at Jerry Moore's old office and archive on the South campus. It will be quiet and away from the summer school traffic. The buildings aren't much, surplus Quonset huts donated to the University, but all the equipment that you will need for the inventory and packaging is in place. The portion of the collection, which was in my lab, has already been moved and all the other lab site locations, specimen ID numbers per site and contact people are on the Casco CD file waiting for you. I need you to round up the sections of the collection, which are currently under study in various labs around the Northeast. Most will be shipped, one or two you might have to pick up. There are seven inventories from those sites that need verification. Once you have all the material logged back in, it's the usual packaging; bones wrapped in unprinted newspaper, each individual numbered, all biodegradable stuff, no plastic and the outside of the box labeled with sex and age of the contents to aid in any custom or ceremony. There's really nothing new, Max. The problem will be compliance with immediate return during the summer. You may have to do some traveling to make sure it all comes together. So you stay here, sit the house and I'll leave you a credit card for the house and road trips. I realize that it's probably too much to ask for you to keep receipts, but please try. And we'll settle up when I return for the reburial."

He smiled when she noted his poor reputation with credit, but otherwise, he waited.

Max was waiting for the reason why she chose him to perform a task better suited to a grad student or post-doc. Sandra also knew this look. For a mutually uncomfortable moment she did not respond until the quiet obliged her to speak. Leaving the rational of the law and searching in areas of herself, to which she rarely adverted, she struggled with her words.

"Maybe it's guilt? I stretched the ambiguity in the relationship with Casco and the use of the Collection many, many years…to the point where maybe I believed they wanted us to keep...keep it indefinitely. Ah hell, maybe it's my good old genetic Irish guilt making me feel that I have done something wrong, that it's obvious they wanted the specimens returned and I should have done it years ago. I may have made a mistake and I need protection. This repatriation has to be smooth and without incident, political or otherwise. I need you to resolve this for me."

Sandra Walsh, the professional had never addressed or expressed her guilty feelings regarding the Casco. She was relieved. Confession had its place, even to Max. She said no more but her relief was short lived. Sandra Walsh knew that she stretched and manipulated the NGPRA law in her study of the Casco bones. She recognized that she exploited the ambiguity and passivity of the Casco people, what was left of them. But, it was her most recent insight that stirred her soul. She had obviated Casco beliefs. She denied them. Sandra Walsh violated a part of the Casco she chose not to understand. Casco beliefs exist; she knew it and she repeatedly chose to desecrate them. This she shared with no one. It was for the resolution of this quiet and ironic atrocity she needed help. To persevere in her search for reconciliation, she needed, of all people, Max Sorensen.

The extent of Max's perception into her turmoil was the simple misplaced thought that self-doubt was not a sole possession of middle aged men. With very little compassion for Sandra's torment, he gave it another try from a different angle.

"Did I ever tell you my plan for my body when I die?"

She was confused by the tangential response, shook her head no and implied she didn't care.

"If I'm physically interesting enough I plan to be dissected. But, if it is an ordinary run of the mill death, I'd like to go straight to having my flesh boiled off. You know, my bones cleaned and bleached, put in a box and sent off to join a skeletal collection somewhere. Maybe here!"

Sandra, on edge, burst into nervous laughter. Max continued.

"I'm serious, because when I'm dead, it doesn't matter. I know what's left is not me. It's just data."

Controlled, she answered, "Max, you mean you believe what is left, is just data."

He stared at the now demanding expression in her eyes and twirled his wedding ring.

The early arrival of Sandra's cab to the airport was a welcome sight to both of them. He never said yes to her request but no was impossible. Their good-bye was genuine and heartfelt with Max assuring Sandra he planned to keep the appointment already scheduled with Margaret Garret for the next morning. She also gave him very specific diplomatic instructions for what was expected to be the follow-up meeting with Charlie Bay Burningwater. He listened but had no intention of taking her direction and she knew it.

Alone in the house, Max sat at her desk and set up his laptop. He scrolled through the files on her memory stick and a CD for all of the information necessary to repatriate the Casco. Also on the desk was her credit card. Sandra was organized. He thought of her as an intense, focused and singular thinker; one direction, full throttle, no brakes. And that quality he knew to be a saving force in his career and in his life, somehow always roaring in when he needed it most, grabbing him for the ride. Picking up the plastic card, he smiled at how difficult it must have been for her to leave him with uncontrolled access to money.

His record was not good; poor budgeting and poor management. Threatened by his own limitations Max, years ago, gave himself a general absolution for his financial inadequacies, attributing it to no math skills, but that didn't stop him from spending. Everything Max owned was borrowed and Sandra knew it. To leave the credit card was significant; to leave the data files was leaving her career.

Early that evening, Max took a long walk on the beach and distracted himself with the cool moderate northwest wind and small curling waves. Wading in the shallows made his feet numb. When he returned to the house he performed his usual ritual in the face of confusion. He got a beer, which was always in Sandra's refrigerator, a jar of pasteurized cheese spread, which wasn't, a box of salted crackers, and the TV remote.

Two hundred and seventy-three channels and not one held his attention. He was searching for Barbara Stanwyck on old movie channels. During the past two or three years, he developed an affinity for early Barbara Stanwyck films and an attraction to the young Barbara Stanwyck. Maybe it was the curve of her hips or maybe it was the smooth profile from her forehead past the tip of her chin to the nape of her neck. Whatever the attraction, he found it perplexing that he was sexually drawn to an image of a vibrant young woman who, off screen, had been dead for years. Generally, he let the oddity ride because he enjoyed her energy and found her beauty in black and white soothing when he was stressed. Not as soothing however, as cold beer, saltines and high sodium cheese spread.

Gazing at the food on the coffee table in front of him, he thought of how repulsive the combination was to his wife, who viewed the ritual as slightly more acceptable than a barn yard salt lick.

Max had not seen his wife in almost seven months. He drifted through the divorce four years ago to clarify the monetary chaos, but viewed their marriage as continuing in separation. He kept wearing his wedding ring. Twirling it occasionally but with no intention of taking it off. Max didn't know what happened in the dissolution of their relationship, other than he was impossible to live with, never satisfied, too quick to jump to the next project, the next town or the next thing that was going to turn his life, their lives around in a weekend. Irreconcilable differences was a haunting phrase. For the longest time, there were the boys and the bills. Then everyone and everything went away, including their wants and desires for each other.

Pondering the work ahead, all in the next ten weeks, Max reached for another beer, cracker and more cheese spread.

Chapter Five

The human beings seated in the circle surrounding Charlie Bay were silent. As before some eyes fixed to his, others stared away. Charlie Bay sat in the center and faced the Ancient One. And like so many other times, he took this moment of contact to engage those who surrounded him. One by one, Charlie Bay met the ancients. He met them in silence. He met them in this faded room with strength and an edge of arrogance. He held firm his past choices as the right ones, the only choices he could have made at the time. Then Charlie Bay came to the empty chairs; those seven empty metal chairs, staggered between the dozen or so human beings circled around him. It was the empty chairs that made his jaw tight, his stomach turn and his defiance flee. The vacancies haunted him. They were seats of the missing, ancients who broke the circle and whose circle was broken. Each empty chair bore witness to the choice he made years ago and the choice he made moments ago. Each empty chair pressed his obligation.

Charlie Bay tried to speak. But he was without breath.

Burningwater woke up choking for air. His pillow was soaked and his moist hair was matted to the back of his neck. Twice he gasped raw and wheezing gulps of air. He labored to breathe. As his lungs filled, the skin of his back separated from the damp sheets. The room was dark and cold. Charlie Bay continued to breathe heavily. He savored each breath.

The window on the northern side of Charlie Bay's bedroom rattled with the surge of a strong northwest wind. Lying in bed, he listened to the howl and felt the vibration of the outside wall against his headboard. Some gusts were higher, but he figured the wind was blowing about thirty-five. Remaining still, he waited on the rain. The sheets of water rapping the glass panes had their moments but he knew the weather was more wind than water. In this breeze, with the moon high tide, Charlie Bay also knew trouble for the fragile water sculptured sand walls of the Western Door. Today, he was not going to be digging clams. At high tide, in this air, waves were going to be carving into the sacred ground of his ancestors. The bones of his people were unprotected from the wind and the water, unprotected from two indifferent beings.

The beads of sweat hadn't left the back of his neck and chest before he was up and headed to the stairs; naked and cold. Passing through the kitchen to the basement door in the back hall, he grabbed a flashlight and moved down the narrow stairway into the stone-walled cellar. A hard packed dirt floor was five feet from the cobwebbed covered ceiling beams. There were stacked boxes and five gallon clam buckets in the center of the room and three wide plank shelves set against the four fieldstone walls. Charley Bay moved quickly to the far right corner and set the flashlight to shine on a large wooden Clementine crate. He removed the box from the shelf and withdrew polished stone figurines and clay pipes from its center. Placing these objects, in order, in the space left by the crate, he whispered a prayer until only a blue silk cloth liner and one small Obsidian stone remained. Charlie Bay returned to the kitchen, placed the Clementine box on the table and considered the tide.

At high tide, with a southwest wind, the water lapped meekly against the base of the sand and sea grass wall on the western tip of Eagle Island. At low tide the right angle formed by beach and dune sand enabled Charlie Bay to walk the borders of the Western Door burial ground. He routinely searched the stratified wall for ancestral remains. A flood tide carried the water above the wall and into the sea grass. The northwest wind brought the high water waves edging and cutting into the layers of sand that held the bones of the Casco. As the wall melted away, the remnants of his ancestors poked from the ground. If uncollected, the bones were in danger of dropping into the river. Charlie Bay had to get to the tip of Eagle Island as the water left the wall. But he knew his patience was to be tested for another hour. It was going to take at least that long for the water to recede far enough for him to wade the beach and hunt for bones.

The draft from the back hall that brushed across the skin of his shoulders and thighs reminded Charlie Bay that he was naked. He scanned the kitchen and living room for clothes, a pair of khaki pants left in a heap at the end of the sofa and a torn navy blue sweatshirt draped over the rocker were enough. With his boots from the back steps and cradling the Clementine crate, he was on his way to the Western Door. He planned to sit at the water's edge until the moment the tide allowed him onto the beach perimeter of the island's tip.

The gray early morning light of the eastern horizon left the western mound of Eagle Island connected to the night. The beams of the pickup headlights reflected off the blades of swaying wet sea grass and dropped into watery white-capped darkness as Charlie Bay eased the truck to the edge of solid ground. The northwest wind shook and rumbled around the cab. He leaned forward over the steering wheel to check the tide. Straining to see the water level, he knew it was still too soon for the beach. He was angry. He was angry at the moon and angry with himself. The moon he forgave.

Max slept past seven in the morning, which was unusual, and awoke dehydrated, which was not. After drinking all of the available non-alcoholic fluids in Sandra's refrigerator, he showered, shaved and felt generally renewed from his travels and professional headaches. He checked his e-mail for the first time in a week, which for him, was the norm. Messages on his cell he figured he'd check with coffee. Voice-mail from his office and apartment land line was another matter. Learning the technical skills required to playback messages from a remote location escaped him. Underlying the block was his belief that to be away from home and office was a reprieve from the ordinary cycle of activity and responsibilities so he skipped it. Sitting, once again at Sandra's desk, he found the page of instructions for the day's appointment. At eleven, he was to meet Margaret Garret near Eagle Island at the junction of routes 1 and 9 in the parking lot of a golf driving range; from there it was onto Burningwater. The range on Rt. 1 was easy to find; Max needed it simple. Sandra also gave a detailed physical description of Margaret and her expectations for their discussion. Marveling at Sandra's powers of observation, he disregarded the agenda topics but Margaret Garret sounded attractive.

Max was early at the driving range and hungry. Wandering over to an adjacent take-out restaurant, he talked one of the waitresses into grilling him a hot dog before they were supposed to open. He sat on a bench overlooking the empty range, ate and pondered golf. There was plenty of time.

Max had neither the talent nor the temperament for golf. As a result, his experience on the links was short, filled with frustration and eventually abandoned. But he retained an appreciation for the Scottish origins of the sport and the assimilation of golf into American society.

From his perspective, golf's greatest asset was as a sport integrated into the lives of either gender at any age. Women and men playing the same sport throughout theirs lives, sometimes even together, was remarkable. His wife liked golf. So from time to time, even he succumbed to a bucket of balls as a hopeful and relaxing distraction. He finished the hot dog and wondered when the range opened.

She was uneasy walking up to a stranger with ketchup all over his napkin in an otherwise empty parking lot to introduce herself, but Max was her only choice. Margaret didn't hesitate.

"Dr. Sorensen, I'm Margaret Garret. I spoke with Dr Walsh about meeting with you... the reburial of the Casco."

Max stood, grunted a yes as he wiped the corners of his mouth and extended his right hand all in one awkward motion.

"Please, call me Max."

Margaret was uncomfortable with the immediate informality. He was the anthropologist designated to return all of the Casco skeletal material and, in that sense, an ally. But, he was also the representative of the University that withheld the bones of Charlie Bay's ancestors for decades. To Burningwater, he was the enemy and she was cautious. For his part, Max was astounded at the accuracy of Sandra's description. She was a beautiful woman. Margaret Garret viewed Dr.

Max Sorensen as an out of shape contemporary of her father.

"Would you like to talk here for a minute first or do you have something planned?" He gestured toward the bench.

Margaret had a script, a short one. Her first goal was to get Dr. Sorensen and Charlie Bay together in order to set a date for the return of the Casco bones. Mediation was foreign territory for her and she planned to keep it simple. She expected to write whatever Charlie Bay needed and assist in a rapid reburial. She was also making it up as she went along.

"Charlie Bay Burningwater is the man that you need to speak with." Margaret had thought about her opening lines, but only her opening lines. "He lives on Eagle Island. He has no phone and an unpredictable schedule. I thought today, we'd just have to find him. I know the places to look and then, we can go from there."

"Sounds good to me. Do you want to drive and I'll leave my car here?" Max grabbed his knees and moaned as he rose.

Nodding, Margaret walked to the SUV, "I'll drive."

This somewhat pudgy, graying man, sitting on the passenger side in rumpled khaki pants and faded blue cotton shirt, appeared to be likable. The casualness of his manner was unexpected. Margaret was wondering how he ended up in charge of the repatriation for the University.

"So Margaret, how did you end up with this mission for the Casco and Charlie Bay Burningwater?"

Margaret smiled. “Charlie Bay’s a friend and he asked for my help in dealing with the University. I think I’m the only one he knows who went to college. I met with Sandra Walsh and made the request, she connected me to you...Charlie Bay wants the return done now. The reburial of his ancestors is long overdue.”

“Oh, so Burningwater and I pick a date.”

Boundaries, sequence and relationships now established, in Margaret’s mind to be followed and in Max’s to be changed.

Driving down route 9, she explained their first stop was to check the fishermen's co-op on the Casco River for Charlie Bay's pickup. It wasn’t far and the most likely place to catch him.

She thought maybe a public space might keep Charlie Bay in check. Burningwater’s volatility was a given, Sorensen's was an unknown.

Scanning the parking lot for Charlie Bay's truck, Margaret squinted and felt her heart pound. It wasn’t around, no sign of the pickup. She didn’t recognize anyone who might know where he was and gave up on the waterfront. Unconcerned about the failure and unaffected by the gray and blustery day, Max enjoyed the Maine coast, enjoyed the smell. He sat in the passenger seat and smiled. Margaret was annoyed. Her next choice was Charlie Bay's home on Eagle Island.

The rickety rail ties got Max's attention as they crossed over onto the island. Margaret noticed he let go of the dash once they bounced onto solid ground. He was alert, excited to be on this land of the Casco.

At the crest of the second knoll, she sighed and mumbled under her breath. Her hope for a calm meeting and date was dwindling, no truck at the house. He was either at the Western Door or the liquor store and neither was good. Watching her reverse direction and assuming that Charlie Bay wasn't home, Max wondered where to next. He was relieved when they didn't turn onto the rail tie bridge, but hung onto the dash as they drove across road-less, boot high chrome green grass of another small mound to nowhere.

"There's his truck. He is out here." Margaret satisfied, at least she found him.

Max felt his heart pound. As the gentle rolling hill dropped beneath them, he knew this was the earth which held the Casco bones, the ancestral burial ground that Sandra harvested so many years ago. He knew this was a pristine and fertile resource to reconstruct extinct lifeways. He knew that giving up the skeletal material of the Casco Collection wasn't going to be easy.

The meandering footprints in the moist sand that on occasion bumped into the north dune wall of the Western Door were clear and easy to follow. The uniform convexity of the shoreline made it impossible to see to the outermost tip. Without discussing it, they both expected to find him somewhere on the beach.

Walking in step, it wasn't long before Margaret and Max saw Charlie Bay's dark silhouette against the gray-green horizon of the marshland. As they approached, he glanced away from the sand wall and in their direction. Margaret waved her right arm. Charlie Bay saw the motion but did not respond. Returning to his work, he scraped the sandy surface for human remains. The two visitors increased their pace without a word.

Since his April discovery of an ancestor on the sand bar in the Casco River, Charlie Bay frequently patrolled the perimeter of the Western Door. Once in awhile, he found a few unidentifiable bones and he cared for them as remnants of his people. Burningwater buried all the recovered remains in sacred ground located on the ocean side mound of Eagle Island. Today, his early morning distress with the wind, the water and the moon proved true. The blue silk liner of the large Clementine crate was covered with bones. The five hours, searching the sand, brought him bone after bone. Each piece of the ancients spilled from their earth stung his soul. He was tense and tormented.

Now beside him, Margaret introduced Max. "Charlie Bay, this is Dr. Sorensen, the representative of the University."

Charlie Bay didn't remove his eyes from the sand or acknowledge Dr. Sorensen. Max leaned forward to greet him with his right hand extended but pulled it back after no response; even he felt the hostility. Rather than withdraw further Max went academic. Without a word, he focused on the brown-gray remains that contrasted dramatically with their soft blue silk cradle. He quickly identified some animal bones, probably dog. He also identified a few nondescript fragments, likely human, three prepubescent thoracic vertebrae, definitely human, and a scapula, likely the right shoulder blade of an approximately ten year old individual. Max was excited. If the scapula and vertebrae were from the same individual and if that individual were buried in a traditional flex position, the knees pulled to the chest and head tilted forward. And if the curve of the spinal column faced the northwest wall of the island, the angelic shoulder blade and vertebrae, found by Burningwater, were the outer most portion of a convex spine. Max expected those bones would be the first to erode through the surface, followed by more thoracic vertebrae and a second scapula. From these assumptions he postulated the presence of a complete human specimen and that got him talking.

"Could you show me where you found those two bones right there." Trying to be as calm as possible, he leaned closer and pointed into the box held in Charlie Bay's left arm. "I believe that they may be components of a complete skeleton, including the crania...that's the skull and very close to the surface, long bones and all!"

Margaret and Charlie Bay didn't share in his enthusiasm. A stoic Charlie Bay continued to search the sand. Margaret rolled her eyes, mumbled something that ended with idiot and fixed a glare toward Max. She was incredulous. The measure of his insensitivity was remarkable. Recognizing he was overzealous, Max attempted to justify his interest and kept talking.

"The remains of the child, the one whose shoulder blade you found, can tell us the story of how he or she might have lived, maybe even how they might have died. These bones can talk to us; they can talk to us about the

Casco past. If I could see the other bones of the child it might help re...."

Charlie Bay interrupted, "Bones don't talk. They don't tell stories. The bones of my people belong in the earth. Their circle has been broken...their journey broken and they all, all that you possess must be returned now. I won't speak about it any more."

Margaret was astounded at Max's lack of diplomacy. Any sense of professional hierarchy and cooperative assistance vanished. She saw in an instant, Max Sorenson operating, on his own, with an academic agenda independent of Casco repatriation. He was as difficult and unyielding as Charlie Bay. Finding herself thrust between two diverse and stubborn men, she tried to stay on track.

“We need to set a date for the return of all the Casco ancestors and plan for their reburial. If it's OK with you Charlie Bay, I'll work on that with Dr. Sorensen and you and I can talk, so that you have the final word. OK?"

Charlie Bay didn’t respond. To press him further was useless. Right now, the only common ground between the two men was their affinity for the ancestral Casco and the same wrinkled khaki pants. Turning without so much as a glance to Max, she walked back along the shore. Max hesitated for a moment, but followed in sync, one step behind. On their way down the narrow beach he attempted, on multiple occasions, to draw even to her side. But, it didn't matter how fast he walked to catch up, she maintained the distance. Earlier, he received the look and now, it was the walk. Max was familiar with both.

On the path through the sea grass back to the truck, he found a yellow range golf ball. He picked it up and put it in his pocket. Margaret Garrett started the SUV and told Max to hold on.

By early afternoon, the wind shifted to the southwest and the rising tide erased all evidence on the beach of the visitors. As the water lapped against Charlie Bay's boots, he found himself inching ever closer to the location in the sand that brought the pieces of spine and shoulder blade. The words and suspicions of Dr. Sorensen didn't leave him. He was torn. To disturb the bones in the earth was an offense, but to abandon them, to let them be washed into the sea, was a violation. With his best recollection, he scraped the spot of his past discovery using the crescent edge of a cohog shell. The enemy was correct. Bone after bone tracked into the wall. The Clementine crate was overflowing. Charlie Bay's uneasiness rose. He knew the skull was coming. He wanted to stop but the tide was surging toward the one bone that remained. Water began to tumble in over the top of his boots. He placed the container in a sheltered section of sea grass above his head and pushed it away from the edge. Leaning against the sand wall, he fought the suction, pulled off his boots and threw them high into the grass. Charlie Bay dug with bare hands. The sand was moist and smelled of salt. The grains packed together under his fingernails spreading the tip of skin from the nail bed. The cold ocean crept to his waist. His lips were dry and craved gin.

The small globe Charlie Bay teased free from the earth was encrusted with sand. Holding the human skull with two hands, he gently submerged the bone into the water, washing away enough debris to know it was all there. His eyes filled with tears and his nose ran with clear liquid. Water rushed into the gravesite collapsing the sand above. Cradling the skull and lower jaw in his left arm, he scurried up through the eroded opening to solid ground. Cold and wet, Charlie Bay sat down and used his sweatshirt to clean the face of this child. As the sand fell away from the upper teeth he recognized an unmistakable sign. The edges of the two front incisors were broken at an angle toward the middle of the face. The chips formed the shape of a triangle. Charlie Bay Burningwater knew this boy. This was his uncle's son; his uncle's son, Flat Stone. Charlie Bay wrapped both arms around the skull and pulled it to his chest. He rocked front to back, chanted with soft breaths and remembered.

Flat Stone was in his eleventh year and Charlie Bay was in his nineteenth when an uncle brought his only son back from the city to the Casco homeland. The boy had sores on his skin, his neck was swollen, he was red, drenched in sweat and then he was no more. A grandfather, his uncle and Charlie Bay dug the grave before the ground froze. They listened as his uncle spoke of the heart's pain when a father must bury his son. How was this so? All those years ago, Flat Stone's grave was far from the water. There were others, many others to the northwest; the northwest corner of Eagle Island, which was no more.

In his mind's eye, Charlie Bay saw the seven empty folding metal chairs encircled about him. He looked skyward, cradled the skull of Flat Stone and chanted.

"Sondaqua, Sondaqua soaring high above me.
Look down upon a son of the Nations
and call to Mother Earth that I might be forgiven.
I make this prayer to you Sondaqua, Sondaqua."

The departure of Margaret and Max at the driving range was business-like; exchanging cell numbers and possible times for contact. She was annoyed and needed a break before connecting with her theatre people. He needed to check out the lab's requirements for supplies and equipment before his return trip to Boston. Their good-bye included a date and positioning for the next encounter. There was no date for repatriation.

Sandra was correct. There was no one around on the South campus. Jerry Moore's old lab was the last in a row of six corrugated galvanized steel Quonset huts along a dead end dirt road. It was an arched tunnel, with few windows and green double doors on each end. The paddle lock and hinges on the parking lot side were rusted and the wooden swinging doors were patched and peeling. As he gingerly opened one to his right, Max held both outside and inside handles to make sure it didn't fall from the frame. A second set of doors in the entryway were closed but unlocked. The main room of the building was one long half tube, painted gray with blood red patches of rust splashed at irregular intervals. Dust was everywhere. Max figured Jerry Moore was the last one to use the lab and smiled. He hit the lights. After a few seconds of flashing, humming and buzzing seven of the eight florescent lights in the sixty-foot long room were on and flickering. Makeshift shelves lined both sidewalls to the seven-foot high curve of the roof. The shelves were filled with file-sized boxes of papers and skeletal material. The end of each box was labeled in black marker for their contents. He recognized Sandra's script on the majority of containers.

In the center of the room were three large old oak library reading tables, their surfaces well worn and scratched with student names, numbers and sketches all associated with the boredom of study. On the last table were five file cartons labeled J. Moore. Each box was packed with papers and articles; the cherished documents of a career, a lifetime organized into five containers. The work of Max Sorensen wouldn't fill half a box.

Jerry Moore died three years ago. Max didn't know until a month after the funeral. Their relationship was professional. They were colleagues and not close. But Max always enjoyed Jerry Moore's spirit. Despite the thirty-year difference in their ages, the professor's spirit was forever a source of humor and energy for Max. It was energy he used to combat institutional and political processes in which he was routinely overwhelmed. Jerry Moore called dealing with university administration "counting coup"; a reference to the Native American Plains warrior who got close enough to his enemy to touch him, preferably with a slap below the waist. This act demonstrated bravery and skill. In his last contract negotiation with the University in nineteen eighty-nine, Jerry requested and received lab space on campus until the millennium. He chuckled every time he told the story of the administration's neglect to designate, in writing, which millennium. Jerry counted coup. Max found laughter, inspiration and most of all energy.

It was Sandra who saved Jerry's research. She heard rumors, not long after his death, that the University, in an attempt to satisfy an ever-expanding need for space, was sending all paper materials from Dr. Moore's office and lab to the recycling center. Climbing into the dumpster left outside the lab for collection, Sandra retrieved most of the discarded material. She cut her hand in the recovery and later implied multiple OSHA violations at the laboratory site. She controlled and occupied the building ever since. Sandra counted coup. Now this marginal surplus building sheltered the writings of Dr. Jerry Moore and the skeletal remains of the Casco.

Walking around the far end of the laboratory and archive, Max examined the catalog numbers on row after row of boxes marked with the heading, Casco. He made a list on his PDA of the material and equipment required for the repatriation inventory until the battery went dead.

He finished off the list with scavenged sticky notes, stuck them all to his PDA screen, shut off the lights and left for Boston.

Chapter Six

Serving plate after plate piled high with fried clams and French fries, even for just the occasional shift at the Blue Lobster solidified an aversion to fried foods. Grilled chicken and spinach salad was Margaret's routine alternative to grease. For Jim Garret the choice was also simple, regardless of restaurant, time of day or appetite, it was always steak, preferably medium-well. Jim chose a restaurant as a good location to discuss career paths and family history for safety. He thought raised voices, emotional responses and loss of control were less likely in public and during a meal. But, he also knew, for Margaret, historically anyway, dramatic outbursts in such places were always possible.

Based on their last late night exchange, Jim began on offense. After they ordered, he brought up his first objective. "So Margaret, I know you've thought about it. Would you like me to make a couple of calls to set up the research assistant spot at Fitzgerald and Reynolds? Ah, you know, the firm I sent you all the info on...the Governor's firm...pretty much connected to everyone and everything in state government...I could set it up for the rest of the summer?"

If he had waited until the food arrived, there might have been an opportunity to discuss it. But, because of his impatience, her answer without food was direct. She was hungry. "No."

Jim Garret, father, mentor and self-appointed architect of his daughter's career, was affected by her sense of assuredness. He wasn't sure whether the change was in Margaret or in his own ability to recognize it. But it was there and she was clear. On the first point, he conceded.

"OK, OK so...what are you going to do?"

Surviving Philly, surviving producers, surviving directors, she was hardened enough to know when to tap the edge, "I'm going to workshop the play...*Overturn* in Ogunquit, waitress a few shifts at the Blue and help Charlie Bay Burningwater rebury his ancestors."

"You are going to what!" Jim raised his voice, responded emotionally and lost control. Everyone within shouting distance turned in his direction.

Margaret, knowing that Burningwater was the primary source of aggravation, didn't miss the beat, "That's right I'm going to keep writing and waitress." Fortunately for both, their food came. Jim was no longer hungry. Margaret smiled; dove into large chunks of grilled chicken, bacon seasoned spinach and reveled in a moment of change.

"Where in the world did that come from...this whole business with Charlie Bay and burying ancestors?" Jim leaned so far toward her, in total disbelief, his tie folded onto his steak. A mushroom stuck to the silk. As he cleaned and repositioned his tie, he slid his plate aside, regained his composure and mumbled about his strategy for a luncheon meeting. After a sigh, he gazed at his daughter who was enjoying her meal and waited for her to explain. He waited awhile, she was thinking about when she could dictate the tie sequence into her phone.

"Remember when I told you that I saw Charlie Bay at Casco Point, on the island, during your trip to the Carolinas?"

Now prepared to listen, Jim nodded.

"Well, he asked me then, for help. He said he needed a writer. When the river was dredged a long time ago, all the work they did uncovered the burial grounds of the Casco tribe. Graves were exposed and the State University was called to take care of the bones. All of this stuff they took from the Casco Indian cemetery on the tip of Eagle Island was supposed to be returned, maybe thirty-five years ago." She continued to crunch spinach. "But it wasn't and Charlie Bay asked for my help to get it back to be reburied. We wrote a formal request. I met with the University's representative, an anthropologist, his name is Dr. Sorensen yesterday and I'll work with him to get everything returned."

Her casual tone, ability to eat and talk at the same time and indifference to a professional career plan annoyed him. However, he was a man who built success on the principles of recognizing the positive in each circumstance and developing it to the maximum. He passed on the judgment of time wasted and focused on the potential of the work, if there was any, as a resume builder.

"Is it possible that this could be considered a consulting job or some type of university affiliate position...maybe you could stick it on your resume somewhere?"

Margaret smiled at her father, appreciated his constancy in the struggle to direct career choices and requested more rolls. He went deeper.

"Why are you doing this?"

"I'm doing this as a return favor for a friend and for Molly, because she would have done it." She also came with an agenda and she wanted the story of her aunt now.

"Ah, Molly, I never finished did I?"

"No, and I have waited patiently, for me anyway."

Jim acknowledged, but only to himself, that she hadn't pestered him about his half sister. He appreciated it without admission. Tentative, he chose his words.

"Molly was nine years older than me. My first real memories of her were as a sister who had already left home. I didn't know about the half sister part till later. She came back to visit us for a few weeks at a time, during what I found out was between jobs or boyfriends or bouts with the bottle. I believe she truly loved my mother, but even then, looking back on it, I think she was sick. In those years, I don't know if she was ever treated. My mother protected me and didn't say much, I guess because of my age. Growing up I never really knew Molly until my mother passed. I was fourteen and as you know I was raised from then on by Aunt Mary and Uncle Kevin. I worked a lot to do my share with that whole crowd in the small house. And during those years, Molly roared into my life from time to time... bringing gifts, probably more than she could afford; great gifts. And not just for me, for everyone... " Jim smiled with the recollection. "She always wanted to take me some place, whisked me away to the ocean usually, even in the winter. We'd get plenty of food, all of my favorites and I ate the whole time. It was great. No responsibilities, no work, just food. Then when I was about seventeen things didn't go too well for any of us. Aunt Mary passed. Uncle Kevin couldn't handle the crowd by himself and he had a new wife within a year and she couldn't handle Kevin or the crowd. So that's when I quit school, got a job at the fish plant.... but you've heard this story plenty of times, night school, GED all that."

Margaret nodded, smiled, set down her fork and folded her hands on her napkin. She understood every family had two or three key stories, embellished and galvanized into familial legend; the cannery and night school was one of theirs.

"But also during those couple of years, when all this was going on, Molly came less and less. When she did come, she wasn’t well. She was not herself. It was like her spirit had been broken. She was so sad. And then, she didn't come at all. I didn't see her for about two and a half years. I was pretty upset with her for disappearing, for what seemed to me, to be a long time. She was the only family I had. Then, just after I started dating your mother she came back. She started visiting now and then with no real explanation of what happened or why. I was very happy to see her and I was very glad that she was back when your mother and I got married, but she wasn't the same. She disappeared from time to time and then she'd come back, same pattern over again for years. And later on, since we were doing OK, I'd give her some money to get on her feet again. She never asked for it and said that she was keeping track and promised to pay me back. I wasn't keeping track and never expected to be paid back. That's when she started taking care of you. Your brother was too old and wanted no part of a nanny. I guess I wanted a way to get her more money and I guess, for you to know what I knew in her; the goodness, the caring and....her love, because it meant so much to me."

Margaret watched her father attempt to control his emotions. He was a very stoic man who rarely spoke of his youth; other than the GED legend, of the feelings he harbored as an adolescent or of his relationships outside the immediate family circle of wife and children. His eyes watered as he continued.

"But there was a problem. We found out that she couldn't be trusted. Sometimes she didn't take you where she said she did and then she'd bring you home and have the smell of alcohol on her breath, a little glassy eyed...we had to stop. She got gradually worse. She was pretty good when she took her medicine. I'd go and see her from time to time while you were in high school without anybody knowing, but eventually even I could see that her illness, depression or just plain sadness required that she be institutionalized. She never came out. When they called and told me, I felt like I let her down. I was ashamed. I told your Mother and that was it." Jim wiped his nose and eyes with the linen napkin.

After giving him a few moments she asked, "Where was she buried?"

"Next to my mother...she never knew her own. No matter what, family still has to take care of family the best they can."

They didn't say much to each other in the restaurant parking lot and left in separate cars.

Jr. Walker never sounded better. With a pale blue sky and dark blue river as the back drop for crossing the Piscatiqua Bridge to Maine, Max enjoyed the view and turned up the volume on Jr. Walker and the All-stars. "Sweet Soul" was the song; Max practiced it thousands of times. Each attempt was a dedicated and impassioned struggle to reproduce the tenor sound of his musical idol. For Max Sorensen, it never happened. He accepted his limitations as a musician and considered the hours of pursuit; sax therapy. His lack of talent and questionable soul notwithstanding, this song simply seized his emotions, his heart and through the years, never let go. He had Jr. and cruised north on 95.

It took Max a few days to get organized in Boston. Dealing with his apartment was of no consequence other than laundry. Most of his effort was with research equipment. He chose to leave nothing behind. Max packed a portable x-ray machine, digital x-ray hardware, software and a variety of sensors. The equipment necessary for cone beam radiography he placed on reserve at the University's technology center in case he needed it this summer. Rather than trying to find a system in Maine to run all the photographic capture and 3D imaging software for the temporary lab, he packaged and boxed all the hardware and took backup software from his own lab. And without any hesitation, he loaded up a brand new digital micro video camera and digital video recorder and hoped that no one in his department missed it. He brought his stuff, his Anthropology Department's stuff, his University's stuff and his hope that he might find a reason to need it all.

There were two choices on the rollers of the small stainless steel rotisserie cooker, regular and foot-long. Max remembered the store from his last trip. It was a converted gas station tucked away at the end of the Maine State University exit. With Jr. Walker's "Sweet Soul" still playing in his head, he chose regular and considered himself a man of discipline. As he ate the hot dog, he let his eyes drift around the remodeled building.

High above the food shelves, display cases and coolers, mounted in a ring around four the walls, was a row of chrome hubcaps. It was fitting to Max, the structure that maintained the big American cars of the sixties and seventies, now a convenience store, displayed hubcaps as if medals of past performance in the battle lost. At one point in his career, he toyed with the idea of a book on the symbolic aspects of hubcaps in twentieth century American culture. This was just before his separation and a few months later, even he thought it was a bad idea. For Max there was still beauty hub caps but they had to be chrome.

Now wandering, he headed to a soft-serve ice cream counter and the adjacent bay door with choices in a colorful mural of sundaes and toppings. He felt like dessert. A bulletin board near the ice cream menu posted business cards, various used cars and boats for sale and a one page printed announcement with information for the Casco Nation Census. The Census was scheduled during the third week in July for five consecutive days. This was an official notification to all those who wished to be recorded as members of the Casco Tribe and listed on the Tribal Roll. It looked legal but the document had no letterhead, logo or signature. Max read it twice and considered it out of place and odd. It confused him.

Ethnicity and belief systems in general confused him. Contemporary America was built of communities of people who, for the most part, believe they were from somewhere else. They were individuals, living in cities and towns across the country, who identified with their ancestral populations. This was ethnic identity defined by belief not by genes or geography.

In this case, Max knew in order to be a member of the Casco Tribal Nation, the individual must demonstrate one-quarter lineage in the ancestral line. To be listed on the Tribal Roll, they had to be one fourth Casco. But he never understood the requirement. Was it a cultural affiliation? Was it a genetic relationship? Or was it parts, not necessarily equal, of both?

Max recognized if he drifted further wandering the convenience store, a headache was not far off. There was a lot of unpacking to be done. Buying a small banana boat, he again thought of himself as disciplined and left for the final ten minutes of his drive to the summer lab with "Sweet Soul" loud and the windows down.

For the remainder of the afternoon, Max unloaded the research equipment into the long large room of his summer laboratory. He spent the evening walking the beach.

According to a hastily constructed timetable, the task for his first full day was to organize and setup all of the equipment for a functional lab; wrestling with the base of the x-ray machine for over an hour threw off his plan. He acknowledged that he needed another pair of hands, skipped the x-ray machine and moved on to the next section. Conceptually, he wanted to take advantage of the long room and large oak tables. To do so, he planned a sequence of recording and documentation stations that ended with the packaging for reburial of each specimen. The easiest part of the setup was to place an examination bin on each tabletop. The exam bin frame was about the size of a door and constructed of two by fours. Max lined the frames with plastic and filled each with a layer, about three inches thick, of fine white sand. The examination bins provided a stable, safe location to place and orient the skeletal material for x-rays, photographs and video. With a restless spirit and short attention span, this sequence allowed Max to examine, record and catalog more than one individual at a time. He could move from station to station as his interest and energy dictated. Along with the still disassembled x-ray unit, the station sequence included: an unpacking and log-in area, a skeletal orientation bin, an x-ray station with digital radiographs, a skeletal analysis bin with digital imaging and 3D scanning, a prepackaging skeletal inventory bin and the Casco Collection's final packaging area. Start to finish, Max's repatriation stations rambled on for fifty feet straight down the center of the arched building.

On the outside wall, halfway down the room was a desk-sized table Max used for his laptop and printer, all his other supplies and materials went on the floor. In order to test his cell service and WiFi connection, he left a message for Margaret and sent her an email that he was in the lab. To test his printer and avoid returning to the x-ray machine, he found an Indian Law web-site, located the Passamaquoddy vs Maine Settlement Act, downloaded the documents and printed. He glanced at the pages to make sure they were legible but didn't read the text. Scanning the room, Max twirled his wedding ring and went for Casco bones.

From the Casco archive, Max randomly selected a storage carton that contained the human skeletal remains of one individual. Setting the carton next to a sand bin, he lifted a number of light brown long bones from the interior. Plastic bags of additional bones followed, each segregated components of the skeletal system; hands, feet, spinal column, pelvis, ribs, were all numbered and labeled. The skull and mandible, wrapped in unprinted newspaper were uncovered and placed at the head of the bin. The stained brown cranium, with empty dark orbits and a lower jaw set askew, appeared to be surging forward from the sand, a record of former life, waiting to be made known. Max passed from the practical and pragmatic aspects of the day's setup to the overriding sense of a presence in generations of human existence. The beauty of this specimen made his breath short. This was a treasure. With moist palms, he aligned all of the material in anatomically correct order. The result was a male specimen in excellent condition. Max estimated the individual's age at fifty-five, plus or minus five years. For him, this was spectacular.

Without examining the specimen further, he selected another box from the shelves and unpacked this material at the second sand bin. Again, the bones were in excellent condition. Examination of the pelvis led Max to identify the sex as female. Age at death he estimated to be forty years, plus or minus three. There was obvious scaring and remodeling on the skull. Scaring was also present on the long bones of the legs. Max noted that both specimens were designated on their box labels as prehistoric; however, there were no date estimates. Once the female was laid into the exam bin, he was hooked. She had a story and it needed to be told.

For the third bin, Max selected a specimen from a co-mingled burial site marked historic. The individual he assembled was male with an estimated age of forty-five, plus or minus five years. The thoracic vertebrae of this specimen demonstrated multiple lesions and there appeared to be generalized osteoporosis in key locations throughout the skeleton. The world around Max was fading away. It was only the distant rhythmic pounding that brought him back.

"Sorry, how long have you been here? It's not locked, just jammed." Max mumbled into the door as he glanced through the dirty glass at Margaret's back-lit silhouette on the other side. After freeing the hinge, he invited her into the lab. Max waited for her purpose. He perceived and appreciated Margaret as a woman intent on reburial and all business. He saw her intensity as similar to his own but in a different direction. He didn't expect repatriation of the Casco to follow the route Margaret planned or happen as fast as she and Charlie Bay wanted. He finally said, "So what's on your mind?"

"Now that you've had a look at the archive and know what it will take to inventory, I came by to set a date for the reburial ceremony. It needs to be set soon to give Burningwater a straight answer and settle him down a little. He has every right to be impatient and he certainly is angry."

"OK, sure. Come on over to my make-shift desk and we'll take a look at the calendar on my laptop and I'll show you the lab." As they walked down the vaulted room Max probed, "While you are here, could you help me put the base of this x-ray machine together? It's really a two man job; you know, easy for two, impossible for one." He needed the help and was already stalling on the repatriation date. Margaret wasn't surprised.

The assembly was easy for two. They needed only a few minutes to place the unit in sequence on the skeletal pathway. Margaret was overwhelmed by the examination and inventory process. She had no idea it would require so much equipment and wondered why. Catching her eyes drift to the human remains situated in the bins, Max was ready to shift to the hard sell.

"Could I show you one of these?"

As she moved to a close-up view of human bones, the old Ash Wednesday prayer, "from dust thou art and to dust thou shalt return", came to her from an experience long since forgotten. As the words tumbled through her mind, she stared at the gray-brown remains of a human being. This was a foreign experience for her. She needed to dictate, to record these feelings, let the words spill out to be remembered. Margaret was also hooked but for a different reason. Before she could get to her thoughts, Dr. Sorensen the educator camouflaged Max the pitchman.

"This specimen is male, about, oh I'd say early to mid fifties at death. He lived in this area prior to European contact, but I don't know the carbon date for this burial site. If there is one, it's in the file on the collection. This skeletal material is a great baseline specimen; complete, in excellent condition and prehistoric. Take a look at this. See how worn the teeth are but with no decay, no European sugar, molasses or whatever. There is an unbelievable amount of wear." Max reached into the sand, removed the intact mandible with a full complement of teeth in the jaw and moved it toward Margaret in order for her to get a better view of the chewing surfaces. She looked more closely, but didn't reach to touch or hold the bone. Sensing her hesitancy, Max continued. "This fellow, by the look of things, was a marine hunter-gatherer; fish, clams, crabs, small game, deer and any nuts, berries or the like. You know, any consumable he and his band could find, most of it was probably mixed with sand. If you look closely at the joints in his arms you can see the difference in the amount of degenerative joint disease between the right and left side. There is quite a bit more degenerative change on the right than the left. He was probably right handed. He was evidently a hard working individual, at least based on the boney wear and tear. He was a hard worker."

"He is a Casco ancestor. He was also someone's grandfather. He is waiting to be buried."

Without acknowledging her comment, Max paused. She was driven, possibly an even match, but he had more. He drifted toward the next bin in sequence.

"This specimen is female, buried in association with that male and of course also prehistoric." Margaret was drawn to the skeleton and stayed by his side. Max looked for her attention and closeness out of the corner of his eye. "Pretty straightforward if you take a look at the pubic bones. She was around forty when she died, also apparently marine hunter-gatherer. But this is an interesting finding." He removed the skull from the bin and rotated it in his hands to the best angle for light. "See in the floor of the orbits that pitted appearance, perforations and up around the eye brows as well? And all the bony remodeling on the forehead; these lumps and bumps on a surface that is generally smooth?"

Margaret nodded, uncertain as to what, but she knew she saw something unusual.

"Tertiary Syphilis. The disease was likely present throughout this population."

Margaret's urban world was inundated with information on sexually transmitted diseases; syphilis was on the list as another STD out there linked to bad choices. Margaret wrinkled her forehead and winced.

"Yes, somebody's grandmother with syphilis." Max smiled at Margaret. "Try to put yourself in a different place and time; her time, there was no treatment. The moral code was relative to her community, her lifeway, which is unknown to us. Our codes and creeds didn't exist in her world. As tempting as it is, and I am guilty too, we can't reconstruct lives to judge them, only try to understand them a little better, ultimately with the hope of getting perspective on our own." He paused and gave her a chance to collect her thoughts.

The ongoing, everyday struggle not to observe human history from an ethnocentric viewpoint was so engrained in Max that his casual and non-judgmental tone regarding both Margaret and the specimen left her taken aback. She forced herself to refocus on a date for burial. Max refused to let up.

"Now here's where this gets interesting and has the potential to make a contribution to the literature. Let's you and I say, for the sake of academic discussion, that the Casco sample includes a number of individuals with osteoporotic sites, cranial vault perforations and scaring as well as long bone remodeling, all of which are consistent with Tertiary Syphilis. And who knows, maybe Sandra has already done this, but I haven't read it...or maybe I have. That doesn't matter, just think about this: with prehistoric radiocarbon dates on such terrific findings as in the Casco, well, this whole debate as to whether Syphilis came with Columbus from Europe to the New World or it came from the New World back to Europe with Columbus becomes much clearer. Here is more evidence to support the latter right here in the Casco Collection. Spectacular!" Taking a deep breath he became more pensive. "Unbalanced reciprocity, that's all it is; unbalanced reciprocity. Our ancestors unintentionally and intentionally gave Native Americans more than their fair share of bad bugs." Max grunted at the disproportionate devastation brought forth by European diseases upon unsuspecting and biologically defenseless Nations. His rapid thoughts of yet another project in another world distracted him from Margaret's presence. Catching himself, he set the skull gently back into the bin. "Sorry, I ah..." Pressing forward, reached for another bone. "Let's just check the tibia. Look at that, the changes are classic. We just established the pre-contact presence of syphilis in the Casco. Perfect."

Pointing to the osseous changes on the surface of the shin bone, he assessed her disposition. She wasn't where he hoped, but he thought she might be close and pushed.

"Using these two specimens, as a prehistoric baseline of bony conditions for marine hunter-gatherers, we can compare those individuals to this historic male specimen. Look at some of the differences European contact may have made on the Casco. How it changed their lives."

"Max we need to..."

Sensing the opportunity was about to be lost, Max continued with his pitch's finale. He picked up the skull of the historic specimen.

"Notice the increase in the pathology of the jaws... all these abscesses and perforations in the upper jaw. The assumption is that with a dietary change, presumably more refined sugars, their health changed for the worst. Look at this." Max pointed to the holes in bone. "It's hard to know whether it hurt or not. The response to pain is so culturally mediated, it's something we'll probably never know, but diet sure did have an impact."

This time, as he held the bone toward Margaret, she touched the crown of the cranium. It was cold. She wouldn't forget cold. Exchanging the skull for a vertebra, Max kept going.

"Tuberculosis is a disease which was present in North America prior to contact, but it was population density dependent. So that meant that before the Europeans arrived, it only showed up in samples of individuals who lived in close permanent quarters; horticulturists, you know, farmers, sedentary peoples. And the skeletal evidence for TB is a lesion that looks a lot like this one on the thoracic vertebrae. Chances are this fellow didn't catch TB while living as a Casco. He might have moved to town, worked in a mill or a fish processing plant, got sick and came home to die. A tough life for people, the ones who left and tried to fit into a different world, the Euro-American world, it was tough."

Margaret found the depth of Max's sensitivity and compassion incongruous. How was it possible for him to have such empathy toward the Casco plight as a result of European contact? And at the same time, he was so insensitive toward Burningwater and the repatriation of the bones of the Casco people. She was now another woman who struggled with Max Sorensen's incongruities. Margaret pressed him back.

"If he came home to die, shouldn't he be buried with his people?"

"By the looks of things he's going to get there. The question is when? I'd like just a little more time with the collection than for a simple inventory and repackaging." Before she responded, he continued with his rationale. "You can tell in a heartbeat that this is an absolutely spectacular collection; a treasure. There is so much more to be learned. So here is what I thought...

By the way Margaret, what do you do anyway?"

"I'm a writer ... a playwright."

"Ah writing, not one of my strengths...so you've got plenty of time and flexibility. Perfect!"

"Not really, I already have a project for the summer...two projects...plus Charlie Bay."

"But no deadlines?"

"Self imposed and we have to set one for this."

"A writer with discipline, also not one of my strong points,...but what do you think of this idea? And in it there will be lots of time for you to write.

I thought with some help, and I was hoping you, and with this equipment, we could digitally record an examination of each specimen as it is inventoried and prepared for reburial, right here, right down this whole assembly line; radiographs, video, all of it. In a short time, we can archive the entire collection as a digital record for researchers and students to study long after we're all dead and buried. There are funds available, you'd get paid as a research assistant."

It was hardly a truthful offer, but Max did have Sandra's credit card, she would have a title and he was desperate. Unable to speak, Margaret was astonished.

"I'll need to round up three or four components of the collection at other universities and museums, that's going to take some time. Before they arrive, if we work together, I bet we could have what's here digitally archived. Together, we can be as fast as I could be just doing the inventory by myself. What do you say?"

His proposal of a digital archive as part of the inventory was suspected when she saw the recording equipment. She figured he was up to something, the offer to be paid as an assistant was a surprise and absurd. Margaret was quickly coming to realize that Max Sorensen operated on his own repatriation agenda, not Sandra Walsh's. She couldn't turn him loose in the lab with a date and expect the reburial to get done as scheduled. He was slippery, scattered and needed to be watched. As a way to complete the inventory more quickly and with consistency, it was a good idea. She did have flexibility and she could still write every morning. Anything that was going to speed up the reburial and keep an eye on Max was a good idea, good for Charlie Bay.

"It wasn't what I had in mind for the summer, but as long as Charlie Bay says that it's OK, I'll help you to prepare the Casco, but no pay. To postpone the reburial for more research projects is another matter and as far as Charlie Bay is concerned, not possible, no, absolutely not. So whatever else you have in mind is not going to happen.

Dr. Walsh knows about this plan?"

Max looked guilty. Lines of authority were something her father taught well.

The phone in Sandra Walsh's living room rang the programmed four times before the caller came over the speaker. Max made no attempt to get up from the winged-back chair to answer. He knew who it was. Holding his sax, he remained still and listened for the message.

"It's me and I know you're there Max, so pick up. I left a message on your cell which was useless. Come on Max, pick up. We have to talk about this incredibly ridiculous stall that you're trying to build into the Casco repatriation. I know you're listening to me, in my living room, probably with your sax, trying to play that same song as ever and with a stack of your tapes of old Bette Davis movies."

"Barbara Stanwyck," Max whispered as he waited for her to call him a jackass. He touched the reed to his lips and wasn't disappointed. Under stress Max's mind meandered to familiar places.

It was December of 1977 when Max first heard Jr. Walker's recording of "Sweet Soul". He was in Detroit after a paleopathology conference at Michigan State. On his way home, an unpredicted lake effect snowstorm stuck him in an airport bar for three hours with ten dollars and a jukebox full of old Motown. By accident, he punched for the flip side of his first choice: the All Stars' version of "Come See About Me" and three minutes of "Sweet Soul" later his world was never the same.

Through the years other tenor sax players like Boots Randolph and Illinois Jacquet inspired Max, but none like Jr. Walker. For him, "Sweet Soul" was a personal anthem that took him to places otherwise impossible to travel. Sandra was correct on two counts: he was with his sax to play "Sweet Soul" and it was a stall. He had no choice but to pursue both.

"Ball of Fire", "Meet John Doe" and "Double Indemnity" were the extent of his traveling Barbara Stanwyck film collection. Fred McMurray was such an impediment in "Double Indemnity" that sometimes he questioned whether to include it at all, but the back lighting and Barbara Stanwyck's radiance in black and white was matchless. Tonight he chose "Meet John Doe". He accepted Walter Brennan as necessary baggage to experience Barbara Stanwyck's exuberant energy. It was her energy that he found most attractive. It was the same quality that he found so attractive in his wife. He loved his wife; he loved her energy. At times like these, when he was drawn into circumstances he thought he understood but didn't, he missed her jolt of clarity. Their last good kiss was on a Monday afternoon four Junes ago. He knew that was it the moment it ended.

Max disconnected the DVD player, put the tape in Sandra's old VCR and twirled his wedding ring.

It was the initial six months of the separation that he found the most difficult. Alone for the first time, he had a constant longing for balance. He missed hearing the other side.

Now he was accustomed to being alone, almost desiring it. He was afraid of disruption. Rationalizing the solitude as a necessity, at least at this stage of his life, he tried to convince himself he needed it in order to produce; to produce something scholarly, something of quality and value to his profession. Even from Max's perspective results were mixed.

From the very beginning, it was not easy to produce. Years ago, during the writing phase of his dissertation research, he was up most of one night, alone at the kitchen table, writing and rewriting a small, two page section of the first chapter. Frustrated and insecure, he pushed through hour after hour of dissatisfaction with his work until he finally achieved what he thought was reasonable. When asked by his wife at sunrise to care for the boys, he fell asleep. This, in turn, prompted a defining moment in his struggle to produce. She threw the two precious pages, along with his electric typewriter off the front porch, into the picturesque center quad of the graduate housing apartments and accompanied the thrust, at the top of her lungs with the phrase, "this is not a dissertation, this is just masturbation". To this day, along with the expected early morning rumbling and grumbling of residents, he swore that she received spousal applause from other graduate couples in the neighborhood. For at least a year after, Max's greatest fear was that the only productive aspect of his research was its association with that nightmarish phrase and its catchy potential to be immortalized on a bumper sticker.

Sitting in the darkness, interrupted by Barbara Stanwyck's voice and the flicker of a black and white film, with his wants and desires for the Casco, the strife continued.

The land line rang for a second time, Max didn't move.

"Max, it's me and this time you had better pick up. Put down the beer and the cheese spread and whatever other high sodium products you have to comfort you in this chaos you're creating and pick up."

Max stood, walked to the machine and muted the voice. He decided to see Burningwater in the morning.

Chapter Seven

The files of papers, names and numbers contained every document and bit of information, some in hard copy, some scanned, concerning the Casco excavation except the one Max wanted. After searching through the stacks and doc folders at least three times, he decided that for some inexplicable reason, the compulsively thorough Dr. Walsh forgot something. Whether the oversight was intentional or not didn't matter. He needed a copy of the Casco agreement. He needed burial ground excavation details: who signed what, where and when for the removal of bones. Despite the early morning hour, Max worked online applications and email requests. Before nine and after five, when dealing with Federal and State bureaucracies, web pages and e-forms had their advantages. Without speaking to a single human being, he requested from the Bureau of Indian Affairs, the State

Historical Commission and the State Archeologist's Office all of the transaction records and Tribal Council agreements regarding the Casco excavation. Sitting back in the desk chair, he looked at his notes, thought about his completed requests and wondered if any information was ever going to show up.

The strategy for his backup plan was a simple one; find out who, on the Tribal Council, signed the release for the excavation, convince one of the members to support the continued research on the Casco Collection and enlist their assistance in overturning or at least postponing Burningwater's request. However, in order to stall Sandra on the other end, he first wanted to get Charlie Bay's permission for an examination of the collection to go along with the reburial inventory. Even with Margaret's help, the process would last long enough to find a Casco ally. He thought this tack had a chance.

Deciding to speak with Charlie Bay and finding him were two separate matters. He retraced Margaret's search path with no luck. As a last resort, he elected to park at the fishermen's co-op and ask anyone who bothered to listen where he might locate Burningwater; still no luck. Max observed that most lobstermen spoke a few well-chosen words and gave little information. With each inquiry and to his amazement, he usually gave more than he got. Figuring that he had outsider, tourist or maybe even anthropologist written all over him, Max chose to explore, without help, the one remaining possibility. He headed on foot up the river shoreline toward the anchorage's only boatyard.

Small wooden rowboats, scattered in a palate of colors against the white sand, lined the narrow river beach. Each boat had an anchor line that stretched up into the chrome green grass dunes. Max hopped and stepped over the taught ropes as he walked west along the leeward side of the river. Two hundred yards beyond the skiffs, he reached three long, parallel and barn red boathouses. The air was humid, the sand was soft and sweat beaded across his forehead. He was wet and winded. To catch his breath he sat on a launching railway that extended from a bay door into the river. He felt his heart pound, out of sync with the rhythm of pounding hammers. Collectively, the boathouses echoed with the sounds of boat building and repair.

Looking into the shed from the bright sunlit riverfront made identifying anyone working inside impossible. Max was unable to see anything but shadows. He gathered himself, walked past the waterfront railways, around the far building and searched for landside access. On the west corner a ladder led from the beach to a large open-air work dock. As he climbed to the top, Max peered at eye level onto the platform's surface. Gray weathered two by sixes were rough and worn. Missing or rotting planks had been repaired in a patchwork array of plywood caps. A few bait barrels stood on the surface along with two stacks of lobster traps. There were no railings on the waterside edges. With a ten-foot tide, from some locations, it was a twelve-foot drop. Max didn't look down. He looked straight ahead and beside a wooden dory, he found Charlie Bay Burningwater.

Charlie Bay was poised next to the overturned boat with a large crank hand drill. The wood bit at its tip was only inches from the faded red dory bottom. Charlie Bay didn't move. He didn't push the drill bit forward into the hull or pull it back to look up as Max rustled his way onto the dock. Charlie Bay Burningwater was too busy praying for forgiveness.

The boat stretching out in front of Charlie Bay was the Alton built dory he fished from for almost sixty years. He and Earl Alton built the boat to row. It was never meant to hold an outboard motor. But for the past two years or so Charlie Bay was not strong enough to row and during that time his boat never touched the water. Expecting to get over this backache or that arm pain and expecting at this stage in his life, to get stronger rather than weaker, Charlie Bay was postponing the inevitable. He hated outboard motors. He hated gasoline. And, he hated the thought of cutting a hole in the bottom of his boat for an outboard well in order to use both. The wind, the tide and time overtook his strength, but not his loyalty to the principles of his boat building master.

At seventeen, with a hard body and adolescent drives, Charlie Bay knew about sex. Earl Alton taught him about women, Scotch whiskey and wooden boat building; especially boat building. A master craftsman with an appreciation for voluptuous women and fine

Scotch, Earl Alton lived his whole life next to the boat shop on the tidal flats of the Casco River. What he knew about fishing and boat building he learned from his father and his father's father. For some unknown reason, during the last year of his life, he chose to teach some of what he knew about women and much of what he knew about boat building to Charlie Bay Burningwater.

It was a strange apprenticeship to those who drifted into Alton's boat shop for a warm seat by the wood stove and some gossip. Earl rarely spoke a word to young Burningwater, he worked and they were always together; the young man's eyes glued to his every move. The result was Charlie Bay's Bank dory, maybe Earl's one hundredth and last; for Charlie Bay, his first and only. Earl told his pupil that a man's dory was the same as his wife, to stick with her in good times and bad and only have one. Earl expected the dory to last longer than both of them, wives and all.

Alton's boat shop was the last building on a dead-end road that followed the Casco riverbank west from the fishermen’s co-op. Parked alongside the peeling white shop was a rusting yellow school bus, with no engine and no seats. It was always filled with long lengths of white pine. Next to the bus was a make shift wood-fired boiler constructed from an oil tank. It was used for bending oak frames and steaming knees. There was no sign. Folks in search of a dory were told to just look for the bus and the boiler at the end of the road. The door to the two-car garage sized building was never locked. If someone came by and borrowed a tool while Earl was on the water, he knew what was gone and generally had a good idea who took it. In the fifty-eight years that he ran his shop only a few tools were lost and none were stolen.

Alton's shop was outfitted with only two power tools: a band saw and a table saw. An electric drill and Earl's big firm hand never met. There was an assortment of hammers, planes, chisels and screwdrivers but the hatchet and jackknife were Earl's favorites. The plans for each boat were in his head and he rarely drew a line.

Most of the tools in the shop were kept in the row after row of different sized fruit boxes that lined the four shelves on each wall of the building. There wasn't a draw or cabinet in the large room but every tool had its place. For years, Earl collected the solid wooden crates left by the traveling Fruit Man. Every Thursday, during the summer; the Fruit Man cleaned his truck and deposited the best boxes under a light pole at the fish pier. From time to time, Earl left him a bucket of clams. Charlie Bay continued picking up the crates after Earl Alton died and did so until the Fruit Man died. Clementines were his favorite.

The Bank dory that Earl and Charlie Bay built was nineteen feet, five inches in overall length. On the fifteen foot white pine bottom the five planks ran stem to stern. In each piece chosen for the dory, the grain held the line and Charlie Bay gradually understood in the daily scouring of the wood piles an unspoken principle of Earl's life; the board showed the builder. Each plank in the lapstrake hull told them where it belonged. Earl

Alton listened, Charlie Bay learned and for almost sixty years the result of their work served him well.

Thanks to Max Sorensen the long planked bottom was going to remain intact a little longer. Looking for any excuse not to cross cut the dory's hull for an outboard motor well, even if it came from an enemy, Charlie Bay stopped praying to Earl for forgiveness and set the drill on the dock.

Max approached Charlie Bay and saw the uneasiness in his face. Charlie Bay was upset. This was not a good time, this was the fisherman's domain and the self-absorbed Dr. Sorensen refused to acknowledge it all.

"Hi, remember me, Max Sorensen, from the other day, with Margaret, on the beach?"

Charlie Bay didn't answer or turn toward him. He dropped his eyes and mumbled, "damn".

"This your boat?"

Charlie Bay nodded yes.

"It's a Bank dory isn't it? Built in Nova Scotia or some place in Massachusetts, Amesbury maybe?"

Max was showing off. Charlie Bay was surprised but he had no intention of crediting Max's familiarity with wooden boats. The Mystic Seaport Museum Marine Bookstore was on Max's regular rounds. He read a lot, had no woodworking or carpentry skills and consistently wrestled with any tool, nails and screws. Blood was the usual result. Charlie Bay looked at Max's callous-free hands and pride got the better of him.

"Built here."

"Did you build it?"

"Some...an Alton Dory, his last one." Charlie Bay was searching for the upper hand. "So it is a Pipeboat for the dream journey."

He succeeded.

"A Pipeboat for the dream journey?"

Charlie Bay again nodded but this time with one singular dip of his chin and didn't say a word. Max wondered if he were about to enter an area in which he had limmitted experience, the dance between the ethnographer, the trained participant observer and the informant, the local knowledge willing to divulge cultural traditions. Was it about to unfold? Or, was Burningwater teasing him? With very little to lose, except control in a relationship that was, even from his optimistic perspective, marginal, Max took the chance.

"What makes this a Pipeboat?" There was no answer. "Who goes on this dream journey?"

After pursing his lips and squinting, Charlie Bay answered, "The Pipeboat People."

"Where do they go?"

"The spirit world."

"And you need a Pipeboat to do that?"

"It helps." Charlie Bay hadn't enjoyed himself this much with an outsider in quite awhile.

"Is it because it was the builder's last boat before he died and he was as close as he would ever get before crossing over into the spirit world? Is it what makes this a Pipeboat?"

Removing his pipe and tobacco pouch from his breast pocket and then pinching a small amount of tobacco, Burningwater made an offering to the four directions and to the earth and sky. Max felt his heart rate increase and the blood pound through his neck.

"Among the Nations, there are those who, even though they are of this world, live also in the spirit world. But because they live in both of these worlds, they need a means to travel between them. For those among the Pipeboat People, the journey must be made in Pipeboats."

In the lee of the boat shed, the smoke from Charlie Bay's pipe drifted skyward as his eyes stayed on Max. Why was he here?

"They travel skyward, like the smoke from your bowl. Is this a Casco Pipeboat and you are the Pipeboat People?"

Max caught himself, considered the moment as a rusty old anthropologist duped by a shrewd Casco and got back to his purpose.

"I have a request."

Burningwater shifted to the hull of the overturned dory and clenched the pipe stem tighter in his teeth.

"I would like to have your permission for some additional documentation of the Casco Collection. I'd like to record their examination as we do the inventory for reburial. I have it set up so it won't take any longer." Max didn't wait for a response. "Those bones have a tremendous story to tell about the way your people lived years ago; before and after the Europeans arrived here. They can talk to us and tell us a lot about lives, diseases, deaths, about how people worked, what they did and what they ate. What do you say? Can I have your..."

Charlie Bay interrupted him with a hard edge to his voice. "I told you before, bones don't talk. They don't tell stories. They don't tell anything. They have nothing to say. They must be put in order; in their proper place, in the earth. It has to be done so that the spirits of my people can take their rightful place, make their journey. Removing them from the burial ground has broken the pathway. Their journey has stopped. The bones are a part of my people. They're connected to their spirits."

"But Burningwater it's a great chance to learn. Chances to learn come in spurts with glimpses of our past that we had no idea about before. Most of the past has just been built over or plowed under...just lost and forgotten, no connection to us. We are great at saving the moments in a sculpture or a painting but we are awful at understanding the people. Bones tell us things, just like the tools that your people made, the wood they carved or the boats they built. We can learn an awful lot about them, your ancestors, your past. By understanding what happened, hopefully, we can get a better handle on where to go for the future. And here, right here with your people, is an unbelievable opportunity to do just that; to get a glimpse, a chance to know the past of the Casco to improve your future, all our futures by not making the same mistakes, by not repeating the same injustices."

"Time is not a straight line."

"What, what do you mean?"

"You're talking about the past and the future as dots on a line and we stand between them. You say my ancestors are the past and you will help me understand my future. The past is yesterday, the past is today and the past is tomorrow."

For a second Max understood, until his stubbornness, his education or his inability to surrender blocked the insight. He was confused. "I don't understand."

"Time is a circle. Time isn't a line. Time is a circle." Seeing Max remained lost, Charlie Bay's patience was fading, "My ancestors are yesterday and they're tomorrow. They're with me today. But some aren't going to continue on the journey of the Pipeboat People because their bones are in boxes on a shelf instead of in the earth. Don't you see that they must be reburied? They must be in the earth!"

In his anger and frustration, Burningwater came very close to grabbing Max Sorensen by the throat.

Recognizing the threat, Max strengthened his voice, "I'm just asking to examine and record the bones as we do the inventory for burial. Those specimens will all be reburied. I just need your permission. No one is trying to keep them ... so much can be gained. To bury all that information away, so much will be lost, lost forever!" Leaning over the dory hull, Max was also tempted to go for the throat.

"You don't want your history lost. I don't want the spirit of my people lost. If bones are not buried, spirits are lost forever." Charlie Bay leaned in, inches from

Max's face. "Spirits are lost forever unless; unless we act in their favor, unless I act in their favor." His voice trailed off. He lowered his head and their conversation was over.

Max realized that the loud and angry voices of the argument resulted in a headache for him and a crowd of friends for Burningwater. Five fishermen drifted into view behind Charlie Bay; young, strong and disturbed by Max's presence on the dock.

No one spoke. Looking at the six men bound together by the ocean, Max realized how different his world was from a lobsterman's life on the water. Their weathered faces and large strong arms carried an allure of romance; lives dedicated to harvesting the sea. But, this was not a time to romanticize. Max knew he was being threatened without being in danger. It was a time to leave.

On his second step backward, in a casual attempt at a dignified exit, he tripped on a plywood patch, lost his balance only to regain it at the dock's edge. Even with his clumsiness, Max didn't remove his eyes from Burningwater. He was holding to the hope that he might receive a nod or a glance; just some slight indication for the possibility of extension, nothing. Charlie Bay's eyes never left the red bottom of the dory.

Half way down the ladder, Max finally looked to the sand and found an incoming tide, water to the second rung and not a speck of riverbank beach clear to the fishermen's co-op. He wondered which was more humiliating, the water or the return. He decided the water was not only more embarrassing but colder and climbed back onto the dock. Shaking his head at Max's reappearance, Charlie Bay mumbled, “damn”.

The fisherman closest to the road pointed in the direction of the co-op. Max followed without a word. He kept his hands tucked in his pockets and meandered to his car, all the while, reviewing his options.

The sound was recognizable but not the song. As she came closer to the open outer doors, the tenor sax was amplified by the laboratory’s metal arched roof. Slipping through the second doorway, Margaret searched the long tunnel of music for a source. Her eyes found a shadow tucked among the stacks of cardboard boxes that held the remains of the Casco. The dark form was swaying to the music. Unnoticed, she moved closer. As she watched Max playing, she saw performance. He gave everything to the music. At the song’s end, she was silent. He stared at the skeletal specimen displayed on the exam table. It was as if he was waiting for a response.

"Do you think they heard you?"

Identifying the voice, “Margaret, come on over." He motioned with his sax for her to sit on a nearby lab stool. "That was "Sweet Soul" by Jr. Walker and the All Stars, or as close as I can come to Jr. Walker." Max smiled. Margaret was unresponsive. "You have no idea who Jr. Walker is, do you?"

"None"

"Motown; the late sixties...a sax like nobody else on the planet, Jr Walker? Here's the way that it's supposed to sound. Jr.‘s dead but his music lives on; digitally remastered, zeroes and ones, ones and zeros or whatever, numbers into the future."

Withdrawing a plastic case from a small canvas bag of supplies, he loaded a disk into his laptop and clicked play. Watching him, with his eyes closed, hang on every note and connected to some other place, she wondered if he had beer with lunch or, as the song continued, for lunch.

"I don't expect this song to do for you what it does for me. That's not fair to you or to Jr. Walker." He spoke softly, the song faded. "But the amazing thing is, when I first heard that song, it was an analog recording. You know on a record, a forty-five. It was the B side on vinyl. Then I had it in my record collection, you know, albums with liner notes and photographs. One of a kind album covers you could hold in your hands...big jackets you could read, over and over while you listened...vinyl."

“I know vinyl, Dean Martin.”

Max froze for a second trying to figure out the Dean Martin reference and couldn’t. “So you know it’s a recording technology that wore out, scratched, broke, melted or just plain deteriorated with time.

This I downloaded myself and burned the disc, not bad, huh?

But Margaret, what you and I can do here, with all this stuff that we have, ah now, that's a very different story. We can record and document the whole Casco

Collection digitally. In theory, and hopefully in practice, this is a method of archiving that won't let the data wear out; keeps it in zeroes and ones indefinitely. And to me, that seems to be a pretty remarkable thing when you think about it. Of course, if I think about it too long, well..."

Max was beginning to ramble and loose her, but the wonderment and enthusiasm with which he approached what he describe to her as, routine documentation and inventory, was genuine and not induced by beer.

"What do you mean Max? I'm a little lost. I thought this was standard but maybe it's not."

“It is. It is. In my book, it is.”

Gazing at the specimen nestled into the sand of the examination bin, Max continued to reflect aloud, "It's unbelievable really; the chronology of my life and my professional life, how it courses the transition from an analog world to a digital world. For you, its only been numbers; that's ordinary everyday life. For Burningwater its never been numbers; its never been quantified. I'm some where in between, a liminal being, in a quiet cultural and global revolution that's almost incomprehensible. Thinking about it, before you came I ended up having to take some sax therapy.

I got very excited at the possibility of creating a site on the Internet that would make available all these data of the Casco specimens we are going to document; accessible by anyone for research, comparative studies, to just look, to stimulate interest; the works. We could just put it out there, what you and I are going to record, for the world to see. But then I panicked...felt like a jerk. I got the blues."

Puzzled, she raised her eyebrows and shoulders.

"In the latter part of the nineteenth century, as the so called Indian Wars were drawing to a close, the U.S. Surgeon General ordered the military; some of the Civil War generals, you know the famous ones, to have their soldiers collect Native American heads and an occasional complete skeleton. The rationale was two fold: to measure cranial capacity for some state of the art supposedly scientific racial comparison which verified the intellectual supremacy of Euro-Americans and to display aboriginal skeletons in museums for anyone who desired, to see, study or simply experience the soon to be extinct Indian. If I were to put the Casco Collection on a Website, digitize the whole thing and put it out there in cyberspace, am I any different, other than a century or so older? Am I just creating a digital museum with the same crass and ethnocentric ignorance and arrogance five generations later?" Max paused, now considering the question. "Troubling questions, huh, all in the name of science and cultural understanding, possibly not such a great idea from another lost academic, so...I got the blues. I went to an old friend, Jr. Walker and suddenly...you're standing here."

The lab was still. Amid the dust, the boxes and the bones sat a man overflowing with incongruity. At one moment he was charging relentlessly toward the ideals of accessible knowledge on the Internet for the greater good and in the next he was questioning the narrow local cultural context of the greater good. Fortunately, for Margaret to clarify the repatriation and for the oncoming pain in Max's head, his ability to grasp, ponder and hold an expanded reality was short-lived.

"There's one other thing I should tell you. I went to see Burningwater this morning to ask for permission to..."

"I know. I already heard."

Max was surprised at the rate information traveled. "For a group of people who don't say much, a few words spread awfully fast."

"Even to me."

"And you still came?"

“I came because we had an agreement. I understood that I was the one to talk with Charlie Bay so we could avoid what happened the other day on the beach. Charlie Bay is a very angry Indian and with good reason. I agreed to meet with Dr Walsh and at her request to work with you. I did this because of an old friendship and because of someone I care about. Charlie Bay needs protection from you and people in the University system like you. He needs my help to get back the bones of his people as fast as possible. He doesn’t want to talk with you any more. He just wants the bones back and he expects me to deal with you as the school’s representative to do it. Now is that the way it’s going to work or not?”

Margaret was flush. She knew he was scheming. Max was sheepish.

“Ya, that’ll work.”

Having gained some ground she wanted more.

"So what was so important that you had to see him about...that you couldn't discuss with me? What are you up to? What do you want to do?"

"What I want to do? OK. I'll tell you what's on my mind. This lab is set up to document, record and inventory all the material before repatriation. What we are going to do, starting today is digitize the whole thing; on DVD, radiographic images, microvideo images, the works. Together we can do it as part of the inventory and it's not going to take additional time. And that's got great potential but it's not enough." Max twirled his wedding ring. "Do you see those boxes stacked against the far wall and marked DNA?"

"Yes, the three smaller ones."

"There are a couple of techniques, which have been used successfully for a while now, and they're being refined all the time. Anyway, they allow the extraction of DNA from ancient bone. It's really not all that complicated but we would have to consult a DNA lab and follow their protocols. I have a friend, a colleague of mine in Pittsburgh, who's in the field and he could work with us. There is a standard for harvesting uncontaminated samples of bone from each specimen and sending it to a lab for whatever state of the art analysis. Collecting the samples from the Casco bone would be our job and those boxes contain the necessary materials; all the stuff to harvest and ship the bone."

"No Max, absolutely not, no more research!"

“But Margaret, it’s not research. It’s harvesting DNA! The key is archiving the DNA, stuff you could store and pull as new techniques come along. This could go on for centuries! Now, that's got some research potential, stuff you could store and pull for centuries!”

Max unclipped his sax from the strap around his neck and set it on the exam table.

"The other thing is there’s the chance to compare ancient DNA with living people, particular groups. You’d be able to tell if people are who they say they are.

But, the whole thing, it takes time and that's why I went to Burningwater this morning. It takes some time."

The ring of the land line phone interrupted Max’s academic ramblings. Standing close to the desk, Margaret reached for the receiver. But Max, with his arms outstretched and palms pressing toward her, tried to stop the pickup.

"No, don't! I know who it is! I don't want to talk..."

Margaret also knew who it was and she did want him to talk.

"I've already gotten three e-mails from her today. I shut off my...I know what she's going to tell me. Just take the message." Max started to walk away.

"Hello", she shook her head no in his direction, hit the speaker phone button before he got too far and gave him the look. "It's for you. Dr. Walsh."

"Nice touch" he mumbled as he walked to his sax, clipped it to the strap and held it for protection. "Sandra! What a surprise!"

Margaret rolled her eyes, dropped her head and sat on the stool next to the phone.

“Max you jackass, you’re acting like an idiot! I don’t get it Max. Why does the bumbling jackass show up when I need perfection? Where is your head? Don’t tell me I already know.” There was a pause.

"So, having gotten that off your chest, what's on your mind." He winced and a few more idiots and jackasses followed. Margaret liked this woman.

"Now listen carefully Max. I don't want any other research projects with the Casco. I don't want you dragging your feet while you try backup plan after backup plan to postpone the repatriation and most of all, I don't want any incidents like this morning. If this type of confrontation ever got to the press, the University would take a public relations beating. It's an absolutely no win situation. It would be a disaster. Do you hear me Max, a disaster! I want the reburial to go smoothly and quickly and remember, no incidents. Do you understand me Max? Am I clear enough even for you?"

"Clear as a bell, Sandra, clear as a bell." He was giving in to Sandra's orders but Margaret suspected by the look in his eyes that he wasn't giving up.

"Good! Now do it! Just do whatever it takes to repatriate the collection. That’s it!

Now you can turn your cell back on." were Sandra Walsh's final words.

Shutting off the speakerphone, Margaret looked at Max as he spoke.

"You set me up for that call."

"You saw Charlie Bay this morning without me."

He smiled. "Tunnel vision can be discourteous."

The self-deprecating aspect of his personality was, at times, disarming.

Although, still unsure about Max Sorensen, Margaret was sure about Dr. Walsh. His response and readiness to move forward needed to be pushed. "Can we get to work on the repatriation?"

"Sure, I guess now's the time." Tucking one hand in his pocket and holding his sax with the other, Max swayed his way to the first inventory station humming "Sweet Soul".

Chapter Eight

Even in an unfamiliar community, Max possessed the ability to find what he always claimed was the best bakery in town. During his stay at Sandra's home, about two miles from the beach he discovered a small, storefront bakery in a private residence. A stout woman in a big apron served hot blueberry muffins in the morning and pie by the slice in the late afternoon. With a good portion of the summer away from his home routine, finding one of his Boston staples in Maine was essential. For Max, it was bakery food. He was a daily sunrise and a sometime late afternoon customer.

The scent of fresh baked blueberry muffins filled his car only seconds after opening the bag. He ate one before starting the engine and saved the rest for the cemetery. It was over three weeks ago Max first noticed the small classic New England burial plot. The site was located just off a secondary road and occupied less than an acre. High grasses surrounded stained, moss covered gray granite markers. There were no miniature American flags stuck next to headstones, no plastic baskets of flowers and no visitors. For almost a month, a neglected cemetery of tilted headstones and unmowed lawns caught his eye and his curiosity.

Finally arranging the schedule with Margaret to free a morning, he was anxious to investigate this Euro-American record. The inscriptions on the first tier of headstones didn't disappoint him. Most of the markers listed mid to late seventeenth century birth and death dates. As was a common tradition of the era, spouse, children and parents were recorded with the deceased. By the dates, Max knew these individuals buried in rows of orderly plots were contemporaries to many of the specimens in the Casco Collection. The gravestone inscriptions indicated that most of the people were of Western European descent. The markers gave a written record of their existence in time and space and described their relationship in a family. Each stone connected the individuals to a lineage, a lineage of North American families, potentially traceable through town and Baptismal records to living ancestors.

For Max, at times such as these, it all seemed so remarkable. He was in a laboratory on the coast of Maine, attempting to reconstruct the unwritten record of a people who occupied the same earth as their European counterparts. The Casco, who also had mothers and fathers, brothers and sisters, sons and daughters; all remained unknown. And again as a scientist, he was pushing forward, in a different part of the world than the Nile Valley, to trudge his way through physical morphology. Attempting to compare and contrast the lumps and bumps on bones, he sought an understanding of the Casco people. He sought to know the Casco lifeway, a lifeway all but extinct. According to Sandra there was only one known lineal descendant left on Casco land. The remnant of the Casco people was Charlie Bay Burningwater and he was the obstacle.

Finding a large fieldstone at the border of the burial ground, Max sat on the hillside facing the July morning sun. The evaporating dew left the scent of tall grass and the bag at his side the aroma of fresh blueberry muffins. His thoughts drifted around the traditional pathway of recreating a lineage; the family tree. Reconstructing from bones and words, assigning names and numbers, Max usually built a tree or a bush or some ascending schematic to objectify generations of life. But with the Casco, his mind had shifted to a component of available technology, a method that resolved the morphological reconstructions of the past one hundred and fifty years with microbiology. It was ancient DNA. For the last six weeks, bathed in the allure of Casco bones, Max was unable to let the prospect of ancient DNA go. Seated in the warm sun among the markers of passed lives, he ate two more blueberry muffins and twirled his wedding ring.

Despite the majesty of handling human skeletal material, even the most remarkable encounters, with repetition, were now routine for Margaret. But the reverence and dignity with which she approached the repatriation inventory never waned, a fact that wasn't lost on Max. To him, she was a novice assistant with remarkable instinct and sensitivities. Her work, over the past weeks had settled into a rhythm of performance and responsibility.

For her part, Margaret wondered if Max, without her help, was capable of completing the job. She respected his expertise and tolerated his occasional lack of focus but in the back of her mind, she always felt he was on to another project. However, between the extraordinary experience and her almost daily opportunity to inform Charlie Bay of the progress, she considered her place in the reburial process fortunate. It also allowed her time to write. She finished the re-write of *Overturn* and thought it was better, not where she wanted, but better. The storyline for *Shadowcatchers* was blocked out, the ending surprising her. Her habitual dictation files were organized and thanks to Max, she plunged into Motown, mainly the Temptations and the Four Tops. All in all, Maine agreed with her.

Left alone in Professor Moore's building for the first time during the repatriation inventory, she enjoyed the quiet and the solitude. Over the past month and a half, she and Max documented, catalogued and prepared for reburial all but eight of the entire Casco Collection. Those remaining specimens were on loan to a Native

American research project underway at a small college in eastern Connecticut. For the up-coming weekend, Max planned to attend the Glastonbury Lacrosse Tournament in an area reasonably close to the school. Arrangements were made for him to pick up the material on the following Monday morning. Their inclusion into the collection was set for Tuesday.

Because more cargo space was needed for transport than was available in Max's Volvo, Margaret offered and he accepted her family's SUV for the trip. The exchange of car for truck was planned for later this morning. But the switch was complicated by Jim Garret's need to tow a newly purchased twenty-three foot, fiberglass power boat from the dealership to his office. The center console model with a two hundred horsepower outboard engine, loaded with extras was headed to her father's parking lot for temporary storage. Expecting Max back from the cemetery around eleven to go for the swap, Margaret used the time to organize the boxes of Casco bones for their final trip to the new burial ground on Eagle Island.

The number of individuals in the Casco Collection was well over one hundred. In order to facilitate handling and moving the skeletal material at the final station, complete specimens, juveniles and partial remains were placed in large foot-locker sized cardboard boxes and labeled on the outside. Fragments, small bones, loose teeth and unidentified bone, all of which were associated with ID numbers, were placed in small brown paper bags or wrapped in unprinted newspaper and packed in the cartons alongside the skull and larger bones. The end result was seventeen boxes whose contents varied in combinations of age, sex and skeletal components.

Two weeks ago, before making the final decision on the packaging, Margaret wanted to check with Burningwater for his approval. She brought him to the laboratory for his OK in the way in which his ancestors were to be returned to the Island. When they arrived at the parking spot adjacent to the lab's entryway, Charlie Bay took one look at the building and refused to leave the truck. He told Margaret to handle the job in whatever way she saw fit. He didn't speak to her for the next three days and never gave a word of explanation.

As she stacked the boxes by the far door, Margaret thought about the incident. She was still uncertain why he came to oversee the preparations, but never came inside to view and check the bones. Placing the last box near the doorway, her thoughts were interrupted by clatter at the opposite end of the building. She looked over to see Max banging his way through what was now a familiar, noisy and ungraceful entrance.

"Did you move this?" Max asked, as if startled by a small table and trash barrel that he bumped routinely. Margaret shook her head no.

"Want some blueberry muffins?" an offer which he made daily and which daily, she refused.

"No thanks. How was the cemetery?" This was a question, odd to anyone but Max Sorensen. She was beginning to enjoy his eccentricities and she was one of few.

"It was terrific; just a spectacularly beautiful and interesting plot. Thanks. I appreciated the time to make the visit." His enthusiasm was genuine. In his mind, they were co-workers, the Casco bones were common ground and he was free to express the pleasure of what might be perceived by others to be an odd attraction to the dead. Placing the bag on the desk next to a bag from the day before, he walked to the far end of the building and to the piled boxes of the Casco. Extending both arms around the stack, as if to hold them just a little longer, he mumbled, "Damn, I hate to see you go."

"But, go they must Max."

He heard her and raised his shoulders and eyebrows in submission. Margaret thought this gesture a bit much.

Testing him, "Max, tell me again what you wanted to do with the equipment over there. The stuff we never opened." She pointed to the containers labeled DNA.

"Ah, remarkable that you should ask, chasing that thought occupied the majority of my morning."

"And what did you think?"

"After all this time together and you're still asking me open-ended questions. You are a courageous woman." With a broad grin and without any hint of manipulation or desperation, he gestured for her to sit down; this was going to take awhile. "You know if you go through the anthropology literature, there is an underlying trend, kind of a theme to the whole thing. To questions answered and unanswered, there always has been and still is, this nagging issue of origin. Here we are, humans, struggling through, with more or less relative success in the human condition. We have our bodies, our minds, our beliefs and our spirit. And, we have this drive as individuals, as families, groups of people; cultures of people to figure out, to understand where it all came from, this humanness, this human condition."

Other than picking up the SUV, her work for the day was done. Max certainly wasn't and she wondered how long this was going to last. They were scheduled to drive in his car to her father's office to make the switch for the truck by noon. She saw the appointment as an escape deadline.

"So, those of us dealing with the physical; the human body, we try to reconstruct the trail, bit by bit, the best we can with what technologies are available to us along the way. We create this latest and greatest taxonomy, the latest family tree. Then we argue, discuss and debate. We rethink, retest and discuss and debate all over again. But we have done it, for the most part, with morphology; shapes of bone, bits and pieces of this or that, measurements, images, for a hundred fifty or two hundred years, essentially the same way, through comparative anatomy."

Recognizing a look in Margaret's eyes as similar to one in his wife's and sons' eyes just before they found any excuse to leave the kitchen table during a lengthily, rambling discourse, Max focused his thoughts. He loved an audience.

"OK. OK, more to the point. North America, with European contact, is a terrific model for change. We have five hundred years of wave after wave of cultural intercourse, with society after society altered irrevocably as Europeans and then Euro-Americans and African Americans expanded into already occupied environments. What the hell happened? The historic record paints the European perspective, with all its ethnocentric biases. Later, that same historic record gives us the American perspective, with its manifest destiny and a justification to exterminate aboriginal peoples. The oral record of Native Americans only begins to balance the inaccuracies and enormous voids in the written record, but it is so sparse. And the physical material fills in a little more about Native American death and diseases and populations. But how many people were living on the east coast of North America when the Europeans arrived? Two million? Three million? Four million or more? What happened to them all, their descendants? Sure, most are aware of the tragedy engulfing horrific events like the nineteenth century relocation of the Nations in the southeast with the Trail of Tears, or the Plains Indian Wars and Wounded Knee but what of the life and death and suffering of others whose story is unknown? Where are those who remain?

There are three federally recognized Tribes in Maine: the Penobscot, the Passemaquody and the Casco. Where are the rest of the vibrant and growing communities that inhabited this territory in the sixteenth century? Obviously, disease, warfare, and politics took their toll, but what about assimilation and relocation in the seventeenth, eighteenth, nineteenth and twentieth centuries? Where did they go? And what happened to their culture; their ethnic identity, all they believed?

Ancient DNA!" Max spoke as if released.

Margaret knew this was coming, was surprised at how he got to it and had no idea where he was going.

"Ancient DNA. Not back to DNA again!"

"Ancient DNA, I can't stop thinking about it. We've been trying to accomplish with morphology, with ethnography and all the rest of it, something that may be best answered at an intracellular level. I think we'll be able to reconstruct the trail genetically. I don't know much about the methods, but the prospect of such a huge leap forward is driving me nuts. I haven't been this excited about an idea in years! I've always been a little obsessive, but this is a frontier almost beyond comprehension and the Casco can be right smack in the forefront.

Here's what we do. We take ancient DNA samples from the Casco Collection as a pristine and distinct Native American Nation, say thirteenth and fourteenth century radiocarbon dates which we already have, and the DNA guys identify genetic markers specific for the sample, which I think they can do. Then, follow the amplified marker through time to the living Casco of this latest July census. It's beautiful. These boxes of bones are a genetic gold mine. We can trace the relocation and assimilation of the Casco with microbiology and overlay the results with a known cultural history. Spectacular!"

"They aren't just boxes of bones, Max. They are Charlie Bay Burningwater's ancestors."

"I know! I know! Don't you see, that's the beauty of it!"

Margaret dropped her head in disbelief and glanced at her watch. “I can’t believe that you’re back onto ancient DNA.”

The ride to pick up the vehicle was in silence. The annoying smile on Max's face intensified as they pulled into the parking lot and her father's latest acquisition came into view.

"Well, take a look at that. Nice boat huh?"

Still upset about his scheme to skirt the issue of outright compliance with the Casco reburial, she didn’t answer.

"I'd just like to use the men's room inside and I'll meet you back here when you get the keys. I gotta take a close look at this boat. That design and hull shape is one of my favorites; beautiful “Pointer” lines like those, that Downeast flare, even in fiberglass is an art form."

The childlike quality of excitement and the appreciation of esthetic elegance in a boat, for which she had none, left her holding a generalization about men, regardless of age. Max followed one step behind Margaret on the walk into the lobby of a six-story contemporary office building and parted company without another word.

Jim Garret's suite of enterprises occupied the entire sixth floor. One of his real estate companies owned the building, but there was no mention of his name or promotion of his businesses anywhere. The street number, twelve fifty which stood on the lawn in stainless steel and JSG and Associates on the Directory for the top floor were the only public forms of identification for his corporations. Familiar with security and catching an elevator, Margaret was out of sight as Max, out of place and underdressed in the corporate environment, headed across a polished marble floor for the information desk and directions.

"Hi, ah could you direct me..." Max was distracted by a group of three women and one man passing by the counter whose physical appearance was dominated by what he perceived as extremely well defined Native American morphological characteristics.

"Direct you to the Casco Tribal Role registration in the main reception room?"

"Ah, no, to the men's room." He remembered that this was the July week of the census and didn't listen for directions to the rest rooms.

Expecting the secretary to have the keys at her desk, Margaret wasn't planning to see her father and was surprised to be led into his private conference room. Jim Garret was alone in the large beige chamber and hunched over a stack of collated folders.

"Margaret! Come on in. I'm just getting ready for a presentation this afternoon. Good to see you up here, it doesn't happen often."

Jim extended his left arm to direct Margaret's eyes to the center of the oval shaped conference table and a glass encased model of what looked to her like one more of her father's hotel and resort complexes. She nodded and smiled.

"I can see that you are taken by the project." He grinned, knowing that his daughter had little interest in his work.

"Well, you know I am but, they all look the same ..."

"Yes they do but, this one is different. For one thing it's bigger. You see that...."

"I see...it looks great, I know you do great projects. I hope it goes through and it's like always very successful." Margaret smiled at her father.

"All right, all right, enough. Here are the keys. Where is the anthropologist? Sanderson? I wanted to meet him." He set the keys on the table.

"Sorensen, Max Sorensen. He's out looking at your boat."

"Sorensen huh, well I was close."

Both drifted toward the wall of windows and observed Max bobbing and weaving his way around the boat and trailer.

"Curious guy."

"Dad, as you would say, just the tip of the iceberg" letting her exasperation show in tone.

"So, how's it going with him? Are you ready to finish up the project?"

"Ya, I think that we're doing OK. We have the remaining portion of the Casco Collection that Max is supposed to pick up this weekend with the truck and that should be inventoried and everything ready to go by the middle of next week.

But now he's rambling on about some ancient DNA archiving and DNA screens of living Casco tribal members, so who knows the exact timetable. He is one idea after the next...it's endless with him."

"Ancient DNA? Where did that come from? I thought that this was a University reburial for Burningwater."

"It still is, but Dr. Sorensen seems to get distracted with additional research pretty easily. I don't think it's ..."

Their conversation was interrupted by the voice of Jim Garret's secretary on the speakerphone informing him that one of his attorneys; Sam Mitchel had arrived.

"Thanks. Send him right in." Taking that as her cue to leave, Margaret picked up the keys. "Wait a second, I'd like you to meet Sam, a nice guy and bright, bright lawyer. Stay just a couple of minutes."

Sensing a political connection or a law firm employment connection but not a social connection, she stayed and expected some of her father's networking in the opposite direction of theatre.

"Sam, come on in. I'd like you to meet my daughter, Margaret."

Attorney Sam Mitchel was a head taller than Jim Garret. He had shiny jet-black hair that was combed straight back and met in a wave just above his starched collar. His stomach was flat and he had a great tan. After spending most of the summer with a rumpled academic dressed in solid T-shirts, khaki pants and sandals; a silk shirt and tie, tailored suit and Italian leather shoes were captivating. Whether it was Sandra Walsh or Sam

Mitchel, Margaret recognized and was attracted to the energy of powerful people. Jim Garret looked for her instinctive response. Margaret looked for a wedding ring.

"Margaret was just telling me about her reburial project. Fill Sam in...on a little of your work with this skeletal collection and about this ancient DNA."

"Sounds fascinating, I'd like to hear about it."

"Well, it's the repatriation of a Native American skeletal collection housed at the University. I've been working with an anthropologist from Boston. We're about ready to rebury the Casco Collection but now, with Max Sorensen, he's the anthropologist, there's some talk about DNA from bone and archiving it to trace Casco genes in other collections, maybe even living people. "

"That's amazing work. Can you really do that?"

"If he has the time to collect the Casco DNA, and from what he has said, once the samples are archived, it seems that you can.

I'd just like to get the bones back in the ground... but he wants to get the DNA before the reburial, hold it in an archive and make it available for later research."

Jim was proud of his daughter even if this wasn't how he wanted her to spend the summer. Knowing full well the look, Margaret was embarrassed and wanted to leave.

"I really should go, nice to meet you..." Uncertain whether to call him, Sam or Mr. Mitchel, she let her sentence tail off and turned to her father. "Thanks Dad."

"See you later Margaret. Oh, you were down a quart of oil in the truck. So I filled it and left a spare in the back."

Margaret was gone. Despite his desire to support and sponsor his daughter, even in the simplest ways, he still wrestled with the principle that sometimes the most mundane things between a father and daughter are better left unsaid. He wished that he never mentioned the oil.

Checking to insure that his Jr. Walker CD sat in the consol tray was the last thing Max did before a long trip. Some of his travel, usually the beginning and end, was devoted to "Sweet Soul", the rest varied. Max was excited; two days of lacrosse and more importantly two days with his son. The lab work through July with Margaret was productive but long. He was ready for a break. Removing his shirt, he climbed into the 4x4 and headed south for the turnpike.

Driving shirtless, during the summer months, was a carry-over tradition from the years of beach trips with his boys; before adolescence and air conditioning. Traveling with the windows down, they were always cool, toll booth attendants laughed and his wife, comfortable with the boys, was embarrassed for Max. His shirtless ritual was now more entertainment than comfort. He refused prepaying on an EZ Pass scanner to maintain the tradition.

Today, at the Hampton, New Hampshire toll, a smiling woman with Sally scribed on a nametag that rode slightly inclined above a full bust, leaned out to the truck and casually glanced down to his thighs. Max thought she was looking for pants and wondered if she was disappointed. He also wondered if it were ever possible to let his old family traditions go.

The past two years of following his son's collegiate athletic career provided Max a positive distraction from his sometimes disjointed professional life. Sports brought them together and gave them the chance to talk. The evolution of sport's conversation between father and now adult child reminded Max of the growth in the relationship with his father. He was beginning to see with his son how he once was, the attitude change, the tolerance and the affection. As the wind blew on his bare chest, he was happy, on the move and looking forward to the time ahead.

Passing through the gate onto the early morning sun-drenched athletic fields, his concerns with the Casco drifted away. For the next forty-eight hours, he was going to immerse himself in the skills, the lacrosse competition and the endurance of college athletes, all without leaving the bleacher seats. There were thirty-six teams, three divisions, one game per hour running time, on six fields from eight in the morning until seven at night. The only food available was grilled chicken and sausage with peppers. The grill opened at nine and he wasn't thinking about chicken.

Max viewed events such as these as pay back to a father, sometime coach and always chauffeur to games, tournaments and practices for two boys during a decade of youth sports. He had his son's schedule and his own love for a game he never played. Once again, he was the consummate participant observer.

The sidelines to each fresh cut field were bordered by competitors of similar demeanor; this time of the morning, young men of few words. Most carried equipment bags packed with sticks, pads, helmets, spare shafts and T-shirts. There were more college, company and association logos than Max knew or could track. Interspersed among the players, were young women, fewer in number, most with coffee and most in conversation. Other support for the tournament came from a small collection of mid-fifties and overweight parents carrying coolers and lawn chairs; fathers reliving their own reconstructed athletic past and mothers clinging to an adult son's ever dwindling athletic future.

And with all this stuff was an aspect of the game that always caught Max’s attention, the technology. Titanium shafts, injected molded helmets, custom pads and shoes for every surface; all of it seemed far from the hand-carved wooden sticks and rawhide pockets of only a generation ago.

The photo of a purification ritual with members of the Iroquois League, the players dipping their wooden sticks into a sacred brook for spiritual power, surfaced in Max’s mind. He looked at titanium and thought of wood. He wondered what was lost. Were the players still connected to the spirits of the game? The question reminded him of the moment he tried to define the spirit of lacrosse for his son. Max sat in the sunshine, remembered it like it was yesterday.

It was over six years ago, during his son's sophomore year in high school. The team's lacrosse season was off to a slow start, dropping their first four games. After the fourth loss, on a rainy day and a muddy field, Max sat in the car with his frustrated son, both soaked to the bone. Cold and wet, he imparted what little knowledge he had of the game. In humble tone, he affirmed that lacrosse was physical, intellectual, social and emotional, and all played their part in wins and loses. But the game was also spiritual. Lacrosse was a sport that benefited from the spirits of those who played in the past, generation upon generation. He explained to his son, it was time for him to tap into the experience and skill of those who came before, to connect with the legends. Without questioning his timing, Max lifted the short sleeve of the school uniform to expose a portion of the shoulder pad. He took a pen from his briefcase and drew the Native American symbol for a Thunderbird on the fabric. As he pulled the sleeve back over the pad he remembered whispering, "to play on the field with the spirit of the Thunderbird."

Max listened to his son sigh but the Thunderbird stayed. The next game, Max watched with pride as he scored three goals to go along with four assists in their first victory. The high school team ended their season that year fifteen and five with a regional tournament championship. Young Sorensen was the MVP. Max and his son never spoke a word about the conversation that day in the car or the symbol of the Thunderbird. As far as Max knew, his son didn't touch the image or change shoulder pads but he never looked.

After enjoying the first game, despite a loss, Max had an hour before the second. He found a seat on a small sunlit six-tier bleacher beside one of the playing fields, removed his shirt and basked in the warmth of a mid-morning temperature serge. The current game was between two clubs from Baltimore, apparently well known to one another. Their fans and friends remained on the player's sideline opposite the bleachers. They mingled among the coolers, equipment and substitutes. Two or three kept yelling nicknames and inside jokes to laughter from players of both teams. Max assumed these guys were older, maybe much older. The "Has Been Farewell Tour" on their shirts was a give-away. The four or five people who sat with Max on the bleachers disappeared at half-time and he was joined by a beautiful young strawberry blond wearing highly cut tan shorts and a white, tight T-shirt. At the end of a twenty-foot black polypropylene leash held in her hand was an Alaskan Husky. As she sat near Max, both watched the dog crawl under the stands for shade. Once again, feeling closer to thirty than seventy, he sucked in his stomach and struck up a conversation about something authentic and at this stage of his life, sincere; the weather.

"Great day for the tournament."

The woman smiled and nodded. Age, physical condition, athletic ability and lacrosse skills aside, he was connected to this event. He was invigorated by the atmosphere and without any intention of letting the moment go, regardless of how incongruent, he kept going, "Ya, just a perfect day for it. Do you get to many games?"

"No, not really, this is new to me. I've been dating one of the guys with the green shirts for just a little while. I don't know much about the game."

Relationships and boundaries established Max had time, plenty of energy and most important an audience.

"Lacrosse is a Native American game."

Her bright hazel eyes and fair skinned brow expressed surprise and interest at his statement. That was all he needed.

"Ya, the game was played by many of the Nations up and down the east coast of North America; probably with the Iroquois and the Cherokee the most well known. Often times disputes were settled by Lacrosse games and that is why it is sometimes called the "Little Brother of War". It was played on huge fields, maybe a mile long. And sometimes games lasted into the night and sometimes with many, many players running around under a full moon, playing in the moon shadows."

Now Max was surprised. She seemed genuinely interested in the historic background and her response was an invitation to carry on. "For other tribes the game also had a spiritual context. And the game between groups was often played as part of a bigger ritual and seasonal celebration. There were all kinds of pre and post game ceremonies and rites to empower and protect the players. Along with that, of course, was the game's tie to the culture's mythology, some great origin myths."

"Origin myths? What do you mean?"

"Well, I don't mean origin myth in the sense of human beings but more like stories that you heard as a kid, tales and legends of how things came to be; plants and animals; you know."

She understood and smiled. He took a quick breath knowing that half time in a one-hour game was short.

"My favorite of the lacrosse myths is *How the Bat Got It's Wings.*" He didn't wait for another signal. He intended to get this story in before they started the second half. "You see, it seems that on a particular day, the four legged animals with teeth were challenged to a lacrosse game by the flying animals without teeth. They were all set to play, when this scrawny little four-legged animal came over to the birds; to the leaders of the birds like the hawk, the eagle and the Thunderbird and said that the four-legged animals didn't want him. They said that he's too small, too weak, can't run fast enough and can't see well; all the usual reasons to be cut from a team. So the flying animals had a discussion, then asked the bear and the wolf if they could take this castoff for their team, to which the bear and the wolf laughed and agreed that the flying animals can have the weak scrawny little four-legged being. So the birds adopted him. Now, the Thunderbird decided that since they have adopted this animal, who calls himself a bat, they must enable him to fly.

In order to achieve this, the hawk hooks some of the bat's skin from his stomach to the bat's front claws and tried to get him to fly. It doesn't work. There is not enough wing. So, some other birds, especially good at building nests, took some hide from the sacred drum which was used to announce the game and sewed it to the bat's wings for strength and speed. The bat flew, although somewhat erratically at first.

As the game progressed, he didn't play much because it was a very close game. And when the sun went down, both teams were boasting of their superiority but it remained undecided well into the darkness and shadows of the full moon."

Max saw the players beginning to warm up. The referees were at mid field. He figured that he had about twenty seconds to finish. "It was then, because of exhaustion of so many of the players and the darkness that the eagle put the bat into the game. Amazing! It was remarkable! The bat darted and flew in and out of the moon shadows and caught the ball in his teeth and scored the winning goal! And that is how the bat got his wings."

Both were laughing, Max's arms were waving, the Husky woke up and the second half was uneventful. At the end of the game, the dog and the strawberry blond ran onto the field to be greeted by a tall, rugged and sweaty defenseman, each with a kiss. The Husky was first. As the couple walked arm and arm across the open field, the young woman turned and waved to Max. Delighted, he smiled and waved back but she had already looked away, tugged by a wandering Husky and the broad arm of number thirty-four. Max flashed to Margaret, thinking she was maybe three or four years older than the strawberry blond. Then he thought how both were young enough to be his daughters.

A great day followed. At its end, after a tailgate dinner with son and friends, Max returned to his hotel alone in search of a Barbara Stanwyck movie on cable and looked forward to getting started all over again with the rising sun.

Finding the biology building and the basement physical anthropology lab was not a problem, finding someone, early on Monday morning, with a key was. Eventually, two floors up in the Microbiology Department, Max stumbled onto a staffer who was able to help. Max never received the message that his contact in physical anthropology started a vacation this week and had left the key and the paper work in the Micro lab. The young, full bearded researcher in the laboratory, wearing jeans, an extra long white coat and extra large plastic safety glasses, apologized for the miscommunication. After appropriate introductions, with Max neglecting to mention his failure to check email over the weekend, he signed the forms and followed the microbiologist to the skeletal material. Promising the researcher he planned to return to the Micro lab with the key when the inventory and loading were finished, he began packing the final segment of the Casco Collection and felt guilty.

As Max saw their silhouettes, facing one another, framed by the counter tops and hoods, he thought that they were twins. Startled, he froze in the doorway and then set the key on the closest counter.

"Don't worry he's my brother. And no, we're not twins. Most people do a double take."

"Sorry I thought you were ...ah...I didn't want to disturb your work." Max thought about a clone joke but passed.

"My brother is also a microbiologist, from Pittsburgh, but he's into DNA. I was just showing him one of my projects, trying to broaden his perspective."

Max perked up, "Oh really, that's great, Pittsburgh? Hmm, that's interesting. Ever work with Cliff Patterson and any ancient DNA?"

"Yes some, he's a departmental colleague of mine. Why, do you know Cliff? And better still do you have any ancient DNA?"

"Yes and possibly."

"What have you got?"

Max eased his way into the room and extended his hand, "Max Sorensen."

"Alan Decker."

"It's Native American collection, archived, radiocarbon dated and I've been wondering about a specific protocol for harvesting a sample."

With knowledge and his brother irritated, Alan Decker was interested. "Well, the biggest problem with archived collections is contamination."

Max sensed this individual was a good source of technical information and pursued him.

"So, what would I use? A core from long bones; drill a hole and then go into the shaft and scrape around?"

"You could. How are the teeth?"

"The teeth? They're OK. Why?"

"The methods to analyze ancient DNA are growing and changing all the time. The key is how, and where, to get the stuff.

You need a sterile, dedicated environment. You know, sterile gloves, filtered air, UV light, the works and the best place to get a sample of material is the inside of the teeth; the hollow part, the nerve chamber. It's got great stuff." The microbiologist also enjoyed an audience.

"The teeth, how do you get it?" As the discussion progressed, Max began to twirl his wedding ring.

"It's not too difficult. Under a hood, you take a sterile surgical mallet and chisel, split the molar teeth in half and curette out as much material as you can into a sterile, labeled, 5ml polycarbonate tube with a good twist tight cap and send it to us. Some anthropologists have told me, the good thing about the technique is that, when they get good at breaking teeth in just the right way, they can glue them back together and no one can ever tell that they harvested the stuff.

I'm telling you, the methods and technology for analysis are on their way. The future looks remarkable and it is truly unbelievable what we're going to be able to do. The hard part is getting hold of good ancient samples even if it's just to archive."

Neither brother understood the few disjointed mumbles of Dr. Max Sorensen, but both caught the word Casco. Max remained untethered.

Chapter Nine

The human beings seated in the circle surrounding Charlie Bay were silent. Some eyes fixed to his, others stared away. Like before, Charlie Bay sat in the center and faced the Ancient One. As he considered those who encircled him, he stared back into the eyes of his ancestor. He was drawn to this man and poured over his features.

The Ancient One's shoulder length white hair was parted in the middle. It fell in an arc that paralleled the downward curves of his brow, his eyes and his lips. Each formed the cascade of distress, distrust and displeasure. The expression was sealed into his face. The Ancient One's arms were folded across his chest and pressed an eagle's wing to his left shoulder.

Charlie Bay let his eyes drift to the woman seated inches from the wing's tip. A dark blue scarf covered her forehead. A red woven blanket sheathed the curves of her body. Her beauty had hold of his heart. The sorrow in her eyes made Charlie Bay uneasy.

A grandfather sat alongside the sad eyed woman. His weathered brow was shielded by a brown felt hat. There was a dried starfish pinned to the front, just above the brim. Beneath the hat his hair was bundled at the ears by shreds of a blue cotton kerchief. The two streams of grey slid down the back of his shoulders and clung to his faded navy jacket. The grandfather's eyes were tired and glazed. His lids puffed.

One by one, as always, Charlie Bay met the ancients. He met them in silence. He met them in this faded room with strength and an edge of arrogance. He held firm his past choices as the right ones, the only choices he could have made at the time. Then Charlie Bay came to the empty chairs; those seven empty metal chairs, staggered between the dozen or so human beings circled around him. It was the empty chairs that made his jaw tight, his stomach turn and his defiance flee. The vacancies haunted him. They were seats of the missing, ancients who broke the circle and whose circle was broken. Each empty chair bore witness to the choice he made years ago and the choice he made moments ago. Each empty chair pressed his obligation.

Charlie Bay tried to speak. But he was without breath.

There was nothing like the smell of a southwest breeze blowing straight off an incoming tide on a sunny

July afternoon. As they turned to walk along the south side of Burningwater's home and the ocean wind hit them square in the face, Margaret smiled. The wind blew back her hair. The wind carried a raspy gasp and choking cough, a last breath.

"Did you hear that? Sounds like death!" Max spoke Margaret's thought and was first up the stairs to the porch.

Pushing open the screen door, he found Charlie Bay curled on the wicker couch, his left arm raised above his head, stark naked and laboring for air.

"Are you OK?"

As Charlie Bay nodded, Max stood still. Margaret bumped his shoulder and knocked him out of the doorway as she rushed to kneel next to Burningwater. Max didn't know what was happening.

"Where are his clothes? What's going on?"

Grabbing a small quilt from the back of the couch, Margaret covered Charlie Bay from the waist down. Max stared at the scared skin of the fisherman's chest and stomach. Regaining his breath, Charlie Bay pointed toward Max, "In on the floor next to the sofa." He sighed and rolled onto his back. "I got hot sleeping in there. I move out here."

"Would you get his clothes, Max?"

Max entered the house without taking his eyes off Charlie Bay's scars. "Sure."

Margaret turned to Charlie Bay, "You're OK, right?"

"Fine...ya fine." He cleared his throat.

Returning with his clothes, Max handed them to Margaret who, in turn, handed pants to Charlie Bay. Without any concern for modesty or hint of embarrassment, Charlie Bay stood naked before the two of them and began to dress. Unsteady in his attempt to step into his khaki pants, Margaret reached toward him and held his elbow. He entered a foot into each leg and pulled up his pants. He thought underwear was useless. Max studied his scars.

After he dressed, Charlie Bay sat back on the wicker couch and looked to Margaret.

"We thought you were choking. It sounded like you couldn't get enough air. It frightened us, the sound I mean."

She leaned back against the rail of the porch. Max sat in Charlie Bay's rocker, which received a look from Charlie Bay that went unnoticed by Max. Turning back to Margaret, who observed both, he chose his words carefully.

"I can't get breath in the dream."

Neither Margaret nor Max understood.

"Was it a bad dream? You mean like a nightmare?" She was uncertain but surprised that Charlie Bay volunteered any information about something so personal. It was unusual.

"It's a spirit dream that I've had for many years; over and over. I can't breathe in the dream. I'm like the others. I wake up trying hard to get air...get air to speak but I can't. I have no air."

"Oh, you mean a recurring dream." Max interrupted. "I get one of those. It's about this archeology course ..." Margaret interrupted him with a look that indicated it was better if he didn't speak. Max understood. They were growing closer.

"Who else is in the dream? Who are the others?" Margaret wanted more of the dream.

"My ancestors are in the spirit dream, the Ancient One...many of my people stuck, in the same place, in the same way. There are empty chairs... spirits waiting for the bones, taken from the Western Door, to be found and returned. I believe it's their bones; those ancestors in the dream, their bones must be returned and their spirits will be freed. We must act in their favor. We must rebury them all.

For a long time, they haven't moved. The missing bones halt the spirit journey. They can't go anywhere without help. As I told you once before Sorensen, it's their spirits, which are lost forever, unless we act in their favor."

Max looked to the floor. Margaret stayed on Charlie Bay.

"The dream also holds me...because of things that I did ...my choices. My spirit is also captured until the bones are returned and buried. I will wait no more. The empty chairs make waiting no more."

Max, now back on Charlie Bay, was finding it difficult to be quiet. A glance from Margaret had kept him silent. Thinking that he had done well in his sensitivity to Margaret's signs and signals, Max asked,

"What empty chairs? Where did the empty chairs come from? And what do they mean?"

"Max please!" The empty chairs also confused Margaret.

"I believe that they're the ones lost; bones lost, spirits lost, my people unaccounted for in this world and in...."

Charlie Bay saw by the looks on their faces that he said enough, maybe too much. He hesitated; he slapped his knees with both hands and changed direction. "Come on, I've finished the burial site. I'll show you where we'll bury my ancestors tomorrow morning!"

And with that stunning declaration, he stood up and hustled barefoot down the front steps. Dumbfounded by his pronouncement for the time of reburial and his abrupt recovery, Margaret and Max were left on the porch staring at one another.

"Tomorrow morning? We can't do it tomorrow morning. It's too soon!" Max continued grumbling. "We're not ready. It's too soon. Margaret come on, talk to him. Tell him we're not ready."

The panic in Max's voice drew a smile, "We are ready Max, everything is done."

Walking about twenty yards behind Charlie Bay and headed west past the blueberry patch, Max was a step behind Margaret and winded.

"Come on Margaret, his recurring dream about some empty chairs can't dictate the repatriation of the material. That's crazy. We can't do that. There's got to be some order to the whole thing. It's going to take a little time to get it organized."

"Like what? Everything is boxed. We bring it over in the morning. Why not? It's done."

Max was desperate, "Sandra! Sandra's not here. She wanted to be here."

"Do you really think that it matters to Burningwater whether Sandra Walsh is present at the reburial? Anyway, if she really wanted to be here, we could call her and she could catch a red eye tonight.

Come on Max, why stall any longer? What are you really after? What do you want?"

"I want enough time to break open some teeth and get enough material to archive the DNA. That's what I want! That's all I want! It'll just take a day or so!"

They walked to the top of a small rise that overlooked the two western mounds of Eagle Island. Across the crest of the hill a trench, approximately three feet deep, four feet wide and thirty feet long, ran from north to south with a sloping entryway on each end. Charlie Bay stood on the opposite side of the burial pit, within the sound of their voices.

Max was, by the expression of exasperation on his face and the tone of his voice, at the end of his attempts to buy time. "You know I can get a lawyer and tie this up for a few days. Then I'll drop whatever legal tactic works before the press can make a big deal out of it. Come on I just need a few days to break a few teeth that's all!"

Both walked to the edge of the trench on its eastern side. Startled by its size, they looked down into the final resting place of the Casco Collection. Across the trough was Charlie Bay Burningwater who heard every word.

"No bones shall be broken. No bones of my people shall ever be burned or broken." He spoke with a vengeance, a vengeance neither had ever seen. Margaret thought of the reference to burned or broken bones in "Heartache of the Hunter". She held her eyes to Charlie Bay's trying to tell him everything was going to be alright. Max lowered his head to the open grave.

Thinking that the driving range was a good place to release some of his frustrations with a minimal risk of injury, he drove directly from Eagle Island to a large bucket of yellow golf balls. Attempting to hit a golf ball as hard as possible without keeping score or chasing after it was supposed to be soothing. Maybe it was for those who were good at it. Max wasn't and his anger remained. Forgetting he lacked talent, he found himself halfway through the container and without any relief. Time after time, he watched the yellow range ball bounce and skid across the ground in front of him. The longest rolled just past the seventy-five yard marker. He wondered if he was ever going to hit one in the air and if he was ever going to get more time with the Casco. Both thoughts fueled his erratic bursts. Max was enraged by knowledge lost.

After the last ball skidded off, he was spent. He sat on a bench with the empty wire bucket hooked to the end of a titanium driver and rattled them both between his legs. Looking due east across the range, the sand landfill and the tidal marsh, he squinted to make out the three small knolls of Burningwater's home. They were one gray green bump against a blue ocean horizon and far away. From this perspective, the landfill and the marsh comprised a huge flat area and a tremendous amount of territory. Recalling the view from the rail tie bridge toward the south and west, it seemed to Max, that there were only two ways to access this enormous tract of land. One was narrow, rickety wood and marginally negotiable and the other was staying straight after the three hundred yard marker on the range. This spot opened onto the whole place.

As the wire bucket spun from the head of the club to rest under the bench, Max lost control of the driver and lost his train of thought. Groping around in high grass for the wire handle, he found another yellow range ball and wondered if Burningwater ever returned to that first site. The site where, almost two months ago, he swore there was a complete skeleton to match the bleached white shoulder blade nestled into the blue silk liner of the old man's collection box. First impressions were difficult to overcome. He considered in the moment why his lack of diplomatic skill was such a nagging constant and he wondered where the range ended and the Casco Reservation began.

Finally meandering to the equipment return counter, he heard the high volume mid-afternoon summer traffic on Rt. 1. The seafood stand was busy, a bait and tackle shop, a convenience store and the golf all had a number of cars in the combined strip parking lot. Addressing a long faced man with lingering acne who was surrounded by large and small buckets of golf balls, Max killed time and curiosity. He placed his driver on the counter and asked for information.

"Here you go. Say, ah, who owns this place?"

The man with the long face and an even longer body shrugged his bony shoulders. "I don't know."

"Well, who signs your checks?"

"My boss, but he doesn't own it. He just manages all these buildings. I think some company owns all of them."

"All of these buildings, is he around, your boss?"

"He's home. He's the boss." The lower third of the thin face grew horizontally into a smile and he took the club.

"Does your boss have an office or a card, so I could call him?"

It took a minute, but after shuffling through a large under the counter draw jammed with papers and invoices, in no apparent order, the attendant produced a business card.

"Great, thanks a lot." Max glanced at the card, didn't read it, put it in his pocket and walked to the take-out restaurant for a hot dog.

The problem was one that Margaret feared as a necessity from the moment she met Dr. Max Sorensen and one, she hoped was avoidable. Charlie Bay

Burningwater needed an attorney. It was up to her to find one. Pride and stubbornness made her choice to handle the repatriation of the Casco without a lawyer, early on, all the more difficult to find one, last minute. She had two resources; some casual attorney friends that her consulting firm used in Philly from time to time and her father. After a few calls, it was apparent finding someone familiar with Maine law in Philadelphia was a dead end. She already knew her father was not.

Late afternoon was a reasonable time to catch him between private meetings and evening functions. Calling ahead for a time in a crowded schedule was usually ineffective. Just showing up unannounced and sitting strategically between offices, a few moments of his time was never refused. Besides, instinct told her to ask for his help required meeting face to face.

Entering the inner suite of offices through an unmarked side door, she announced to her father's executive assistant that if possible, she hoped to catch him for just a few moments. Cordial as always, his assistant, a professionally dressed woman with blond hair and dark roots informed Margaret that his current meeting was about to end. She signaled with the tilt of her head that a seat on the sofa across from a small conference room was the best chance to intercept him on a tight schedule. Margaret sat, waited and tried not to listen.

"Congressman Bob Shaw please. This is Alice Parker from Jim Garret's office confirming the Congressman's flight tomorrow morning from

Washington into Portland and the car to meet he and his staff member at nine-thirty. Sure I'll hold. Hello, Congressman Shaw, Jim's looking forward to tomorrow and I'm just checking to confirm. Wonderful.

Anything you need let me know...it's a good-sized boat and you'll just be in the river but you could take one if you wanted. The patches are good too, but there really shouldn't be any waves...well, don't eat a big breakfast." Alice rolled her eyes in Margaret's direction. Both women smiled. "It'll be a pleasure having you here tomorrow. Goodbye."

Without a second's hesitation, she hit speed dial for another number and withdrew a blue folder from a side draw. "Congressman Gundermun, please."

Recognizing the names but wanting no part of politics, Margaret was hearing the Temptations' "Ain't to Proud to Beg", the chorus playing in her head, until her father burst from the conference room with four other pin striped suited men in tow.

"Hey, Margaret, this is a surprise. What's up? Everything OK?"

"Ya, everything's fine. I realize you're busy but I want to check with you about something. Maybe a couple of minutes, that's all it'll take."

"Sure, I have a second. Come on back in here. Go on ahead. I'll be right there."

Jim Garret and his daughter slipped into the vacated conference room and Margaret came right to the point.

"Max Sorensen is talking about getting a lawyer to tie up the reburial for a while so that he can do some additional DNA archiving with the Casco. You know the DNA stuff I told you about before. Charlie Bay might need a lawyer to deal with it and I...I didn't get anywhere with my contacts in Philly...so I need your help for a name."

Her last sentence was key and Jim Garret responded in kind. Leaning back through the door and holding his hand in the air to pause their conversation, he called to Alice.

"Alice, grab Sam before he leaves and have him come in here. Would you, please."

To Margaret's amazement he didn't turn and re-evaluate her summer. Pensively, he waited for his colleague.

"He'll be right in," were his first words and after a moment, he ventured his position. "Margaret, this could turn out to be a hurricane. I'll get you the name of a good attorney who knows Maine antiquities law and then as much as I'd like to help, I'm going to have to step back. This is all yours. You're on your own."

"That's all I'm asking. Thanks."

"Ah, Sam great. You remember my daughter, Margaret." Both smiled to one another as Jim kept talking with increased abruptness. "Well, it seems that there might be a problem over the reburial of the bones, the bones of the Casco; the project that Margaret told us about the other day. And Dr. Sandersen, on the University side, wants to stall a bit to do some DNA studies with Casco DNA. So, if necessary, she needs the name of someone to aid in the reburial. Who's out there?"

"Hum, Vince Simmons, in Augusta, has worked on and off with the Historical Society and some antiquities issues..."

"Perfect, he's perfect. Alice!" once again leaning out the door, "Alice, see if Vince Simmons is around for the next couple of days. It might be necessary to get in touch with him. She'll give you the numbers Margaret. Sam and I have to run." He didn't kiss her goodbye and left in a hurry with Sam hustling to remain at his side.

This time, the search for Burningwater was simple. Expecting to find him working on the burial site for tomorrow's ceremony, Margaret returned to Eagle Island late in the afternoon and found Charlie Bay's truck between the blueberry patch and the open grave. Following the sounds of low, rhythmic chanting, she walked down the narrow path to the work dock and fishing shack. Hovered over a large galvanized wash pail, Burningwater was singing in a language unrecognizable to Margaret and stirring a long wooden shaft into a bucket of cloth engulfed by a pool of bright red. Draped over the nearby lobster traps, barrels and hung from the roof, as well as any other location that supported fabric, were royal blue strips of material drying in a light southwest wind. He stopped chanting.

"Don't worry, it's not the blood of Sorensen."

Margaret smiled. She wondered what he was doing.

"These are traditional Casco colors. The silk is from parachutes my Uncle Robert brought back from war."

"Parachutes?"

"Silk parachutes. For years, I used the nylon lines from the chutes to knit heads for my gear."

"Knit heads?" She was lost and dangling.

"Ah, went to college and became a writer. There're things college doesn't teach and writers should know. There're many things universities don't understand."

Margaret nodded and Charlie Bay taught. "Heads are the woven net of a lobster trap. Look over there at that one. The lobster crawls up the head, falls in and can't get out for awhile. That's, if it's knit right." Charlie Bay smiled. He was happy. "I saved the silk. I've been saving it for years. The bones shall all be wrapped in silk of traditional colors. I'll do it first thing in the morning, as soon as you bring all of the bones over here."

"We packaged everything in biodegradable paper and cardboard boxes and tried to return the material with some dignity and respect." Anxious, tired and defensive about her inventory efforts, she wished that she never uttered the word, "material". Charlie Bay bristled. If he was happy, he wasn't anymore.

"Margaret, respect is not calling the bones of my ancestors, material and specimens. It's not taking them from the ground and putting them on shelves in universities and sending them all over the place to be touched and broken. That's not respect Margaret, it is desecration.

The bones are a part my people, people which I helped to bury; grandmothers and grandfathers. Flathead, Flathead's father, Bass Catcher, Gull and Gull's mother, my Uncle Two Moons, my Uncle Hollis and my Uncle Robert of the silk parachutes and Bat Player, even...Bat Player." Charlie Bay's voice trailed off in anger and hurt. Margaret was embarrassed but not confused. She must prepare him for the worst. She worried about his volatility.

"Charlie Bay there's a chance that there may be a problem with having the reburial ceremony tomorrow. Max may try to put it off for a few days, with some legal stalling. I know it's not good news but we are prepared and it won't last long, if it happens at all. It's going to be all right. There will be a reburial."

Charlie Bay stopped stirring the silk in the watery red die. Turning slowly toward Margaret he was stern. "Margaret, you are a woman with greatness, you've a gift, you write. You've done a good job. You've done all I asked. But, as I told you earlier today, I can wait no more. It will be tomorrow." Once again mixing the cloth, he began to chant ending their conversation and Margaret thought her role in the reburial.

The lights were on in Jerry Moore's laboratory. As Margaret suspected, Max also had trouble staying away from the Casco Collection archive. Passing through the unlocked door of the entryway, light from a flickering florescent bulb reflected off Max's tenor sax and caught her eye. The sax was lying on the near corner of the first exam table. It was the only object on the enormous oak surface. Everything else was gone; the sand bin, the digital x-ray materials, all of it gone. Her eyes darted to successive tables, each a bare wooden slab with only an occasional dust outline of its function as a station. He was packed; just about everything was packed. Only the portable x-ray machine remained standing. The makeshift desk, with the exception of some stacks of someone else's' mail, was empty. The hardware was sealed into three boxes on the floor next to the travel cases of the digital video and recording equipment. The frames of the exam bins were stacked against the outside wall. As she walked beside the tables, the echo of her footsteps was more pronounced. The arched building's function was reduced. She thought it was over. Seeing Max's smiling face bounce from behind the cartons containing the Casco, she knew otherwise.

"Margaret! Nice timing. I need your help taking apart the x-ray. Can you give me a hand? Hey, this same thing happened once before, a couple of months ago, didn't it?"

"Ya it did. Sure I'll help Max, but tell me why you look so happy. What are you up to?"

"Up to? Me? Come on Margaret, what makes you say that?"

"I've seen that look before. You're not going to let it go are you?"

Smiling, as a man coming to terms with his own obsessiveness and shrugging his shoulders in submission to his compulsions, he playfully answered, "Would you expect anything less? Help me take this thing apart and I'll show you what I've set up".

After their time together, Max, truly did not view Margaret's position as for, or against, his academic pursuits. He simply enjoyed her presence. She was bright and beautiful. Tonight, despite the day's conflicts, was no exception. For Margaret, with each occasion on which she began to appreciate him as someone other, his unilateral research reminded her, he was still a relentless enemy of the Casco.

"So what do you think of this!" Max beamed and pointed after they finished with the x-ray.

She knew what it was, "What is it."

"It's a portable hood with air filter and UV light. Isn't it great. I talked a guy in the Micro Building into letting us borrow it for a couple of days. Maybe an opportunity will present itself."

"Us?" Margaret scanned a small table set next to the hood and saw all of the material and equipment to collect DNA samples. "Max you are exhausting!"

The words were haunting. Max began to twirl his wedding ring.

The echoing tweeter of the phone left Margaret grunting with disgust as she marched to hit speaker, "It's for you."

The voice was a familiar one.

"Max, it's me. I thought I asked you to keep your cell on."

"Sandra! How are you doing? Bad reception here."

"I'm headed to the airport in Seattle and I'm on a red eye flight tonight. I'll be there first thing in the morning.

I want to be there for the reburial ceremony. So, stall if you have to, just until I get there."

Thinking that now was as good a time as any, Max pursued the inevitable, "Sandra, I was hoping that maybe we could stall things even for just a few more days. I've got a great project all set to go. I'm anxious to go over it with you as soon as you get here. I think that you'll be excited by it."

Margaret saw this coming. Sandra's voice exploded through the speaker phone, "Excited by it! I'm already excited by it! Don't you even think about any more projects. You just wait for me. All I want you to do Max, is wait for me. Understand, don't be a jackass and wait for me."

"OK, we'll talk when you get here."

"We certainly will. Is Margaret there? Margaret can you hear me?"

"Yes, I'm here."

"Margaret, as far as I'm concerned you are a Saint. You lasted two months with this man. You, my dear, you are a Saint! The gates of heaven will open for you! I'll see you both in the morning."

Neither spoke. Max sighed, raised his eyebrows, wrinkled his brow and pursed his lips. It was time for both to go. Margaret walked with him to the doorway. Max shut off the lights and eased the door shut behind them.

Chapter Ten

The first early morning words spoken from Max Sorensen's dry mouth, were in a voice coarse and loud. "What do you mean, they're gone!" He cleared his throat. "Well ya, I came back to get my sax and they were there. They can't be gone! I saw them! I'll be right over, don't touch a thing."

Crashing through the entry doors to the laboratory and knocking the trash barrel clean out of his way indicated to Margaret Max was upset. But she still thought somehow, in some way, he was responsible. "Take a look, there're gone, just the Casco, nothing else. What happened to them?"

"I don't know. Why are you asking me?" His eyes darted around the corner of the lab which twelve hours ago sheltered the nineteen trunk-sized cardboard containers of the Collection.

Margaret didn't go for the innocent look. "Well, you're a logical choice."

"Logical choice? I, ah.. I'm not logical. Why, ah.. well ya, I mean I think I know why you'd think that, but I didn't take them. Burningwater, he's the logical choice. He had more reasons... I didn't do it! He did it!" Max appeared to be dumbfounded. First, the collection was gone and second, she was accusing him of theft. "Look, it must have been Burningwater. He probably got two or three of those young fishermen and they came over late last night and took the Casco...took the burial into his own hands. Who else would? It was them. Did you call anyone?"

"No, just you...I was dropped off. My father has the truck for the boat. I haven't been over to the island or anywhere else. And I haven't seen anyone or talked to anyone but you."

Max was still scanning the floor, for what, he had no idea. But, because of his anxiety and confusion, his nervous energy dictated he do something. Unable to determine whether he was listening or distracted, she moved to block his path.

"What are you doing?"

Without lifting his eyes he answered, "I'm looking for clues."

Margaret was confrontational, "Clues, what clues? Someone pried open this lousy, rusty old lock on this door, came in, took only the Casco, left and closed the door behind them. Police, Max, the police look for clues. We need to find Charlie Bay. Because it was either you or Charlie Bay, nobody else would want these bones! I vote for you!"

"The lock? I didn't see that. You're right, but let's not call the police till we check with Burningwater. I don't want this to become an incident, especially if we can resolve it ourselves."

"An incident? It's already an incident. Dr. Walsh is going to be here in an hour or so and it will be larceny and, by that time, probably attempted murder. And she'll have to get in line behind Charlie Bay and me!"

Despite his concern, she suspected that Max whisked the Casco off to a motel room somewhere, planned to accomplish whatever he desired in the next two or three days and before things got too far out of control, the Collection would reappear. She knew him well enough and believed he was more than capable of such a strange plan.

"Oh, Sandra, I forgot about her, bad timing."

"Let's get going. We have to tell Charlie Bay. You can worry about Dr. Walsh later."

The burial site on Eagle Island was unchanged. Yesterday's footprints in the sandy windblown soil on each side of the grave were the only evidence of activity. There was no sign of Charlie Bay. There was no sign of the Casco. Margaret walked from the crest of the hill to Charlie Bay's fishing shack on the work dock. In silence and one step behind, Max followed without a word. Strips of red and blue silk were piled on two benches and weighted with bricks. The stained maroon bucket sat in the center of the platform surrounded by splashes of the traditional Casco colors. There was a quiet rustle of the oaks and poplars in a midmorning ocean breeze. The air was salty but there was no Charlie Bay.

As usual, curiosity was suppressed only so long for Max Sorensen, "What is this place? And what's all this cloth?"

"It's where Burningwater builds his lobster traps and the silk is for the bones of his ancestors. He's planning to wrap them in it. You know, in bundles. It's parachute silk, dyed the traditional Casco colors."

"Parachute silk?" Max was bewildered.

Margaret was off to check the next waterfront location.

As they approached the tip of the Western Door from the high ground above the beach, there was no truck, no Charlie Bay. Max pulled the car cautiously to the edge of the grass at the outer most point of land and both peered into the flat green water of a near high tide. To their left, on the southern branch of the Casco River, a large white center console was powering past them.

"It's my father. My father's boat, remember?"

"Ya, nice boat. He sure has a crowd on there. Some are in suits with ties. What does he do anyway?" They watched the boat pass without getting out of the car or waving.

"He's in real estate, used to be retail...now's recreational developments...golf resorts...you know, those kind of things. There must be some big deal going on.

Those suits are on Congressmen. I heard the plans yesterday."

"Congressmen? U.S. Congressmen?" Max shook his head. "Hmmm, he's into something."

"He always is. Come on let's check the fish pier."

Never rowing beyond the mouth of the river for almost three years was intolerable for Charlie Bay. Making up his mind in early July that he wasn't going to miss this season's late summer run of soft-shell lobsters, he mustered the courage two weeks ago to cut the outboard well into the hull of his Alton built, Bank dory. He was unable to get over it. Each day, at around high water, he made the trek to the fisherman's co-op where the dory was anchored in the shallows. Resetting the hook from time to time, he picked spots with just enough depth for most of the tide to swell the new seams without letting the boat sink. The joint leaked less each day, but each day Charlie Bay was there, bucket in hand, dressing and tending the wound. Any thoughts of strapping his brand new, two-year-old twenty-five horsepower Johnson motor to the dory were painful. Still feeling he was strong enough to row surged from his heart with each pail of water, water from a boat that had never leaked. And his back ached more with each bend.

As Max and Margaret drove into the co-op, the SUV with Jim Garret's huge empty boat trailer stretched across the parking lot.

"I see why your dad needed the truck. He thinks big. That's one long rig."

Margaret spotted Burningwater's pickup and paid no attention to Max. "Charlie Bay's here. His skiff's still in the dunes!"

"Good, now we'll find out what really happened."

Max's air of confident innocence didn't surprise Margaret. But she realized that her impatience wasn't so much to identify the guilty party, as it was to resolve the whole thing. Burying the Casco and moving back to her apartment in Philly, push *Overturn* and finish her third play, was all she wanted.

They parked next to Charlie Bay's truck and walked to the water's edge. The dory was moored in three feet of water about ten yards to the lee of the fish pier. Sitting on the gunnel of the dory's inland side, Charlie Bay watched the two of them as they approached. He was suspicious. Their expressions were a give-away. Margaret waved him into shore. Watching Burningwater gracefully skull the dory closer, silhouetted behind him, she saw the center console Pointer docking at the fish pier float. She rolled her eyes and dropped her head.

"Oh great, now all we need is to have Sandra Walsh show up yelling jackass. Max, I'll talk. Try to stay in control. There's my father and the Congressmen out there at the dock."

Max squinted toward the float and a small group of people unloading from the outboard. "Look I gotta find out what happened to..."

"Max please! Just give me a chance to ask him. Don't accuse him of anything."

Climbing out of the dory when it scraped the sand and wading in his boots the few feet toward Margaret and the shore, Charlie Bay's eyes did not leave hers.

"Charlie Bay we have to talk. There's a problem."

He didn't respond and stopped at the water's edge.

"The Collection...ah, the bones of your ancestors are missing. They were not in the lab this morning when we came to bring them to you. They're gone."

Max moved into the water, face to face with Charlie Bay; sandals soaked and long khaki pants splashed to the knees. Raising his right hand and pointing at Charlie Bay's chest with his index finger, Max shouted, "Did you take them? You took them because you didn't believe that we would bring them over here this morning, didn't you! You took them! Who else would want those bones but you. You stole them right out from under us because you didn't trust us!"

He was impulsive. He was passionate. And before he took another breath, he was drenched. In one lightening quick swoop, Charlie Bay Burningwater took down Dr. Max Sorensen to roll, grunt and groan in the sandy salt water at Margaret Garret's feet. Her first instinct was to let one, or both, drown. She was angry. She reached into the churning water and grabbed whoever and whatever brushed against her out-stretched hands. As she was turning to shield her face from the cool salty spray and the flailing limbs, she saw her father's form against a light blue sky beginning to jog along the elevated pier. His head was turned toward the commotion and he was accelerating. Knowing things were now going to get worse before they got better, she leaned into the twisting, entangled men and yelled, "That's it! Stop! That's ...ugh! I've had it with both of you!"

Wobbling and stumbling to their feet, they were again face to face. This time, Margaret stepped between the two winded soggy men and pushed Max to one side, "That's it Max. Don't say another word." Her father interrupted her as he ran down onto the beach and stopped next to the disorientated Max Sorensen.

"Hey, what's going on? Margaret, are you OK?"

"I'm fine. Just fine," Margaret's glare was now on the dripping wet face of Charlie Bay Burningwater.

Charlie Bay let his eyes drift from Max to Margaret to Jim Garret. His stare was returned. A few seconds later Charlie Bay turned back to Margaret and announced, "I'm going home." With his boots filled with water, his pants sagging to expose a portion of scarred bare skin and his head high, he sloshed his way to the dory, climbed in and made ready to row across the harbor for Eagle Island. No one spoke as he left. Max was exhausted and unable to speak even if he wanted to, which he didn't. He realized that once again, he said too much.

The silence was broken by a request from Jim, "Margaret, since it looks like this is all settled, can you come over here with me a minute?"

Without acknowledging Max, the two turned and walked up the narrow river beach to the parking lot. Max dragged his wet body to a nearby skiff and sat on the bow in an attempt to regain his strength. He watched the graying form of Charlie Bay and the dory glide through the harbor until out of sight. He watched Margaret meet the Congressmen and other guests. After what Max perceived as small talk, she marched to Charlie Bay's truck, slammed the driver's side door and without so much as a glance in his direction, she drove away. He wondered if Sandra were home.

"Well, what happened to you? Did you fall in the ocean somewhere?" was Sandra Walsh's boisterous greeting through the screen door as Max climbed the back steps.

"I had help."

"Why in the world do you look so forlorn?"

Max hesitated, knew no alternative and looked up to the ceiling as he spoke, "The Casco Collection is gone." Then, cold and wet, he waited.

"Gone? Gone!"

"Missing, stolen, whatever; from the lab last night." Max tried to look innocent.

"But, how could that be?" She whispered the words as she leaned against the kitchen counter with a perplexed glare.

"I don't know what happened. Someone broke in through the back door; pried it open. They just took the Casco, nothing else, no equipment, nothing, just the Casco." Max mumbled as he glanced around the room to avoid her eyes.

As fast as she seemed to loose energy with the news, she regained her vigor and demanded, "Come on Max you're coming with me! Didn't I say no incidents? Didn't I? I want to see the lab and I want the whole story. And then, we're going to see Burningwater. Come on!"

"But I'm all wet!"

"Yes you are and consider that the least of your problems."

As expected, jackass followed and Max followed Sandra.

During the drive to Jerry Moore's lab, to the best of his abilities and with a genuine attempt at objectivity, Max recounted the most recent episode in the Casco saga. He did however; interject his innocence and his conclusion that Burningwater was the culprit.

The hollow steel shell echoed with Sandra's labored breathing and Max's squishy wet leather sandals. Looking for any excuse to be as far away from his mentor as possible, he stopped at the desk as Sandra kept walking toward the Casco end of the building. He checked and shuffled unopened mail as apparently more important.

"Time to check your mail Max? It looks like once every week or two wouldn't hurt. I'm going down here to have a look."

Max wanted nothing more than a hot shower, dry clothes and to be alone. It was too early for a beer, cheese spread and a Barbara Stanwyck movie, although, the thought of disappearing into "Ball of Fire" was soothing. Instead, he chose the mail and a seat on a stool in the middle of the room. Examining the return addresses, he discarded the junk mail and sorted until he identified the long awaited response from the State Historical and Antiquities Office.

The cover letter was a short, simple form message with two enclosures. The first was a copy of the authorization for the skeletal excavation of the Eagle Island site signed by a State official, Sandra, as the representative of the University and in clean block letters, the only signature of the Casco Tribal Council; Charlie Bay Burningwater. Just one signature for the Tribal Council; Max was mystified.

The second document, unrequested, but involving the Casco, described an earlier land transaction. Charlie Bay also signed this document as the sole member of the Tribal Council. On the record, the Casco agreed to a renewable ninety-nine year lease for all of the occupiable land at the western end of the reservation. The deal was made with only one individual; someone named Seal Swimmer. This struck Max as a casual arrangement with no specific boundaries. But it was an intriguing contract. It was dated almost a year before the dredging, the excavations and the huge land fill. The lease entitled Seal Swimmer to essentially all of the buildable land adjacent to Rt. 1...however big that might become.

As he sat re-reading the two documents, he was interrupted by his cell.

"I got it...see cell phone on and ringing", he called to Sandra and followed with a whisper to himself, "at least it can't be you."

Sandra was immersed in something or other and didn't look up.

"Hello". The caller's voice was unknown to Max. The questions were startling but he answered without hesitation. "Yes, I do...I agree to do that and I'm sure Burningwater would, ya, I'm sure...After dark, Pier Twenty-two...by water...I'll be there. How did you get this...?" He closed his phone.

"Sandra, you're not going to believe this. Come on! Come on! Hustle! We've gotta tell Margaret. We're going to get them back! Hopefully tonight, I just have to round up a boat. Let's go! I'm driving."

It was difficult for Sandra to decide which was more disturbing, the odd and obtuse requirements of repossessing the Casco Collection or Max driving across the rail tie bridge onto Eagle Island. As suspected, Charlie Bay, with Margaret at his side, sat in the shade at the reburial site and neither was aroused as Max skidded to a halt next to the elongated grave. Sandra grasped both sides of her head, leaned forward in the passenger seat and sighed one long breath of thanksgiving. Max popped from the car baring a broad exuberant smile. Bouncing his way toward Charlie Bay, both he and Margaret came to their feet. Fearing another confrontation, she grabbed Charlie Bay's arm and he responded.

"It's OK. It's all right Margaret. He didn't take the bones. He didn't do it."

"What do you mean? How do you know he didn't take them?" She let go of his arm.

"You can learn a lot about a man when you wrestle him in the River." Charlie Bay smiled, still following Sorensen.

Max stood before Charlie Bay with such a genuine grin even Margaret almost smiled. "What is going on? Why do you look so happy?" As she spoke, she wondered if her words were interrupting an awkward embrace between the two men. But she considered it out of character for both. Margaret was the only one uneasy with the silence. "Well? What's going on?"

"Just a little while ago, at the lab, I got a call. I don't know who it was, but if we want the Casco back we can pick them up tonight, after dark at Pier Twenty-two on the Portland waterfront. It has to be by water, so we'll need a boat. The only condition was that they have to be in the ground tomorrow. I said we would. They aren't lost. We're going to get them back!" The excitement and joy in Max's voice matched his expression. "So, we need a boat."

"I suppose I could get the center console, which would work. It's in the water." Margaret wondered to herself, who, of the three, was able to run the boat. Her answer was no one.

Max had another choice. "I was thinking maybe, that based on the nature of the mission, ah, that this required a Pipeboat; in a sense, this is now a part of the dream journey. You do have a motor for the Pipeboat?

What do you think Burningwater, can we take the Pipeboat?"

"I have a motor, brand new. I need gasoline. Gasoline, hmm, you, me and gasoline..." Charlie Bay's voice tailed off in a chuckle.

Max joined him and Margaret wondered what was going on.

"Who called? You have no idea who it was?"

“No he didn’t give a name and the number was restricted.”

From inside the car came a muffled voice, "I pass, you three are on your own; only you Max, no one but you Max. I sure can pick'em."

"I'll get you two by boat at the fish pier about a half hour before sunset."

Max interrupted, "Sunset? What time is sunset?"

Pointing skyward, Charlie Bay shook his head, "Look to the west and watch; university Americans. I've a lot to do." He glanced into the burial trough and left without looking in Dr. Walsh's direction.

"Sunset's around eight-thirty. I’ll meet you at the dock at eight. Who do you think was on the phone, any ...?"

Max shrugged his shoulders. "I'll see you tonight at eight. I gotta get a shower."

A rule, generally understood by all and routinely enforced by the harbormaster, was the five-knot/no wake zone of the Casco River anchorage. For the few lobstermen tending to some late day chores, it was an odd sight. To the recreational boaters settling in for the night, it was an annoying disturbance. But, for the bass fishermen enjoying the flat calm of an evening lull and dotting the harbor in their small aluminum boats and kayaks, it was terrifying. As if from nowhere, came a roaring rumbling wooden wedge, with the bow raised so high from the water that a wall of foam crested amidship on the red bottomed hull. Waves from the wake rolled through the moorings tumbling and rocking everything in their path. The tranquil river harbor was set into complete disarray by a clam digger with an outboard, and who, despite his best efforts, was unable to see what floated in front of him. The motorized dory's inability to plane through the water, lower the bow and afford at least some visibility, combined with Charlie Bay's frozen grip on a wide open throttle, left the placid anchorage in watery chaos. The dock was in one direction, the Pipe boat, at full speed, was headed in another. Margaret and Max were left to stand on the fish pier float in disbelief as Burningwater zigzagged his way through the boats and moorings, never hitting anything but coming close to everything.

"Do you think he's going to be able to bring it into the dock?" Margaret was using concern as a mask for amazement.

"This is going to be an adventure. Looks like Sandra made a good choice." Max grinned. "He'll be alright, let's give him a little time."

As Max spoke, Charlie Bay buzzed within fifteen feet of the dock sending everyone on the float to their knees and cutting or tangling every fishing line running from the pier. This sent an array of catcalls from anyone within ear shot of Charlie Bay. His look was brief, but Max thought that he saw a twinkle in Charlie Bay's eyes as he flashed and sliced before the sunset crowd of fishermen.

"He'll be OK, don't worry. He just needs to get close and cut off the engine, then he can row or drift in. We just need to get to him before these fishermen do." Max was chuckling as he helped Margaret to her feet.

"It's really not funny, well maybe it is." And she laughed.

On his next pass, Charlie Bay was headed straight for the float; still at full speed. Seconds before he was to ram the dock and after everyone nearby except Max and Margaret ran for safety, the outboard engine stopped and the dory rolled to the float on the crest of its' own wake. Fending off the bow, Max signaled for Margaret to climb into the boat and he tumbled in over the gunnel behind her. After the less than graceful boarding, Max was left seated on a wet and slippery floor to stare aft at the silhouette of a man poised against the bright red sunset sky.

Charlie Bay was a boat builder, who, in the spirit of Earl Alton, stood indifferently to the presence of his two passengers. Burningwater caressed the inside of the Pipeboat hull and softly chanted a prayer. Taken by the trauma motorization inflicted upon this fisherman, neither Margaret nor Max moved until he was finished.

Finally, Max said, "We should go."

Without hesitating, Charlie Bay pulled the starter cord, held the throttle at wide open and sent Margaret and Max lunging backwards, groping for something solid to grab.

Once he found some stability, Max leaned toward Burningwater and shouted, "You don't always have to run at full speed! There's half throttle you know. She may ride better." Taking Charlie Bay's lack of response as an opportunity, Max reached for the outboard tiller, grabbed the rigid hand, twisted and slowed the motor.

The salty old fisherman grinned, "I wondered how that worked."

In the newfound calm and quiet, Max pointed to the words indicating various speeds and gears on the side of the throttle without any knowledge of Charlie Bay's illiteracy. Burningwater nodded politely and grinned, this time at Margaret.

At the slower speed, they took a moment to organize and center themselves for the journey. Margaret sat on the bow seat and faced forward; a familiar spot, with her legs nestled among the orange lifejackets. Max sat amidships and faced the stern as if to aid in navigation, but without any idea of where they were going. Charlie Bay stood forward of the well and the cove seat, white knuckled and as far from the gas tank as possible. Passing the bell buoy at the entrance of the harbor channel, they were three motionless figures headed seaward.

As Charlie Bay turned east to round the rocky peninsula of Casco Point, both Max and Margaret were captivated by the contrasting view of the brilliant western sky and the dark shadowed edge of the shoreline evergreens. The State Park forest trees melted into the black rolling swells of open ocean and set the foundation of their inland horizon in darkness. They watched in awe as the watery world around them was falling into night.

To alleviate his concerns with dusk and the cold merciless appearance of the sea, Max moved closer to Charlie Bay and asked, "Where are we headed?"

"Right now; Spain." Charlie Bay answered without a change in expression. "Move up toward the bow with Margaret, so we can go faster. I'm going through this gut at Seal Rock and run up along the shore, northeast until we hit the next bay. From there, we head inland."

Passing closer to the ledge than the coastline and once again at full throttle, Charlie Bay piloted the dory through most of the lobster buoys and over a few as they cut Seal Rock. The higher portions of the ledge formed a black crescent-shaped stone mass intermittently protruding from the swells and surrounding a large pool of kelp swaying on the surface. Seal pups, skirmishing around the rock and seaweed, paused to watch the boat and passengers intrude. Max was hanging on as if for his life. The seals caught Margaret.

"Charlie Bay, seals!"

Focused on the waters ahead, Burningwater didn't alter his stare or share her excitement.

"Seal Swimmer, hey Seal Swimmer, look there they are." Margaret yelled again.

Seeing that Charlie Bay was unresponsive, Max took the opportunity to divert his fear of traveling on the open ocean at night. "I think he has seen seals out here before." He waited for the look. He wasn't disappointed. "What did you call him, Seal Swimmer?"

"Ya, Charlie Bay used to be called Seal Swimmer, before the fire and they changed his name. Look there's two more."

"Seal Swimmer," mused Max, as he recalled the lease contract between the Casco and Seal Swimmer. He was puzzled by the possibilities until the surges of much larger ground swells rekindled his anxiety. Seal Rock quickly faded into the distance. The sunset sky turned to the black of a moonless night as the dark gray waves rose and fell beneath him.

The Pipeboat's course traversed the crests of the rollers and slid into their watery valleys. With each upward thrust of the waves, Max felt his gut push into the base of his throat and his frame compress. As the craft fell off and rolled into the following trough, his split second relief was overtaken by a weightless descent until another rising wave initiated the cycle again.

Again and again, as they progressed into the night, the rolling continued. The endless rhythm was finally broken when Max vomited two cheese dogs and diet Coke over the starboard rail. Resting his chin on the gunnel and spitting the lingering bitter contents of his mouth into an indifferent sea, he turned to Burningwater, "I really didn't need the nitrites anyway. Don't worry, I'll be alright, I'm fine."

As the vomiting resumed and Margaret, her hand on Max's back, gazed at their skipper with big dark, apologetic eyes, Charlie Bay shook his head and looked skyward. He wondered how his relationship with the eternal world of spirit beings came to be linked with a seasick university American and big-eyed writer. Returning her stare, he nodded in assurance and turning seaward, he nodded into the darkness.

Chapter Eleven

Charlie Bay slid the dory alongside the rafted trawlers docked on Pier Twenty-two. In the darkness he found a small landing float tucked on the inland side. Max and Margaret were surprised at how fast he had learned to handle the outboard motor in tight places. As they stepped onto the float, eight-foot wharf pilings surrounded them in a forest of moist black columns, visible only one tier deep and echoing with lapping waves. This dark and damp place was unwelcoming to two of the three trespassers.

"You know I almost went to work here once, right here on this fish pier. Couldn't do it for some reason, I don't know, work in a fish plant. I stayed on the Island. Most that did come here to work never came back. If I remember right, there's a shed door and an office at the end of the dock. Now I remember, I couldn't fill out the papers." Charlie Bay looked at Margaret and laughed but not about the job application. He was going to get the Casco home.

Without another word, they climbed the dock ramp and walked to the water end of the pier. There was a dim security lamp at the peak of a warehouse roof. It cast a grainy gray hue over the front entrance and the dock. The door was a six-foot plywood panel set in a large sliding shed door. The shed door was locked but the inset panel door was wedged open. Pulling it toward him, Max stepped back and they all peered inside.

"Where's the office?" Max raised his eyebrows at Charlie Bay.

"Well, it was here. They must have moved it. There's some light over in that direction, further down. It's probably there. Let's go." Charlie Bay's voice was a notch higher than usual.

Max hedged, "I don't know. I got the call. Whoever this is, they are expecting me. I don't want anything to go wrong. Sandra wouldn't forgive me. Why don't you two wait here and as soon as everything is set, I'll get you, and we'll get the Casco together."

"But..." Margaret broke in and Max responded.

"Please, do me this favor. Let me go talk with who ever this is and I'll come back." Max began walking toward the light alone.

Margaret turned to Charlie Bay, "I'm not going to let him go down there alone. Are you?"

“Ugh, ugh.” Charlie Bay shook his head no. Margaret started after Max.

Holding her arm, Charlie Bay whispered, "Wait, give him a minute and we'll follow. I don't want anything to go wrong either."

After he passed from sight, the couple crept to cover, hiding in the shadows, but close enough to hear the noise give Max away.

Knocking over two stacked empty polyethylene bait barrels was easy for Max, catching them as they rolled in different directions was not. As he stopped one, the other came to rest at the foot of a man who stepped in from the darkness.

"Quite an entrance," a voice came from the cavernous warehouse.

"Yours too." Max was not amused but he was intimidated.

"Dr. Sanderson, I'm Jim Garret," were the words that came in a businesslike manner along with an extended right hand.

"Sorensen, Max Sorensen," Max corrected firmly in tone and grip.

"Sorensen, I'm sorry. I'm usually pretty good at names, sorry." Jim was upset with himself at the discourtesy and embarrassed. His sincerity was Max's first impression as both men picked up their barrels. "Come on over to the office here, so we can talk."

"My father? What's he doing here!" Margaret started to stand up until Charlie Bay restrained her.

"It's best that we just listen."

Margaret stood for a few seconds thinking about it and slid back to cover.

Switching on two desk lamps to light up an office which was nothing more than a few chairs, file cabinets, a small refrigerator and a paperwork counter in an otherwise enormous storage space, Jim offered Max a seat.

"Not the way I remembered it," mumbled Charlie Bay.

"Well, the world around Eagle Island does change." She was angry with her father but Charlie Bay was closer. “What is he doing here?”

Walking toward the refrigerator with a coffee maker on top, "Would you like coffee or something to drink?" Jim tugged at the artificial wood grain door as if by habit, but never looked inside.

Max was surprised by the invitation and felt for some unknown reason they were about to settle into conversation. "Ah, do you have ginger ale?"

"Ginger ale?" Jim was baffled, who asks for ginger ale?

"It was a tough ride over here. It's been awhile since I've been on rolling seas; you know..." Max patted his stomach.

"How about a Diet Coke?"

"Diet Coke, sure. Why did you steal the Casco Collection?"

The question and Max's directness didn’t disrupt Jim Garret. The tolerance for small talk had expired in both men.

"You can't steal something that already belongs to you." His affect was flat, matter of fact and passionless.

"Seal Swimmer? You are Seal Swimmer." The lineage fell into place in Max's mind; a son, in Native American tradition, named after his father.

Jim Garret nodded a deliberate yes.

“Named before he became Bay Burningwater.”

"You are Burningwater's son," Max whispered, as he grasped the relationships and their implications. “The bones are your people.”

Jim Garret spoke clearly. "By blood."

Margaret's knees buckled. She sat back onto the bottom of an overturned work skiff. "He's your...that means I'm..." Her words were in short quick breaths; words buying time to understand.

With his mouth grinning broadly, with his eyes twinkling and rolling open the palms of his weathered hands, Charlie Bay looked to Margaret, "So my granddaughter, you too, have rolled three times on the ground and been turned into a buffalo!"

"You are my grandfather."

Sitting in an office chair directly across from Max, Jim Garret clarified the conditions of the Casco's return. "You agreed on the phone that the bones would be buried tomorrow; no more studies, no more research."

In their previous conversation, Max didn’t recall the stipulation of no further study. To the best of his recollection, it was never mentioned. He was hesitant. One last time, he was waffling, still unable to accept the commitment to rebury.

Anxious to resolve the issue, Jim ended, once and for all, any more research on the Casco.

"Right now, the bones are set to be run through the fish waste processor first thing in the morning. They're going to get broken and crushed and end up in bags of fertilizer on the shelves of home improvement stores all over the country. You want them; they are to be buried in Reservation ground tomorrow morning."

The thought of fertilizer made Max cringe. "You went to all the trouble of taking them; you've got'em. Why ...?"

"Some overzealous colleagues arranged to have them removed from the lab and I..."

"But why?" Max was frustrated, "Why do that?"

Max was asking why they were stolen. Jim answered why he was offering their return.

"I had seen rage in him before. The damage it caused our family; my mother's suffering...it was all so aimless. But today on the beach with you, I saw his rage and experienced his fire." Jim paused as if amazed by the insight. "For better or worse, the fire is in the hunt for those bones. And despite it all; my lack of understanding of his ways, his life and everything he has done, I owe him. I have to act in his favor. You want them or not?"

"Yes, ya of course I do. I'll take them. But why did you take'm in the first place?"

Margaret moved toward an opening in their camouflage and whispered, "Ya, and I want to know why you never told me..." Charlie Bay cut her off abruptly with a firm hand over her mouth and a restraining hug.

He said into her ear. "Be patient granddaughter, on this night, he's doing all he can. There'll be a time."

Margaret relaxed into his arms, knowing from experience that her father's ability to divulge family history came in bits and pieces.

"Why we took them? The DNA stuff panicked us a little."

Max looked at Jim and decided to give it one more try.

"You know I could do cone beam radiography, create a 3-D file of the skull...reconstruct it in resin with laser polymerization...no bone whatsoever, no DN..."

"No, now do we have a deal? You choose; crush or bury?'

"Deal, we bury." Max let go.

Both men acknowledged a deal, Jim extended his hand, the tension in his body gone.

Max remained seated, shook and looked back to the floor. Suddenly slapping his knees, arching his back and looking up into the darkness, Max repeated the reason, "Ah, the DNA stuff! You mean, one of my less than sound research ideas, which was driving me crazy, along with everyone around me, panicked you! The DNA?"

It all came together for Max; the marsh landfill acreage off Rt. 1, the resort development project and the Congressmen.

"Casino. A Casco Casino. You're building a Casco Casino! That's it! It's gambling!" Max burst into uproarious laughter. "Ah, you're unbelievable. You are recreating a Casco gene pool from who knows where!

Because there's no one left, so you're reconstructing it. A new genetic Nation with an old name." Feeling the blood pound through his heart, Max was off and running. For a fragile ego, anticipating the confirmation he had figured it all out, was energizing. "All I am, with those bones and a archived DNA Casco profile, potentially accessible to any one, is someone to mess it all up!"

"Well, it might. We are rebuilding the Casco Nation with folks who believe that they are Casco. Genetically who knows?" In a conciliatory fashion, with a raised brow and tilted head, Jim acknowledged Max's assessment. "Down the road, with confusing information spun by the wrong hands, it could be a big problem. And there're plenty of problems ahead so things don't have to be anymore complicated than they already are."

"Problems? Ah, one's got to be the Settlement Act. Didn't the Penobscot and the Passamaquady try to pursue gambling on their reservations awhile ago and lose in the State or Federal Courts?"

"I see you know some Indian Law, but the Casco weren't part of the Settlement Act and in the deal with the State of Maine; they were passed over, an insignificant piece of the whole thing. There was no land claim made by the Casco Nation. They were and still are just a Tribe shunted aside and left to die, back then just a handful of members who really didn't matter; no benefits, no help."

"Ah, so you are the mysterious force behind the approval for the Casco of federal recognition. How did you do that?"

“We went quietly through the Bureau of Indian Affairs, not the courts. Once the Passammaquady and Penobscot set the precedent and established federal recognition for the eastern tribes, as long as we didn’t make any trouble, like land claim lawsuits, we didn’t have any trouble. The Casco people have been living on that land for who knows how long before the Europeans showed up. There just haven’t been a lot of them out there lately. But that really didn’t matter with the B.I.A., based on the evidence of occupation, they went right ahead and granted federal recognition without state regulation.”

Max smiled, “So the Casco are a federally recognized tribe and therefore with Congressional specification under the Indian Gaming Act, very eligible for casino gambling."

"Could be a billion dollar a year industry."

"So, your first problem is extinction...that's why the tribal roles. Who's out there that claims tribal affiliation? Who thinks that they are Casco?"

"We got twenty-three people with no vested interest, no idea of what's going on, who believe that they are Casco. The records are terrible. Only five have a slight chance to demonstrate, with birth records, the required one-quarter lineal decendency for federal tribal membership. If we go to oral lineage reconstruction with the others, we're weak, maybe we have eighteen who claim to be Casco by some story or other. If you add that to unsatisfactory DNA comparisons between known Casco bones, the DNA archived by you, and whoever we have and they don’t match, the project dies in Congress as a scam and extinction wins. Now we have what people believe. With the DNA it's too risky; extinction will not win again."

Jim considered the integrity of those who signed the Tribal Role. "You know, these people, with absolutely no knowledge of anything to gain, these folks have said, "I'm Casco." They believe it." Pausing, Jim looked at the floor, "And then there's Burningwater, who is Casco body and soul, and....who has always believed."

Max saw Charlie Bay as a genetic problem.

“What are you going to do about him? He’s the living DNA remnant of the Casco Nation.”

“The irony is that he’s not listed on the current tribal role...the one true Casco. And down the road, if it came to that, someone would have to find him first. By now you know that’s not easy...in today’s world he doesn’t exist.”

"He got you started with the land on Rt. 1 didn't he? I saw the contract."

"Ah huh, land from guilt. With that land I crossed over; nineteen years old and leverage on the other side. I started with miniature golf; built it myself working third shift right here at this fish pier, you know, wind mills, waterfalls, lobster traps. A summer later, it became the driving range and a clam shack. Then it became the landfill, and with that landfill came capital, a lot of capital. That changed everything. And, it was on and on from there. I was in a different world...no longer Casco."

Charlie Bay lowered his head and once again was compelled to recall how, in a moment from which to mark time, he released a son and enslaved a Nation.

Still fuming at her father, Margaret missed Charlie Bay's torment. "Why is he telling Max all this? This is more stuff I knew nothing about..." Her voice tailed off with the desire to know.

"Max is not a threat to your father. He's a teacher, not a businessman. With our ancestors in Reservation ground, your father knows that none of this can be used against him by others. My son has a warrior's way of thinking; he attacks and he protects. He is the Casco lance and shield."

Testing Jim for more of the story, "He was the only one left on the Tribal Council wasn't he? He could do whatever he wanted. There was no one else."

Jim nodded acknowledging Max's grasp of the circumstances, "The death in his generation was unbearable, not just dead bodies; relatives and friends, of which there were plenty. But, it was a death of spirit; individuals and community. Alcohol sucked it out of some people, my sister, Molly and...Burningwater, 'til they all but disappeared. Looking back on it, I think he saw what was coming. And, there was absolutely nothing he, or anyone else, could do to change it; the ancestral ways of being, slowly and sometimes quickly, were exterminated. He was the end of the line. I've often thought that he saw my energy to build as an alternative to booze and depression; an alternative that he didn't have. And... I needed land, which he did have. Ha, it was so lousy nobody else wanted it until they needed a place to dump all the sand." Jim paused. "He gave me the only thing he could give and I took from him the only thing I could take."

Empathy and understanding in the sufferings of one family were never strengths of Max Sorensen. In some ways, personal histories overwhelmed him. He dealt with the emotional consequences of individual relationships by removing himself from the situation and studying the broader biological complexities. He studied bones. Unable to engage in Jim's familial struggle with Burningwater, Max chose safer territory, the reconstruction of a federally recognized tribe with extraordinary potential for extensive gaming.

"So you have all this Casco Reservation land, you control the access and from what I can see, there's an awful lot of space out there."

"Over four hundred and fifty acres suitable for development."

"And now you're rebuilding the Casco Tribal role and Casco Tribal Council from scratch, Congress specifies the sovereign nation status of the Casco so it's within the structure of the Indian gaming regulations, but what about the State?"

"You're pretty good at this. Are you looking for a job?"

"Oh no, it's the design, constructing the whole thing and the long odds on it happening."

"Well, one of the next steps is to enter negotiations with the State. Imagine it; a handful of rag- tag Casco as a sovereign Nation, on equal ground with the State of Maine." Both chuckle at the incongruity of the image. "Basically the negotiations are to discuss the State's share of the revenues. Maine has no regulatory power over the Casco as a federal tribe and there are no restrictions against Casino gaming. There's no ban anywhere on the books because the Casco aren't a part of the Settlement Act. Since there's no State regulation or tax on the gaming, Maine is not going to get anything. We can leave them out and antagonize everyone or we can give the State a share up front. If the pot's sweet enough in profit-sharing, there should be a relatively smooth and quiet agreement before the anti-gambling forces or anybody else gets vocal."

"Who's doing all this, and... handling the money?"

"Casco Casino Board of Directors."

"You?"

"Oh no, not me."

"But you picked every member of the Board didn't you."

Jim smiled and skirted the question, "They're all good, bright and honest people, experienced in the right areas and dedicated to the mission of the project."

"The mission of the project? What is the mission of the project, besides making tons of money?"

Despite his indifference to the deposition fate of the Casco bones, Jim experienced an unexplainable euphoric sense of release with the agreement to rebury the remains on the Reservation in the morning. By solidifying the final arrangement for the collection's return, he perceived a small, incremental leap in his emotional freedom. It felt good. He felt good and the consequences were an uncharacteristic willingness to talk.

Nursing one Diet Coke, Max knew this was a chance to hear more of the Casco story. In an attempt to keep the conversation going, he was just about to ask for another one, when Jim kept going.

"Besides making lots of money... adoption of abandon and lost souls."

Max was stunned, "What?”

"To assimilate orphaned Native Americans who identify into the Casco corporate community. You know, to do with the revenues exactly what the spirit of the Indian Gaming Regulatory Act intended: create opportunities for healthcare, housing, education, childcare, job training... to support all of it; college, graduate school... seed money for Native American businesses. You know the law, the whole thing; redistribution of wealth. We will adopt and educate by creating sound economic resources...rebuild a Nation...hopefully within a generation."

"You are going to have people showing up from everywhere!"

"I hope so!

If I think too far ahead, you’re right, it's a complex project. So I take the steps a few at a time, hold the best I can, our vision for the future.

But, it doesn’t take much to see this is an astounding opportunity! Not so much for those who are with us in the beginning, but for their children and their children's children; because of the capability that this enterprise has to educate. It's all about education... and the obligation is to make it happen. It's the possibility for Casco generations to come, ancestral line after line, to see the world and themselves in it, as filled with hope and creativity. They can compete and contribute with a sense of identity and self-knowledge not just in America, but in the world! These children will have the opportunity to become your colleagues, rather than the subjects of your research.

This is not a quick get rich quick entitlement plan filled with cars, big houses and flat screen TVs. The key is the education of a Nation, developing its identity, its skills and talents. People hear Indian gambling casino and they think money in their pocket. The greatest value of the project isn't in doling out cash but in elevating the knowledge base of the Casco tribal members... give people the chance to become builders, educators, business owners or whatever else...all within Casco culture. Money is not the end! The mission is to build and sustain a Casco ethnic identity with individuals who actively contribute to the strength of a diverse American culture!"

Jim took a breath, calmed himself and came back to Max. "It's education Dr Sorensen, education."

Overcome with the irony of Jim Garret's passion, Max was unable to respond. His life's work was espoused by a businessman with a clarity and conviction dormant in his own being for too long. A humbled Max

Sorensen sighed through the recognition of his limitation and asked for another Diet Coke.

"Could I have another one of these?"

Jim handed Max the cold drink and continued, "You are right, assimilation of various tribes and beliefs is difficult, but it's not without historic precedent in the treatment of Native American peoples during the pan-Indian extermination campaign; "the only good Indian is a dead Indian."

Ignorance is the enemy; victory is collective."

Max recognized the quote and knew of the genocide during the U.S. government's Indian War campaigns following the Civil War. It was apparent to Max that from Jim Garret's perspective, regeneration of native peoples required, at least initially, unification and education. The elevation of Native American cultures was to be found in ethnic solidarity and educational opportunity. There was not a lot for Max to say. This individual was truly much more complex than he initially perceived.

"It is a noble endeavor," Max affirmed.

Having no desire or patience for compliments, Jim returned Max to the pragmatic. "Just because you are doing what you believe is a good work, hopefully for the betterment of many, it doesn't mean that it will turn out alright. That's why I'm so adamant that those bones are not a part of any DNA research or an accessible data base. This is just one step in a very long sequence."

Charlie Bay's moist eyes sparkled in pride. Margaret's lower jaw hung open. Tears ran onto her cheeks.

Stepping this far into one man's vision of the Casco future and with really nothing to loose, Max asked his last key question without antagonism. "What's in it for you? Why do all this? You're not on the Casco Role or on the Board of Directors. You've separated and distanced yourself from the Casco. What do you get out of the enormous effort?"

"It's pretty straightforward. I get to design, develop and build. Then I step away, let somebody else manage and operate. That's it. What more could I ask for? That's what I do! And a casino is like nothing else. It's an extreme environment designed to captivate and transport people into a world that suspends their everyday reality and reconstructs a new reality, one that's dedicated to the redistribution of wealth. They lose and we gain... gambling to redistribute wealth...it's a Native American tradition!

With this work, I can dream and create as far as my imagination will take me. It's up to me. My whole life's been a preparation for this and the entrance is right up through the middle of the driving range."

Leaning forward in a straight-backed chair toward Max, with hands outstretched as if poised to shake his own excitement into a docile academic body, he spoke, charged with energy.

"That whole strip along Rt. 1, almost two miles is going to be wooded, about a half mile thick, east into the marsh. It will be planted with fast growing coniferous trees; white pine, fur to enclose the western border of the Reservation. That leaves the State Park to the north, the Casco River to the south and open ocean to the east. The entrance to the Casino complex will be from the southwest corner, where the driving range is now and another from the northwest corner. The view of the Reservation from the road will only be woods. They'll just be the two service roads on each end and the monorail loop entrance and exit."

"The monorail!" Max,his voice boomming.

"I thought that might perk you up a little.

There are no hotels on the marsh, just the Casco Casino with all kinds of terrific restaurants, any type of food you want and big and small entertainment pavilions for marquee names. The first building phase is a quarter million square feet of earthtone single story domed modules interconnected with loops of an indoor tube system which is basically to connect players to every gaming location in the entire Casino. The monorail transportation, from a string of hotels and parking on the periphery, will take people across the highway, through the woods and out to a Native American gambling village removed from the rest of the world in time and space; to spend money and be entertained. And we are not just going after the drive market from a radius of about a hundred and fifty miles. At one point I was toying with the idea of building another high speed monorail to run directly from the Portland International Airport which is only eleven miles away. But after thinking about it, even

I thought it was a bit much. Instead we're building luxury coaches to shuttle people from the airport and train station."

"But how...no bank today is going to loan money for reservation development because technically the Federal Government owns and will always hold title to the land?

Ah, but you own all that land around the western periphery, where the hotels will go, don't you? That's how you can raise the money to build the casino. Otherwise no private investors are going to put up that much cash for a building on a federal reservation where they can't hold a mortgage. But banks will take a mortgage on the hotels off reservation land and reduce the risk for the casino.

It's going to take a lot of cash. You must be going to leverage everything you have." Max shook his head.

Jim smiled, but again didn't answer the questions. "There's a four hundred room, five star hotel planned for the hill on that northwest corner that will overlook everything. Max, this is a eight hundred million-dollar deal designed for additional resort expansions over the next twenty years. It's a very conservative step-by-step approach... see why they panicked.

In a few years, if growth is good, we're even planning hydrofoil shuttles from the Nova Scotia Ferry that docks daily in Portland and we're going to build them."

"You're going to build hydrofoils to bring Canadian gamblers up the Casco River?"

"It's a shallow river." Jim looked at the dazed expression on Max's face and thought an explanation might help. "I bought a small shipyard two years ago for the hydrofoils and to assemble the monorails but for now we'll use it for the luxury coaches. We'll subcontract most of it. This fish plant was a part of the deal; this and three others; Clam Cakes, Fish and Chips; somebody at the all-night buffet will eat'em."

Intrigue, academics and curiosity aside, the drive and accomplishment of the man in front of him overwhelmed Max. He was also overcome by his own inadequacies. For some unknown reason, it wasn't his professional inadequacies but personal ones, his marriage and his relationship with his wife that hit him. It was true that for awhile he blamed his wife and her lack of support in all his projects and plans. Then he blamed himself for his inability to present an idea to her or anyone else without leaping over all the steps to rave about the expected results. He accepted how difficult he was. He thought that was progress.

Tonight, Max wondered how Jim Garret did it. "Tell me something. Do you drive your wife crazy with these ideas; I mean all these incredibly big ideas? Don't they upset her?"

"What?" Jim was unable to make the connection.

"You know these enormous plans, all the big ideas... one after another. Don't they drive your wife nuts?"

By the look on his face Jim knew that Max was now struggling with an issue different than Casco bones and casino plans. Jim saw in him, only turmoil. He did the best he could to answer.

"Ya they did, at first, but now I never discuss them. I just show her when sections of a project are done. Then we talk about what's coming next, usually just the next section."

"When parts are done, nothing about the whole thing?" Max considered this. "I don't know if I could do that, keep quiet about it. I think that I'm a leaper. I jump. I just never know the direction and can't keep it going once I get there." Max's head ached. He sat motionless; forearms resting on knees, thumb and index finger grasping his wedding ring. His eyes glazed as every ounce of energy was devoted to absorbing Jim Garret's story. It was now too much. Confronted with his own short-comings, he shut down.

Sensing Max was done, Jim stood, walked to his side placed his hand on a shoulder and asked, "Hey, you alright?"

Max didn't answer.

Both men knew the Casco story was safe. It was given and received in the spirit of the Casco reburial. It was entombed in Max and he knew silence.

"Remember the job at hand Max. Get the bones and bury them on Reservation ground in the morning. Come on. Let's get going."

Raising his head, Max nodded and came to his feet. Their eyes met.

"I'd like to tell Margaret about this, about everything myself" Jim mumbled, both as something to say and to verify a secure exchange.

For Max, it was never an issue, "Sure, of course." He smiled at the thought of Jim dealing with Margaret. "This is turning into quite a night. You have my word."

Shutting off one of the lights, Jim shifted the conversation to the information necessary for the retrieval of the Casco Collection.

"Did you tie up at the work float on this pier?"

"Ya."

"As you came to the float, you passed some rafted trollers. The last one, outboard, at the end of the dock, is called the "Rita Marie". In the main hold are the boxes of bones. The hatch is unlocked and you can load from the water. I'll take care of security. No one will bother you. It should take you less than a half-hour. You're on your own. Good bye Dr Sorensen." Jim shook Max's hand, turned away without another word and disappeared into an unlit corridor.

With his eyes still adjusting to the darkness, Max was startled as Margaret and Charlie Bay stepped forward from their cover. "Whoa, were you two there to catch that?"

"We pretty much heard all of it, although there was some mumbling I didn't get." Margaret confirmed, "...but most of it."

"I've had enough. It's between you and your father, father and son, family business...I'm staying out of it OK? I don't want to rehash that conversation, OK?"

He looked at Margaret and glanced at Charlie Bay as they all nodded in agreement. "Now let's get the Casco and take them back to the island."

The deck of the troller was moist and cold. To Max and Margaret the smell of fish was overpowering. Charlie Bay took the hold, Margaret carried the boxes to the gunnel and Max stacked the cartons in the dory. They worked without speaking. Before they left the troller's side, Charlie Bay restacked all of the Casco containers. Max wasn't offended.

The trip back to Eagle Island was a slow one. The size of their fragile cargo and the darkness made speed secondary to safe return. Having mastered the throttle, Charlie Bay stood and looked over the packed dory as if each box were a lobster trap and he was making the traditional August reset of his gear closer to shore. Margaret was cradled in the bow, facing aft and dozing amid swells and bones of her people. Again, Max sat amidships, but this time facing forward, each arm outstretched to his side, stabilizing the load. The breeze of the cool night air erased his headache and the gentle roll of the sea relaxed him near sleep. Charlie Bay, unlit pipe clenched in his teeth, stood at the helm and watched the dark water as the midnight southwest wind began to stir the crests of the ground swells into small splashes of foam. Occasionally glancing under the extended arms of Max Sorenson at the placid face of his granddaughter, Charlie Bay Burningwater whispered a prayer of thanksgiving. For two of the early morning hours, the Pipeboat of the dream journey made its way homeward.

Chapter Twelve

It didn't take long for Max's wrinkled khakis to be wet above the knees and clinging to his thighs. Even in daytime he knew the Maine water was often unbearably cold, a few hours from first light, without the heat of the sun, it was worse. His feet were numb and his body chilled. But that didn't stop him from the quiet and evenly paced task of handing the containers of the Casco Collection on shore to Margaret. With the Pipeboat anchored in the sandy shallows as close to Charlie Bay's work dock as the outgoing tide allowed, Max waded from the dory's side to the water's edge. From there Margaret stacked the remains of her people up on the dry sand. She didn't say a word.

On shore, Burningwater began to organize his preparation for the reburial of the Casco bones. Lighting two old kerosene railroad lamps and placing each on a pole at opposite corners of the platform, he set up a worktable between them in enough light to overcome the early morning darkness. The red and blue parachute silk, tobacco in a sealed tin can and a Clementine crate containing pieces of obsidian were brought from his fishing shack. Laying strips of the cloth, tobacco and the stones at one end of the table, Charlie Bay called to Margaret for the first container long before Max completed unloading even the port side of the Pipeboat. Margaret carried the cardboard box, which she labeled and packed just a week ago, from the sand, up the two steps, onto the work dock. She set the carton on the table in front of him. His eyes sparkled in the reflected light of the lanterns. Remaining still, Margaret watched as Charlie Bay unpacked the first box, carefully setting the packaged long bones of an ancestor on the tabletop. He removed the unprinted newspaper and exposed the contents. Pausing for a moment to view the skeletal remnant of a member of the Casco Nation, Charlie Bay then ran his hand across a light brown shaft at the top of the bundle.

"They haven't been burned or broken." He spoke with relief.

Margaret saw a man approaching peace. She saw her grandfather fulfilling his obligation. And only she heard the splash.

"Whoa! That's cold!" Came the muffled voice followed by a second splash. "It's OK. Nothing got wet...except me."

Margaret turned as both she and Charlie Bay, now aware of the splashing, peered out in the dory's direction onto the black water.

"Max, are you alright?" Margaret was concerned more for the Casco containers than him.

"Ya, ya I'm alright. I just stepped in a hole filled with quicksand and lost my balance. But the box didn't get wet...just my..." His voice tailed off but returned louder, "So I'm wide awake now."

Acknowledging the adventure with Max Sorensen was a constant in the reburial process; Charlie Bay rolled his eyes and shook his head.

Redirecting his focus to Margaret, "I need you to take my truck, go onshore and call Bud Walker before sunrise, before they'd be heading out on the water. Let him know the burial will be mid-morning here on the Island...over by the blueberry patch. He'll know who to tell. Then call anyone else you want to come."

His lack of specification, in extending other invitations with the phrase, “call anyone you want” made her uncertain about her father. Did he want him there or not? She hesitated. The moment passed.

"After you get the rest of our ancestors up here, there's some driftwood kindling and split logs on the inland side of the shack, you know, same as always. You can build a fire at the hearthsite for the Wet One. Be sure you light it."

Margaret smiled. Recalling the feeling of Molly wrapped next to her; tucked together in one blanket, warming the soles of their feet at the hearthsite and curled beside a fire built by the Storyteller, she nodded yes. His phrase “our ancestors” surfaced, she lingered in front of him and nodded again.

Moaning and groaning through the transfer of the Casco from the Pipeboat to the work dock provided Max an opportunity to express his wet discomfort. With placement on the platform of the last carton, Charlie Bay signaled Margaret, by a tilt of his head, in the direction of the firewood.

"She'll build a fire. There's some dry pants in the shack. They should fit. They're not mine." The comparative belly size, by Charlie Bay of his own wirery build to the midriff bulge of Max Sorensen, was enough to get a laugh from Margaret.

Recognizing he deserved it and appreciative of the chance to get warm and dry, he stopped fussing. "You wouldn't have a beer in there too, would you?"

"Might."

Heading into the doorway of the fishing shack, Max whispered to himself, but loud enough for both to hear, "Charlie Bay, you're a man after my own heart."

A short time later, Max reappeared before a newly lit fire wearing dry baggy navy work pants, holding his wet khakis, a gray woolen blanket and a brown quart bottle of beer. The twist off cap was in place but a small light line of foam indicated about a third of the beer was already gone. Kneeling by the fire and adding wood, Margaret watched the sparks from the kindling rise to just above her head and disappear. She began to relax as her cheeks collected the warmth and her breath drew in the pine scented air.

"Ah, this will do my cold bones a world of good," was the grateful response as Max spread the blanket near the flame in a spot with lateral views of Charlie Bay on one side and the Pipeboat on the other.

"I'm going to make some calls and get a change of clothes. Need anything? Or, you want a ride somewhere?"

"No I'm fine. I'd like to stay here." Max looked out onto the water. "Don't worry, I won't disturb him. I'd just like to stick around until they're in the ground. Really, I'm done."

This time, Margaret believed him, "OK."

"Oh, be sure to let Sandra know." He exhaled a deep breath. "That was close, I almost forgot her."

"I didn't."

Max expected the look he often received from Margaret concerning his mentor, but it never came. Tired, Margaret walked across the work dock. Passing slowly but leaving Charlie Bay undisturbed among Casco bones, she found the path back to the house. When she reached the crest of the hill between the new burial ground and the truck, Margaret looked to the east. A line of stars cut the horizon sky from the water's edge to the streaking dark clouds overhead. It was going to be a good day to rebury and she considered her father.

Settling in with a lifejacket for a pillow, the blanket and beer, Max watched Charlie Bay bundle the bones in silk from the corner of his eye. The fire leaped and snapped at his toes. As his belly warmed and the muscles of his legs, bathed in heat, began to loosen, he thought out loud with no expectation of conversation.

"I wonder if he's going to make it happen? It is truly amazing you know. What a dreamer. Your son, what a dreamer. But it's a noble call...educating a Nation.

I've two sons. Two sons. One's in Japan. He's an engineer, working on an elevator that goes horizontally and vertically. You know, like this." Max demonstrated with his right hand by holding the bottle of beer, first dragging it across the ground and then raising it to his mouth. After taking a large swig he continued. "A horizontal and vertical elevator, great idea. It's a very big idea in Japan, very big.

My other son is still in school; college. He's a lacrosse player. You know, the old Native American game." Max assumed that his sarcasm wasn't going to elicit a response and continued rambling. "That kid can run like the wind, especially with some huge defenseman chasing him...he'll run like a bat out of hell. Just like a bat, dashing and darting all over the place. You should see him. Once, when things weren't going so well for him, I wanted to write the Eastern Cherokee word for bat, I think it's "tlaniwa", or something close to that. I wanted to write it on his shoulder pads for the spirit of the bat to guide him, to impart skill and speed. In the moment, even I thought it was too much. So, I drew a Thunderbird instead, just something, anything to get him in touch with the spirits." Max's voice faded as he drew near sleep. "I wanted to get him in touch with the spirits of the game...spirits who played the game before."

Charlie Bay spoke without lifting his head or interrupting his work. "To evoke the spirit of the Bat or the Thunderbird is a serious matter. The power of the spirits can't be taken lightly."

Max was startled. He didn't think that Charlie Bay was listening. Sitting up and turning toward him, he spoke in an annoyed tone, "Yes it is. And, it wasn't taken lightly."

Without acknowledging Max in any way, Charlie Bay continued to bundle bones. After a long silence and seeing that it wasn't going to be discussed any further, Max slid back down against the lifejacket to get the last word.

"It wasn't taken lightly and I appreciate them to be very effective spirits, the kid's been playing great ever since." In a huff, that his understanding was challenged, a tired Max Sorensen folded his arms across his chest, closed his eyes and fell asleep.

The pine coals were still warm but the sand under Max's heels took on an early morning damp chill with the loss of flame and a low sun. As he stirred, the pain in his neck surpassed the stiffness in his back. His immediate thoughts of age and poor judgment were, with an increased awareness of his surroundings, replaced by a concern for Burningwater. Checking the dory, he saw the empty Pipeboat resting at anchor. He looked toward the work-dock and saw the open cartons of silk bundled bones awaiting the final episode in their journey. But, he didn't see Charlie Bay. He rose to his feet and he surveyed the platform corner to corner. Tucked in among the lobster traps, he caught the crown of matted white hair on top of the fisherman's tilted head. It appeared to Max, that the keeper of the dead, who sat limp among the traps, was exhausted and asleep. Easing his bare feet across the platform and working his way through the maze of containers that blanketed the weathered wooden surface, he moved next to Charlie Bay. Max was startled; Burningwater's eyes were wide open and fixed to his lap. Charlie Bay didn't move. In his large strong hands, he cradled the gray brown skull of a child. Max froze.

With watery red swollen lids and rhythmically clenching the muscles in his taught jaw, Charlie Bay Burningwater turned his head toward Dr Max Sorensen and spoke with piercing clarity.

"They're not all here."

"What?" Max knelt down next to Charlie Bay, their faces only inches apart.

"They're not all here."

"What do you mean they are not all here? I checked the inventories three or four times. I marked off every specimen and recorded it. Charlie Bay, I counted the boxes at the troller and when we unloaded. There were nineteen both times. They're here. It's all of them." Max was tender.

"No."

"Well, how could you know that? How could you possibly know...did you dream? Did you have the dream again, the dream and there were the empty chairs...?"

"I didn't sleep. I didn't have the dream this night."

"How could you know who's here and who isn't?"

Charlie Bay hesitated, as if afraid to say the words. Then, he spoke without doubt. "It was the bones. The bones told me. They talked to me and told me that they're not all here."

"But bones can't..." Max was reflexively set to argue, his own words stung him. He withdrew and admitted from his experience "the bones told him", was a profound statement. It was true. The bones told truth. "OK, OK. I understand, the bones told you."

Watching Charlie Bay's hands begin to tremble, Max spoke softly, "It's OK. It's OK." He placed his right arm around Burningwater's shoulders and his left; he gently set atop Charlie Bay’s hand and the child's skull. He pressed his forehead against the white stubble of a leathery cheek and whispered, "I know the bones told you. They're not all here."

"The spirit journey for the missing ones has been halted. I haven't been forgiven." Charlie Bay ended with a whisper, barely audible to Max.

"Sondaqua, Sondaqua soaring high above me,
look down upon me.
Sondaqua, call to Mother Earth
that I might be forgiven."

Sitting back on the deck and leaning against some nearby lobster gear, Max did his best to respond in kindness and to comfort a man in anguish. "Ah, forgiveness, that's a tough one and forgiving yourself, even tougher. Chances are Charlie Bay you are forgiven...even if you can't forgive yourself...maybe someone else needs to lead the way..." Max points skyward, "...praying for forgiveness, I always figured praying was a good thing...trouble is I'm no good at it so I can't...it's beyond you and me...you're headed right..." Max's voice trailed off in this small burst of affection. It was all he had.

"I must persevere. I must hunt until all the bones are returned. I must persevere."

"Persevere, ah, another tough one. I'd pray for that one too, perseverance, by far not one of my strengths." Max shook his head and reached over to touch Charlie Bay, this time on the knee. "Charlie Bay, look, you can only do what you can do. So today, today you rebury the Casco."

Neither man moved. Max felt his heart pound. Charlie Bay continued to stare at the skull until his chest expanded and air whistled through his nose.

Looking toward Max he rose, "Yup, today I will!"

Directing the reburial, Charlie Bay assigned Margaret, Bud Walker and five other fishermen roles in the procession of the Casco bones from the work dock to the burial site. Showered, refreshed and wearing a sleeveless, dark blue cotton summer dress, Margaret had Bud Walker staring as she processed beside Burningwater. Still holding the child's skull in one hand, Charlie Bay carried the tobacco tin in the other and set the pace. In both arms, Margaret held a large bundle of red silk wrapped bones. The six fishermen followed her; each baring an open carton of prepared Casco ancestors. Unassigned, Max gathered his damp clothes and followed off to one side and behind. He was unable to take his eyes off the group as they approached the mass grave. The lobstermen, dressed in work pants and solid colored t-shirts were led by Bud Walker. They marched out of step but in single file to the edge of the burial site. As if well rehearsed, each placed the containers next to the western side of the trough in a row, removed the contents and gently placed the bundled bones at the edge of the grave. They made two more trips back and forth to the work dock for the remainder of the Casco. Without being asked, Max collected the empty cartons. In several trips, he neatly placed them in the bed of Burningwater's pickup and stood apart from the lobstermen.

A small number of visitors arrived as Charlie Bay worked the western border of the grave and made final preparations for the placement of the remains. Those present included Dr. Sandra Walsh, two other members of the Anthropology Department, a photographer from the local newspaper and the wife of T.J. Toomey, one of the fishermen. Jim Garret was not among them. Annoyed with the presence of a photographer, Charlie Bay stated bluntly that no pictures were allowed but allowed him to stay. He asked the largest of the six lobstermen, Paul Flarety, a burly man with huge tan forearms covered in a brush of blonde hair to stand next to the man with the camera. Upon her arrival, Sandra acknowledged Max with a smile and a shake of her head at his motley appearance. She embraced Margaret and they engaged in quiet, private conversation.

Without introduction, Charlie Bay moved to a spot beside Max at the southern entrance of the burial trough. He sprinkled some tobacco in the four directions and to the sky and earth, eased his way into the grave and began to systematically place the bundled bones on the dirt floor. Appreciating that the reburial was underway, the participants moved alongside the remains of the Casco. Indicating to Walker and Toomey that it was almost time to shovel the sand into the section of the grave in which the bone placement was complete, Charlie Bay positioned them on the southeast corner with long handled spades. Each bundle was arranged on the floor of the grave with the skull facing west and the long bones extending in an east-west orientation. As he approached the center of the trough, Charlie Bay signaled with a wave of his left hand and the two fishermen began to fill in the pit with sandy soil. No ones eyes left the trough but Burningwater's as he continued the rhythmic deposition of his ancestors. Situating the child's skull next to the last bundle, Charlie Bay completed the repatriation. He first invited Margaret and then the others to shovel dirt over the final section of bones. As they threw the grainy sand onto the Casco, tears overcame Margaret and

Sandra, each for a different reason. Max remained standing at the southern end, with his hands clasped just below his waist, twirling his wedding ring. Charlie Bay Burningwater moved to the northern border of the fresh soil to stand opposite Max Sorensen. With his lips moving inaudibly, he made a last tobacco offering in the reburial.

Sandra leaned and whispered into Margaret's ear. "Is that it? Do you think it's over?"

"I'm not sure, but I think so." Margaret caught Charlie Bay's glance as he signaled for the guests, the ceremony was over.

Stepping forward next to Burningwater, Margaret smiled, "My grandfather and I wish to thank you for coming. It means a lot to have you here and thank you for your help. We have blueberry muffins and coffee on the front porch of the house for those of you who are hungry. Everyone is welcome."

Charlie Bay was startled by the open invitation for food, "We do?"

"Yes. I brought them back this morning from the best bakery in town. You can't send these people away without feeding them something. I also have gifts for Bud and the men as a sign of our appreciation"

"You do? Where did you get those?"

"I shop...gifts I've saved. Remember I'm a child of retail strip malls, collecting good gifts for the right time...it's tradition."

“It is?” Charlie Bay was lost and surrendered. "OK. Well, I never planned on that either but OK. You take them up. I'll be along in a bit."

As the small group drifted in quiet conversation toward the house, Max and Charlie Bay were left standing alone at opposite ends of the gravesite; bones of the Casco buried between them. Max watched Bud Walker hustle to Margaret's side as the sun attached to the skin of her bare arms. She did have great shoulders. He saw Sandra’s face express relief and quiet joy. He was happy for her. Then, he turned his attention to Burningwater.

Staring at the salty fisherman, Max felt a newfound sense of similarity, somehow, in some ways, they were alike. The two of them shared a coinciding and continuous search for bones. There was common ground in their hunt, granted, to different ends but a hunt with the same intensity and reverence none the less. They were connected to something. Max couldn’t pinpoint it. Maybe it was a link to the dream journey of the Pipeboat people, a journey with an intuitive attraction for both of them. Or maybe it was just the bones. Whatever the source of the union, as Max studied the weathered and worn face of Charlie Bay Burningwater, he saw a kindred spirit.

As Charlie Bay looked back at Dr. Max Sorensen, he saw a tormented soul with a strange job.

After the moment's unspoken exchange, Max waved good bye to Burningwater without a word or expectation. He walked away slowly at first, then picking up speed to catch Sandra and Margaret before the house and the food. Halfway to the small meandering cluster, he glanced over his shoulder and caught sight of Charlie Bay standing motionless on the burial grounds. Burningwater was alone, silhouetted against the billowing white clouds and the blue late morning summer sky. He was a solitary figure, once again, among his people. The singular, framed image of the man was burned into Max. He would always remember.

"Hey Sandra, wait up. Excuse me for a second." Pulling Sandra aside, "Did we get them all? Did we give them all back?"

"Max, what are you talking about? What do you mean?"

"The bones, did we give them all back? All of them?"

"Well ya, sure we did. If you gave him everyone on my master list, we gave them all back. You did, didn't you, check them off the list?"

"Of course, I double checked it a couple of times."

"Then why ask?"

"Burningwater says they're not all here. Some of the bones are still missing."

Sandra hesitated, "Oh....but how could he...."

"Is there any possibility that there are still some out there, that someone else took some material from the site. Were any other University people, other anthropologists around?" A sense of frustration was seeping through his voice with the thought of lost Casco.

"Max, it was almost forty years ago. There were people crawling all over the tip of this Island, in no particular order other than to beat the clock. I don't know, maybe it's possible. But they're sure not mine."

"But possible."

"Ya."

It was a revelation and a circumstance concerning the excavation that Max never entertained; other collectors. His head ached and it was time for him to go. "Ah, I'm going back to your place, pack my stuff, maybe get on the road today. I'll see you later."

Nodding, Sandra left unconcerned as Margaret approached Max carrying coffee and a blueberry muffin.

With his eyebrows and shoulders raised, Max asked, "Your father?"

"Charity golf tournament. He flew out last night. I never saw him."

"Ahhh golf." Max drifted off.

“Max you look a little lost. Are you OK?”

“Ya, I’m OK. Maybe it’s just time for me to go. Maybe it’s time for me to head home. I’ll catch a ride back to the co-op with one of the lobstermen and get my car. I better get going. Thanks Margaret. I'll see you...sometime I hope." Uneasily gesturing in the direction of some parked pickups and a lobsterman’s lone departure, Max leaned forward, kissed Margaret on the cheek and took the muffin but not the coffee.

"Max, here is something to remember us by." Reaching into her dress pocket, Margaret removed a CD in a clear plastic case. "It's a recording of the Storyteller's; my favorite."

Flipping the case over nervously with one hand, Max saw the words "Heartache of the Hunter" neatly written on the label side. He smiled but didn't speak.

"It's important to me and I thought you might enjoy it."

"Thanks."

Watching him hitch up his borrowed pants and hobble his way toward the trucks, she whispered, "Good-bye Max."

Packing was not difficult or long. The lab equipment and supplies were already boxed. His clothes were either in the clean or the dirty pile, stuffed in two kitchen trash bags and all into a duffle bag. Papers, journals and CD files were stacked into one of Sandra's file cartons. Still undecided, the most effort and energy of the packing went into the question of whether or not to leave. For some unknown reason, leaving was not easy.

Max set aside his sax, packed his limited Barbara Stanwyck video collection in his laptop case and put on his bathing suit. The heat from the early afternoon sun was cooled by a strong salty southwest wind. Standing on a kitchen chair in the exact spot of the backyard to see the ocean, he checked the tide and the surf each trip to the car. He was restless, anxious and exhausted. Two grilled hot dogs and a beer failed to soothe his uneasiness. Finally, sitting outside in a sun-drenched corner of Sandra's home, wearing only a generic dark blue swim suit, he retreated to Jr. Walker and sax therapy. The past twenty-four hours melted away.

After over an hour of intermittently playing "Sweet Soul" and wrestling with the power of a solitary Charlie Bay Burningwater standing on the crest of the burial site, Max was jolted by an unseen neighbor. With a voice enjoyed by strong and enormous men, Max was pierced by the command, "Hey, either play a different song or quit playing!"

This was followed by a woman's reprimand, "Gil, we're on vacation. You're supposed to relax. Now, let the kid practice."

"It's not a kid. It's an old guy in navy boxers and he keeps playing the same dam song over and over and over again. How crazy is that?"

Undaunted, the shirtless tenor soloist stood on the chair, hit a few high notes and checked the surf. Luckily for both, the waves were perfect.

The water was much warmer than at the time of his early morning plunge. With an incoming tide, onshore breeze and sunshine, this pudgy man stood ankle deep at the water's edge and estimated the temperature at sixty-five, plus or minus one. However, it wasn't the tolerably cold water but the surf that renewed his spirit and gave strength to a tired body. Age and degenerative joint disease were now irrelevant. These were, by far and away, the best waves of the summer. Max knew it was instinct, ability and endurance that defined a capacity for body surfing. With child-like joy and the belief that he possessed significant portions of all three, he tiptoed into the breakers.

Having no recollection of the age at which the experience of riding a wave passed from an adventure to a passion, Max simply acknowledged to himself that he loved it. Without hesitating, he dove into the first rolling crest of water. Cold, wet and happy, he studied the waves. Through years of body surfing, Max knew Maine waves usually came in sets of threes. In his judgment, the second of the three waves was the best ride. Size and curl were important but the break point was key. Standing in water waist high, he watched as three to five footers crashed to shelves of rushing white water and charged indifferently toward him. Edging deeper for the exact spot to catch, not the first break of foam on the crest, but the thrust of a collapsing arc, he waited. At the precise moment, on a perfect wave, he left his feet, buried his head between out-stretched arms and lunged forward along with the rumbling layer of ocean. The ride in was spectacular. Out of breath and in water only shin deep, he struggled to his feet, tugged at his sagging suit and ran back to do it all again. For the few seconds of each ride that his body was suspended and driven forward with the wave, he relaxed. Max stayed in the water so long that his body fatigued but not his uneasiness.

The steam in Sandra's outdoor shower rose across the rectangular patch of blue sky that bordered the top of the warped wooden door. Standing still on a makeshift grate, Max let the spray beat against his neck and run down his back until all the hot water was gone. He finished packing his car, wrote Sandra a brief thank you note and drove with his shirt on back to Boston. In place of “Sweet Soul”, he listened to "Heartache of the Hunter", again and again, the entire trip.

Chapter Thirteen

The human beings seated in the circle surrounding him were silent. Some eyes fixed to his, others stared away. He sat in the center and faced the Ancient One. As he considered those who encircled him, he stared back into the eyes of the ancestor. He was drawn to this man and poured over his features.

The Ancient One's shoulder length white hair was parted in the middle. It fell in an arc that paralleled the downward curves of his brow, his eyes and his lips. Each formed the cascade of distress, distrust and displeasure. The expression was sealed into his face. The Ancient One's arms were folded across his chest and pressed an eagle's wing to his left shoulder.

He let his eyes drift to the woman seated inches from the wing's tip. A dark blue scarf covered her forehead. A red woven blanket sheathed the curves of her body. Her beauty had hold of his heart. The sorrow in her eyes made him uneasy.

A grandfather sat alongside the sad eyed woman. His weathered brow was shielded by a brown felt hat. There was a dried starfish pinned to the front, just above the brim. Beneath the hat, his hair was bundled at the ears by shreds of a blue cotton kerchief. The two streams of grey slid down the back of his shoulders and clung to his faded navy jacket. The grandfather's eyes were tired and glazed. His lids puffed.

Next to the grandfather was an empty metal chair skewed to the outside of the arch. Dust masked its color. Beside the empty chair was a young woman with pitted skin. A crescent scar marked her right cheek and a moon snail amulet hung around her neck. Her head tilted forward and her eyes were sheltered from view by dark disheveled hair. A child, swaddled in sealskin, stretched across her lap.

One by one, he met the ancients. He met them in silence. He met them in this faded room with strength and an edge of arrogance. He held firm his past choices as the right ones, the only choices he could have made at the time. Then he came to the empty chairs; those seven empty metal chairs, staggered between the dozen or so human beings circled around him. It was the empty chairs that made his jaw tight, his stomach turn and his defiance flee. The vacancies haunted him. They were seats of the missing, ancients who broke the circle and whose circle was broken. Each empty chair bore witness to the choice he made years ago and the choice he made moments ago. Each empty chair pressed his obligation.

He tried to speak. But he was without breath.

Choking for air and unable to breathe, Max woke up. He gasped raw and wheezing gulps of air. His pillow was soaked with sweat. His moist hair was matted to the back of his neck. He was coughing. Max lurched forward and labored to breathe. As his lungs filled, he fell back onto the damp sheets, glanced into the darkness and panicked. For a few disconcerting seconds, Max had no recollection of his name or his whereabouts. As he caught his breath, he was able to bring the room into focus.

"What the hell was that?"

The similarity of inexpensive highway hotels was a comfort for him; the city's location didn't matter. He stood and walked toward the bathroom. The cool dry air chilled his moist skin. Remembering that this was Baltimore and the Fall Lacrosse Tournament, he groped for the two switch light panel on the entryway wall. With the glow of a dim bureau lamp and the bathroom overhead, Max made out the room in faded brick red and beige, sparse with cheap generic furniture. Walking in short shuffle steps, he returned to sit on the edge of the bed. Beads of sweat ran from under his chin, over his chest and collected on the rolls of his stomach. He was breathing heavily as he whispered again, "What the hell was that all about?"

This fall lacrosse trip was planned during his stay at Sandra's place in Maine. It included two days before the weekend games for some time with friends in D.C., visits to the Smithsonian for a little research and the National Gallery for recreation. Leaving Boston on Wednesday morning, he spent Thursday and Friday in the Capitol and made the quick trip to Baltimore early on Saturday for the first round of the tournament.

The first day in Washington, his planned schedule collapsed. By chance, he stumbled on to an exhibit of late nineteenth and early twentieth century Native American photographic portraits by Edward S. Curtis. Fortunately for him, old friends were forgiving and social calendars rescheduled as the rest of the world, for forty-eight hours, disappeared. Max was so enthralled by Curtis' work that he even managed to finagle a pass into the collection's archives. Friday afternoon melted away two floors below ground among stacks of glass plates and prints. The black and white Native American photographs were stunning images, full of physical form; morphology, what he enjoyed most, the lumps and bumps of bone.

After tearing himself away from the Smithsonian Friday night, the first day of lacrosse in Baltimore was terrific. Aside from an early morning shower, the mild mid-October sunshine was a welcome relief from the cold and damp New England autumn. It was a perfect Saturday for the tournament. Once again, he enjoyed time suspended by the athletic expertise and competitive spirit of the young. When his head hit the pillow just before midnight, he was exhausted but content. He put in a wake-up call for seven and expected to do it all again on Sunday.

Now awake, alert and sitting on the edge of the bed, Max was frightened by this dream. It was bone-chilling.

His stomach was tight and his hands shook. Slowly, the tension began to dissipate as he rationalized the dream. He glanced at the bold block red digits on the alarm clock, three forty-eight. He began to match the images of the dream with the photographs of the Curtis exhibit. There were no matches, not one.

Max kept mumbling, “What the hell kind of dream was that?”

Then he remembered. Goose bumps grew on his thighs and his breath grew short.

The flood gates of Max’s memory opened. It couldn’t be. This wasn’t possible. This was the spirit dream. It was Charlie Bay Burningwater's dream. This was the dream that Charlie Bay described. It was the ancestral dream from that summer afternoon on Eagle Island. The dream Max never understood and never pursued. It was sacred territory. It was the spirit dream of Charlie Bay Burningwater.

Max was angry. He paced the room determined to figure it all out. How could this be possible? For the two and half-hours until daybreak, objectifying failed and understanding was impossible.

Despite the warm Sunday sunshine and the festival-like atmosphere of the tournament, Max was obsessed by the images in the dream. Unable to distract himself with the lacrosse games, the food or observing people, he replayed the Native American faces in his mind. He wrestled to link each character in the dream with either the Curtis plates or with something from his professional past. He had to find images in his memory he could make fit the dream. Right off, he knew the faces weren't the familiar Native American photos of popular media and Public Television. They were not Curtis' staged portraits of the noble savage. Recalling other images of aboriginal people, he struggled with the unfamiliar faces. He tried to convince himself the beings of the dream must be individuals whose likenesses he had somehow, somewhere already experienced.

Reconstructing the whole thing as a compilation of Native American images, Max decided it was set off by the days spent with the Curtis exhibit. Using this line of reasoning, he attempted to push the explanation into his heart. There had to be a way to make this something other than Burningwater's dream. He had no success with any of it, waking without breath clinched it.

By mid-afternoon, he was nervously trying to decide between driving to Maine for an explanation from Burningwater or returning to Boston for what, he had no idea. To burn some energy, he tried to use his cell to check his messages and home voice mail. But, true to travel time, he had forgotten to charge the cell. With his phone dead, he caught up with his son between games and borrowed his smart phone. The touch screen was beyond him. He was desperate for information about something, anything that might lead to an explanation. After touching too many wrong buttons and entering too many wrong passwords, Max gave up and gave in. He returned the phone, said a quick good-bye, hedged on Maine and headed for Boston.

In the quiet of his apartment Max listened to his home phone voice mail. There were three messages.

"Max, it's Margaret Garret. Ah...it's Wednesday, a little after three. I've been trying to reach you. The departmental secretary said your cell was useless and my best chance was to call you at home. I'm sorry I can't speak with you directly, but I think you should know. I have bad news. Ahmm... well, Charlie Bay passed . . . he died Monday. I came up from Philadelphia yesterday when I found out. I just thought you should know Max, that's all, I thought you would like to know." Her voice faded. Max sat motionless in the dark. The sadness in her voice was not masked by the background noise on her cell.

He hit the second message. "Max, it's me again, Margaret. It's Thursday, about eleven. I wanted to tell you that the burial of Charlie Bay is on Saturday, sometime in the morning, on Eagle Island. Ah...you know, the Casco gravesite by the blueberry patch, you know the place. Any way, I hope you hear this before Saturday and maybe you would be able to come. Bye Max." A third message followed. "I don't know when you'll be back but, it's me again. The burial was yesterday...and ah, it rained some. I'm in Maine a few more days this week. We need to talk about some things, so ah...if you could call me on my cell. I'm staying at my parent's house. And if you're busy, I could drive down to Boston and maybe meet you some place. It's important we talk. Thanks."

Frustrated and embarrassed that he was unable to remotely check his voice mail, he took his cell, threw it across the room at the couch and listened to the messages again.

After his Monday morning Human Antiquities class, Max was on his way to Maine. Unable to reach Margaret, he left a message on her phone and another with her mother that he was coming. He expected to be at the burial site on Eagle Island by one o'clock. Margaret's mother sounded pleasant, but was confused by the information. Max assumed Jim Garret wasn't the only one in the clan who told only portions of the family history. Either way, he hoped that Margaret got the message and was there to meet him.

The rail tie bridge didn't appear any stronger. Holding his breath, he rattled his Volvo to brown grass and a leafless treeline. Eagle Island looked cold as Max drove to the hillcrest but it wasn't empty. With a sigh of thanks, he pulled up beside Jim Garret's SUV. Margaret was standing next to some freshly turned sandy soil at the northern end of the burial trough. She was wrapped in a long gray wool coat and shivered as a chilling saltless northeast wind tugged her hair. After a cordial embrace, both stared at the rectangular section of scattered dried grass and light brown sand. Max's nose began to water.

"He died last Monday, a week ago...well you know. The way some of the fishermen describe it, he was digging clams on the late afternoon low tide. His heart gave out somewhere on the sand bar. Evidently, he didn't die right away. He was covered with sand. They said that it was all over his face, chest and legs, like he fell face first, maybe crawled before he got in the skiff." Margaret's eyes were watering and she repeatedly wiped her nose with a tissue. As she did, she handed Max a fresh one. "He made it into his boat but, he never rowed. The tide came in and took him up the river into the marsh and then through the night back out into the ocean. No one even knew he was missing. No one missed him." Max reached over and put his arm around Margaret. "Tuesday morning, early, one of the lobsterman, just by chance, spotted the skiff on the horizon. They said another hour and the current would have taken him right out to sea. We never would have found him. He was lying in the bottom of the boat, covered with sand, the oars still across the seats."

Without hesitation Max gave comfort, "He wasn't lost. He's here with his people. You buried him."

It seemed to Max that even the possibility of Charlie Bay's bones missing from this place was disturbing to her. It was to him.

"How did you find out?"

"My father called on Wednesday and I flew right home. Charlie Bay was buried wrapped in silk, the traditional colors, right here, where he asked...beyond the child, over there on the end."

"He asked?"

"Yes he did, that's what I wanted to speak with you about. We talked before I left to go back to Philly.

Come on; let's walk down to the work dock. I have some things for you."

They crossed the wind off the marsh and river. It was cold against their skin. Max put his hands in his pockets and Margaret held his arm, sliding behind one shoulder down wind for shelter.

"Before I left, at the end of August, I came out here to say good bye. There was no small talk; he was all business. I got the impression right away he had a list of things he wanted to tell me. He started with; when I die. I think he knew and was giving me his will. You were first on the list."

"I was?"

"The Pipeboat, he said he wanted you to have the Pipeboat."

Max was surprised, then as the pieces began to fall into place, stunned.

Reading the expression on his face, "That's right the Pipeboat and I was to be sure that you got it. So here you are," she extended her right arm, palm open in the direction of the Pipeboat. "I had Bud Walker and some of the other fishermen at the burial carry it up here to the work dock, because I didn't have any idea when I'd see you."

As they stepped onto the platform, Max saw the overturned dory restored to its original design. There was fresh red bottom paint on the hull.

"There's no outboard motor well."

"That's the first thing he did after the reburial, rip out the well. I helped him caulk and paint the bottom. The whole time, I listened to him mumble about how this boat was meant to be rowed, just rowed...and how he hoped Earl Alton forgave him." Margaret recalled a wonderful afternoon and smiled.

Caressing the new stem to stern plank and former location of the square hole, Max whispered, "Pipeboat for the dream journey of the Pipeboat People."

"The motor is in the shed . . . gave it to Bud Walker but he hasn't picked it up yet. The oars for the dory are in there too. They are yours." Ducking into the building, Margaret returned carrying a plastic bag of eight oar lock Tholepins. "Max, Charlie Bay dictated something to me that he said you would need. I wrote it on a blue index card. It's in the bag."

Max was distracted by his experience of the spirit dream and the mid-summer discussion with Charlie Bay about the dream journey of the Pipeboat people. Now, they were both his, the boat and the dream. "Thanks Margaret. Thanks . . ." Without looking, Max took the plastic bag filled with the wooden pins. The blue index card was in front with the blank side facing out.

"Come on there's more."

"More?"

"Not for you, but there is more, more that you should see."

They walked single file back up the path to the burial ground. As they approached the clearing next to the blueberry patch, Max stepped to Margaret's side.

"You said your father called you?"

Margaret smiled, "Ah, very tactful Max; different for you."

Caught and embarrassed at his probe into Garret affairs, "Well, I know them both as very remarkable men. I wondered if..."

She interrupted, anticipating his question, "There was no reconciliation before Charlie Bay died and my father never made it to the burial.

I made it easier for my father. After the Casco reburial, I told him that I was there the night of your meeting. And, I was with Charlie Bay and we heard the whole thing. We talked a little but not much. He told me how he took his mother's maiden name and why he was always quick to emphasize our Irish ancestry. He asked for some time and the chance to talk with my mother."

"Oh." Max tilted his head and raised his brow.

Margaret didn't volunteer more and Max didn't ask. They stopped walking and stood beside Burningwater's grave. She broke the silence.

"He told me, with the same, “when I die”... he wanted to be buried on the north end about ten yards beyond the bones of the child...in silk of Casco colors, in his work clothes, with a Casco lobster buoy and his bait iron."

Smiling, Max whispered, “... his Casco buoy and his bait iron."

"He also told me that all the bones weren't here. There were still some Casco bones missing. He said you knew."

“That’s why he left the space...for the others. He’s protecting the north side...on the end.” Max pointed to the gap then looked at Margaret. “See...see. Yes, we talked about it that morning on the dock before you came back for the burial."

"Are there?"

"I'd say yes. I believe it's true."

"More bones...hmm...it explains why...he asked me to take care of everything here. It seems I got the house...wait ‘til you see the house."

“Ya and...I gotta tell you...I, I ah, it seems I got the dream."

"You got what? What do you mean, you got the dream?"

"You remember that day on the porch, when we heard Charlie Bay choking and we ran up to find him just waking up and breathing so hard?"

"Yes, I do, but..."

"You remember him telling us about the spirit dream, his dream, his ancestors and the Ancient One, all unable to move until the bones are returned."

"Yes, oh...I... but how could you have his dream?"

"I don't know. And it makes no sense to say it, but I do know it's his dream and I’d say for better or worse, it's mine now."

Staring at one another, Margaret broke into a smile. "So, you too have rolled three times on the ground and been turned into a buffalo!"

"Heartache of the Hunter"

Margaret tugged Max's arm. “Yes Max, Heartache of the Hunter.”

Turning his eyes away and squinting to the east, he struggled with his anger.

"Margaret, I'm not real happy about this dream. Not only is the experience frightening and I’ve already had it a couple of times, but I have, or I should say, had plans. I figured that I was headed for the banks of the Nile next semester or maybe next summer, you know, to continue my Nubian stuff. Instead it looks like, thanks to Burningwater, I'm going to have to deal with the coast of Maine for awhile, maybe a long while. That's really not what I want. I was just here as a favor to Sandra, I owed her. And now for some reason, I owe him, I owe the Casco." He turned to Margaret. His left foot rhythmically kicked loose sand in the direction of Charlie Bay's grave. Max unveiled a small portion of his torment. "I mean how did this happen? I'm stuck with this dream until I find the rest of the Casco? That’s really crazy! It’s not rational...I can’t talk about it with any one...it’s crazier than I already am!

I have no idea what skeletal material is out there or where to look. We're really not dealing with one excavation, but five hundred years of violations, five hundred years of desecration. And it’s not just the Casco . . . pick a Native American Nation . . . any one, any Nation and it’s the same damn thing!

How am I ever going to find a way to break through in one direction if I get pulled so hard in another?"

Max paused. His eyes filled with tears. Shaking his head with a sigh of resignation, “So I’ve rolled three times on the ground and been turned into a buffalo.” He was still bewildered.

In a barely audible voice, he mumbled toward Charlie Bay and then to himself.

Margaret caught the words, spirit dream, and gave him time. "It's a noble work Max, who knows, being attached to this place ... it’s good.

Come on, let me show you what's up at the house...maybe that will cheer you up." Again, Margaret took Max’s arm and they walked side by side down a fall wind to the home of the Storyteller.

"Take a look under the porch, right here, where this opens." Her voice, now excited. Swinging open a section of the grill panels that surrounded the base of the front porch, Max peered into a small dimly lit space adjacent to the stone foundation. On the ruff dirt floor were two overturned traditional Native American canoes and one incomplete canoe frame.

"Canoes, that's amazing. Look at these Margaret...they look pretty old, great condition. I don't think he ever would’ve used them, but he took good care of them.”

"Let's go down to the basement Max, I want to show you more."

At the bottom of the cellar stairs Margaret plugged in an orange extension cord with four caged hook lights hung from the ceiling. The lamps exposed a large room with walls of fieldstone and lined by wide planked shelves. Each shelf contained section after section of shallow wooden fruit boxes.

Lowering his head to remain standing did not prevent Max's chin from dropping. He was speechless. Beginning on his immediate right, Max worked his way along the shelves. Without missing a surface or a container, he explored the archive of Casco artifacts. The carved stone sculptures and the ritual masks were works of extraordinary beauty. Even utilitarian objects; axes, choppers, projectile points, knives, spoons, ladles and serving bowls were so pristine in character, it disrupted his breathing. His heart was racing. Passing the far wall, he examined the bone carvings and the stone effigy pipes until his eyes fell upon a shelf overflowing with lacrosse sticks. Each carved wooden shaft was unique in size and thickness. Each pocket of woven leather was perfectly formed by the curved frame. Studying one stick, he discovered lightening bolts etched and painted into the wood just a few inches from the webbed pouch. White dots of hail ran the shaft. Max's body chilled. He sat back on an overturned five-gallon clam pail.

"I just have to take a minute. I'm starting to hyperventilate. This is embarrassing. This is what's left of the Casco material culture. He saved it. He saved all this. This is generations of creativity."

Holding the lacrosse stick across his knees, Max leaned forward and took a deep breath.

"Max, are you OK?"

“I'm fine. It's all just so remarkable. I never would have figured him for it. It's all..."

"Max, this is not all."

Regaining his strength and lifting his head toward Margaret, "Are you trying to kill me?"

"Bring one of the lights over here to the fruit cellar" Margaret grunted, as she partially pushed open a thick wooden door.

Placing the light in the available space before peering inside, Max was astonished by the baskets and pottery, stack upon stack. The decorative symbols alone were spectacular.

"How large is the room?"

"I have no idea. I haven't been able to get the door open wide enough to get in there. I don't know how he did it."

Max sat on the stairs and gazed at the bundle of harpoons and fishing equipment, attempting to integrate the treasure. "Are we done?"

"No, we have to go upstairs." Margaret wondered how much more he was able to take.

On the second floor there was a center hallway, three bedrooms and a bath. As they reached the platform at the head of the stairs, Margaret pointed to the closed door at the end of the hall, "That's Charlie Bay's room. Just take a quick look in this first room on the left, so that you'll have some idea of what's up here."

The bedroom was devoid of furniture and filled with woven blankets of remarkable designs, rugs with intricate patterns and traditional clothing and festival costumes that hung on make-shift racks across the room.

"It's overwhelming Margaret, truly overwhelming."

"Yes, I know. I got the house remember. But here's the most amazing record of all." Leading Max into the second bedroom, she presented the written and photographic archive of the Casco Nation. "I've just spent a little time here, but it seems to me that he divided it into three sections; photos, family albums, pictographs and paintings in this section, letters, diaries, journals and anything else that look personal in this area and all the legal transactions like agreements, treaties, contracts over here. The most astounding thing is, Charlie Bay couldn't read. He must've just gone on instinct. And here's the best of all, these tapes! "Heartache of the Hunter" wasn't the only story Charlie Bay dictated. There's all kinds of stuff on these tapes. Look, there're Clementine boxes full of cassettes maybe eighty to a hundred of them! And Max, some he did in three languages. There're in English, then what I'm assuming is a translation in Casco and then what sounds to me like Cajun French. He couldn't read or write but he spoke three languages! This stuff is unbelievable! My grandfather was very bright.

I think Charlie Bay recorded the Casco oral history, all he could on all these tapes. He saved and protected it all. My father isn't the only warrior to fight extinction. I think Charlie Bay gave us the Casco story, maybe all the way back from the beginning."

Max picked up a cassette, looked at it and began to circle the room, "since the beginning of time." He caressed the tops of the piles and looked through some of the photographs without another word. They stayed in the room for some time, drifting from section to section.

As the afternoon sun moved further from reach, Max finally whispered, "It's a life's work."

Margaret wasn't sure whether he meant of Charlie Bay's, for her or for himself. But instead of clarifying, she asked if he wanted tea or a beer. Margaret already knew it was for her. Max chose beer.

Sitting together at the kitchen table, Max looked Margaret square in the eyes, "What are you going to do?"

"I'm going to write Max. It's what I do. I write plays. This is my Pittsburgh, my home."

"You mean DNA Pittsburgh...?"

"No, I mean August Wilson Pittsburgh, my cycle of plays, my place, my people, you know, my *Fences,* my *Piano Lesson*. I'm a Casco American."

Max was still a little lost and Margaret just kept going.

"My father has spent his life trying to get away from being Casco. Charlie Bay spent a good part of his life keeping the Casco alive. And I, I have a lot to learn to become more Casco.

Right now, I don't even know what I don't know."

Max raised his eyebrows. He understood and Margaret knew he would.

"I'm starting to sound as crazy as you!

Look, this house holds the Casco story, but not as an archive or a museum. Max this is not a place to visit on a rainy Sunday afternoon. It's a story that's living right now, with a past, a present and a future, now, right here! And I believe Charlie Bay is going to help me uncover, "what I don't know". If I write he'll take me there. He'll guide me.

This place is of a people. It has an identity that lives and a people whose stories must be told. Charlie Bay is going to teach it to me with all those tapes and he expects me to write it and to write it well, to strive for an expression of Casco culture that forces the recognition of the existence and value of the Casco people and their beliefs. The need for strong Casco ethnic identity among disparate and alienated living Casco is profound. And that cultural base, it's all here. The Casco aren't going away!

Writing the cycles of the story is one way, my part. My father has his part, as ironic as that may be and the Casco Board of Directors and the Tribal Council theirs.

But look Max, if we, with efforts on these different fronts and others to come, keep the Casco as a distinct Nation in the present, a Nation with customs and traditions, religion, the Casco colors and on and on and it's lived ...people are living it, it forces fairness. It forces everyone to recognize the issues of American history, the atrocities and injustices, the extermination. The Casco aren't going to disappear, we have a past and a future, right here, in the present. It's a way to hold a line for my grandfather and all the others. This island is the ground of the Casco. This is the place. And we...I need your help."

"You're asking me?"

"Yes."

"I think it's going to be hard to fit the Pipeboat into my apartment." Max was trying to peel the label of the beer bottle off at each corner.

“Max, I need your help with the bones, the missing bones.”

Margaret wasn’t about to let his distraction last. She slammed her open palms on the kitchen tabletop. Max jumped in his chair.

“Max, I know you have Charlie Bay’s dream. I believe you. You don’t need to talk about it with anyone else. We both know Casco bones are still missing. And I need you to flat out tell me you’re going to get them back or none of this is going to work, I believe none of it will happen! The Casco bones must be returned to Casco ground…spirits in order...so they can act in our favor.”

He loved passion and she was overflowing. Max looked up.

“You know I’ve been out of sync my whole life...always a few beats off... remember me and ancient DNA. I was a disconnected academic until Charlie Bay. My whole career I skirted the issue of what people believed. I was always able to bend or twist or sometimes not even advert to other people’s beliefs about human remains. They were there but not that important, nowhere near as important as the bones...as the scientific data. I figured that if what I did was in the name of science ... seeking and acquiring new scientific knowledge, it was more important and the right thing to do. People’s belief didn’t carry that much weight ... didn’t matter. I could justify it ... until Charlie Bay. From Charlie Bay I learned that belief can override science.

Something is happening between us, Charlie Bay and me. I have his dream. And I know they're not all here.

Ya, I will keep looking...hunting for Casco bones...but you've gotta know putting them back in the ground is pretty much the opposite of my whole professional life. It's counter to everything I've done and been trained to do. I recover and analyze bones.

Margaret, I don't want to be a buffalo!

It's not going to be easy to keep up the hunt...to repatri..."

Max felt this was an awful turn. He needed help. He wouldn't look at Margaret and tried not to think about it.

"You have his fire Margaret." The thought of repatriation lingered. "I just hope I'm able to keep up...to keep up the hunt."

The human beings seated in the circle surrounding Max were silent. Some eyes fixed to his, others stared away. Like before, Max sat in the center and faced the Ancient One. As he considered those who encircled him, he stared back into the eyes of his ancestor. Max was drawn to this man and poured over his features.

The Ancient One's shoulder length white hair was parted in the middle. It fell in an arc that paralleled the downward curves of his brow, his eyes and his lips. Each formed the cascade of distress, distrust and displeasure. The expression was sealed into his face. The Ancient One's arms were folded across his chest and pressed an eagle's wing to his left shoulder.

Max let his eyes drift to the woman seated inches from the wing's tip. A dark blue scarf covered her forehead. A red woven blanket sheathed the curves of her body. Her beauty had hold of Max's heart. The sorrow in her eyes made him uneasy.

A grandfather sat alongside the sad eyed woman. His weathered brow was shielded by a brown felt hat. There was a dried starfish pinned to the front, just above the brim. Beneath the hat his hair was bundled at the ears by shreds of a blue cotton kerchief. The two streams of grey slid down the back of his shoulders and clung to his faded navy jacket. A lacrosse stick with dots of hail and lightening bolts carved into the shaft was at his feet. The grandfather's eyes were tired and glazed. His lids puffed.

Next to the grandfather was an empty metal chair skewed to the outside of the arch. Dust masked its color. Beside the empty chair was a young woman with pitted skin. A crescent scar marked her right cheek and a moon snail amulet hung around her neck. Her head tilted forward and her eyes were sheltered from Max's view by dark disheveled hair. A child, swaddled in sealskin, stretched across her lap.

Seated in folding metal chairs, wrapped in skins and blankets were those who came before. One by one, as always, Max met the ancients. He met them in silence. He met them in this faded room with strength and an edge of arrogance. He held firm his past choices as the right ones, the only choices he could have made at the time. Then Max came to the empty chairs; those seven empty metal chairs, staggered between the dozen or so human beings around him. It was the empty chairs that made his jaw tight, his stomach turn and his defiance flee. The vacancies haunted him. They were seats of the missing, ancients who broke the circle and whose circle was broken. Each empty chair bore witness to the choice Max made years ago and the choice he made moments ago. Each empty chair pressed his obligation.

Once more it went on, his contact with the circle of ancestors who were without speech, without breath and without sound. Ancestors transfixed on Maximilian Kolbe Sorensen. They sat and they waited. They waited for him to act in their favor.

Like before, Max tried to speak. But he was without breath.

Max woke up choking for air. He gasped raspy wheezing breaths. His pillow was soaked with sweat and his moist hair was matted to the back of his head. Single trails of water ran from under his chin, through the folds of his neck and pooled on his chest. Max lurched forward and labored to breathe. As his lungs filled, he fell back onto the damp sheets and glanced around the room, muscles beginning to relax. It was his room, his apartment.

Rolling to his left and reaching for the nightstand light, he read the digits on his alarm clock; three nineteen. There was time. He still had time with the night. With the lamp on and the room dimly lit, Max fumbled through a stack of printed articles and books on the tabletop. After knocking his old yellow sport CD player and head phones to the floor, he gently placed a disc, labeled "Heartache of the Hunter," to one side. Moving a hardcover, he found a clear plastic bag containing a single light blue index card. His skin cooled. His breath was short. Angling the card, still in the bag toward the light, he read aloud Burningwater's words, written in Margaret's hand.

"Sondaqua, Sondaqua, soaring high above me,
look down upon a son of the Nations
and give strength to the hunter,
that I might persevere.
I make this prayer to you Sondaqua, Sondaqua."

Max slid the bag back onto the table, shut off the light and stared at a thin slice of moon shadow that slipped between the curtain and window frame. Dropping back to the pillow and still staring at the moon shadow, he wondered about this latest turn in his vocation.

He had hope for the first time in a long time. He knew Charlie Bay was acting in his favor. And he knew he had to act in favor of the Casco.

He had belief. He believed the dream was now his. He believed that the bones were not all on Eagle Island. And he also believed that somehow Charlie Bay was going to illuminate his hunt.

But, he still wondered about his ability to keep going. He wondered if he had the strength...the strength to persevere.

With a fresh breath, Max chanted Charlie Bay's prayer, now his prayer.

"Sondaqua, Sondaqua, soaring high above me,
look down upon a son of the Nations
and give strength to the hunter,
that I might persevere.
I make this prayer to you Sondaqua.

Sondaqua, soaring high above me,
look down upon a son of the Nations
and give strength to the hunter,
that I might persevere...I might persevere."

www.ingramcontent.com/pod-product-compliance
Lightning Source LLC
LaVergne TN
LVHW020537100826
845148LV00010B/1511

* 9 7 8 0 9 8 2 5 8 5 4 8 1 *